2.

CRUSHING ON THE COP

PIPER RAYNE

D1160933

Cover Photo: Wander Aguiar Photography

Cover Model: Andrew Biernat

Cover Design: RBA Designs

Line Editor: Gray Ink Editing

Proofreader: Shawna Gavas, Behind The Writer

Cristian Bianco has two things against him—he's a police officer and he's a police officer in the 18th District...**meaning my dad is his boss.**

Growing up as the Commander's daughter and having his magnifying glass focused on everything I did was more than I could handle.

Now, I'm out on my own, living by my own rules. Well, mostly. The 'job' I created for myself has me in some hot water and my exit strategy isn't exactly working out how I'd hoped.

Which is why when my best friend bids on Cristian for me at a charity bachelor auction, I'm not having it. A man in blue is only going to be one thing for me—a problem.

Except after his brother starts dating my best friend he becomes harder to ignore. The eight-pack abs. The sense of style only a girl like me can appreciate. The way he puts his family first. It all adds up to make him one irresistible prospect and has me wondering if he knows how to use those handcuffs the right way—**by locking my wrists to his headboard.**

Crushing
ON
THE COP

CHAPTER ONE

Cristian

*M*iddle Child Syndrome.

It's not really a thing. At least, not in my family.

Being the middle child of three boys, all a year apart, I should know.

Mauro is the eldest, the first son born into an Italian immigrant family. I came along so quick after him that Mauro needed my ma's arms as much as I did. I wasn't off my Ma's tit before Luca barreled out of her. When I say barreled, it's the truth. The guy was four weeks early, screaming and wailing, already searching for the party.

You'd think it would go Mauro takes care of Cristian, Cristian takes care of Luca and Luca—well, let's be thankful he's the youngest because he'd take care of no one but himself. Somehow though, I ended up with all the responsibility genes. I'm the one who checks on my parents, the one who makes sure Mauro and Luca remember birthdays and anniversaries, the one who organizes the paperwork for our recreation teams and makes sure everyone has paid.

Is that why I became a police officer? Maybe. It's not a lie that I thrive on order and rules. Who wants to live in a world of mutiny and insubordination? Not me, that's for damn sure.

What all that means is that it doesn't add up to why I've been staring at the blonde across the field for the past five minutes. Because she doesn't seem to want to follow rules and she could definitely invoke riots with her presence alone. The worst part about it, and the fact that my dick is overruling my brain, is that she's my commander's daughter, Vanessa Flanagan.

We're all here because Mauro came up with some cheesy way to win Maddie back and we're re-enacting a bonfire from high school.

"Hunt is driving me fucking insane. Did you see her wanting to arm wrestle me?" Luca doesn't even notice I'm distracted. Youngest child—everything's about him. "I mean, she's like a little Energizer bunny that never dies. Does she honestly think she'd have a chance to win? She's so competitive. It's annoying."

I'd take the opportunity to remind my brother that he's no different if Vanessa hadn't just laughed at something someone in her circle said. Because as she lets her laugh loose, she pulls at her hair, sliding it to one side, exposing her long slender neck and my jeans grow tighter and I'm speechless.

"Mauro owes me for this one. He and Maddie disappear now that they've made up and we're left here with Hunt. I should be in those woods with some chick fucking her against a tree like it was high school again. Instead we're here..."

A hand waves in front of my face.

"What the fuck are you staring at?" He must follow my line of sight. "Nope. Sorry, I'm not letting you get involved with one of Hunt's friends. It's bad enough that Mauro is probably popping the question to Maddie right this moment since he's completely pussy whipped now. But not you, too. No way I'm sharing two weddings, and every monumental life event with Hunt. Find someone else." He glances around the area, past the bonfire blazing in the middle of the field. "What about her?"

He points. My gaze drifts to a redhead who is attractive but more his type than mine. I've always loved blondes and the fact Vanessa's tall only increases her appeal.

I give him an indifferent shrug.

"Okay then, screw her, have some fun, but no wedding shit. You hear me? No way I can be with Hunt all the fucking time." He shakes his head, arms crossed over his chest.

I do remember this from high school—him and Lauren Hunt. The king and queen of jockville at St. George. Each one played four different sports and I don't even know why they grate on each other's nerves so bad. It's not like they ever had to compete against the other.

"She's the Commander's daughter," I say. "She's been refusing to go on a date with me since Maddie won her a date with me at the bachelor auction. The commander's on my ass to know why we haven't gone out. What am I going to tell him? Your daughter has something against police officers? She's giving me the cold shoulder? I might as well admit I rescue stray cats."

"Lie. Fuck, Cristian, just lie." He smacks me on the shoulder, downing half the beer from the red Solo cup.

"Yeah and that will go over well when he finds out the truth."

Damn, she is gorgeous though. Picturing her long legs wrapped around my waist is my first thought when I look at her.

"Stop living in the fucking right lane, dickhead. Slide on

over to the left and enjoy the ride until you have to go all slow and shit for kids in the backseat. You're like an eighty-year-old in a twenty-eight-year-old body. It's a shame you work out so much. A waste really."

I quirk an eyebrow. Not that I can refute what he says. He's right. I take my life way too fucking serious. Do I want a family? I do. I want a woman to come home to, to make a life with. A woman to carry my kids. And Vanessa is not her. She's the female version of Luca in the dating department from what I can tell.

When Vanessa visits the district, rumors fly about her like she's a Kardashian. She's so gorgeous you can't take your eyes off her, but you know she's not the bring-home-to-mom type. Guys like Luca crave girls like that. Me, not so much.

"Listen to the right head this time." Luca glances down to between my legs. "The one who knows what he wants. You just have to listen to him." He tips his Solo cup again. "Fuck. I'm out. You want one?" he asks, already stepping away.

"Nah." My gaze is still glued to Vanessa as she pulls a ponytail holder from her purse and secures her hair low at the bottom of her hairline.

Luca laughs as he walks away. "Just get her out of your system, man." He points at me with a stern expression. "But no going back for seconds."

Once Luca's gone, I weigh my options. He's made some valid points. Fuck Mr. Responsibility, for once in my life I'm taking what I want without thinking of the damn consequences. Downing the rest of my beer, I head across the grass not willing to accept the answer Vanessa loves to give me—no.

CHAPTER TWO

Vanessa

A new guy I just met who's on the fire department with Mauro carries on and on about how romantic Mauro is. Yeah, I didn't need that confirmation since I'm standing dead center in a re-enactment of a night that happened ten years ago.

And that's not jealousy in my tone—it's envy. I love Maddie and I only want her happy, but no one has ever put in an effort like this for me. Not that I really care that much because the last thing I need in my life is another man thinking he owns me and can run my life.

"He is sweet," I say with a smile and nod.

"Yeah, one day he'll be captain at the firehouse. Maybe after I retire."

His wife touches his arm in an affectionate pat. "I doubt that day will ever come." She smiles.

What must it be like to love your job so much you don't want to leave.

"We have three kids and they're approaching college. Someone has to pay for their education," she says.

Patel, as he introduced himself to me, stares down at his wife with a smile that matches hers.

"Scholarships," he says to his wife.

They laugh like it's a conversation they've had a million times.

It's nice and yet it still makes me want to throw up about as much as Mauro setting this whole thing up for Maddie does.

Again, envy not jealousy.

"You know I have this cousin," the wife whispers in my direction. "He likes blondes. He'd love you."

Patel shakes his head. "Excuse my wife."

She slaps him on the shoulder in a friendly 'stop' manner. They're cute and the fact that they're married with three kids and still civil to one another proves that marriage works for some people.

"No, just think, we wouldn't have met if it wasn't for Raj."

Patel nods in agreement at his wife. The sweet look shared between them tells even a bystander like me how much in love they are.

"Patel," a deep voice interrupts our conversation.

Thank God, I needed a clear path to escape from yet another set-up.

"Cristian." Patel places his hand into the hand of the large figure to my left.

Great, tonight just got even more intolerable. I down the rest of my flat keg beer, ready to excuse myself to go for a refill.

"I was just telling this lovely woman what a romantic your brother is." Patel gestures to me.

Like Cristian didn't know I was here. I swear he's embedded a chip in me like they do to dogs and cats. The guy doesn't understand the word no. I could still kill Lauren for giving him my number. What kind of friend is she?

I search her out with only the glow of the bonfire flames to light the surrounding area. She's nowhere in sight. Great because I'm about to ask Mrs. Patel to drive me home even if I have to hear her brag about her cousin's dating resume.

"I hope him and Maddie are happy. They seemed it when they left." Cristian smiles. One that probably leaves most women he comes in contact with, weak in the knees. Uniform or no uniform.

He's a good looking guy. Okay, okay, he's hot. Like mysterious hot. Always more stern looking than his brothers are. Maybe it's the police officer in him. Assessing the scene before he can relax and be himself. My dad has the same trait. On guard most of the time in public. Never able to settle until his back is to the wall so he's able to see the entire place and prepare for anything that might happen.

"Hey, Vanessa," he says to me, sipping from his own Solo cup.

I want to roll my eyes at his pretend surprise at finding me here, but Commander's daughter and all that.

"Hello, Officer Bianco."

A smirk tilts his lips.

Patel and his wife's gazes are poised on us with curiosity.

"You can call me Cristian," he says.

"No. That's okay." I shrug.

"Okay, Miss Flanagan." My gaze snaps to his and he raises his eyebrows, his smirk growing more prominent.

Touché Mr. Bianco.

"Well." I drag my eyes away from him although I have to say seeing him out of uniform is doing crazy things to my libido. Isn't it supposed to be the other way around?

For such a stiff do-gooder he sure has a sense of style even in the decade-old clothes we're wearing. "It was a pleasure meeting you. I'm going to refill my cup."

"You too," Mrs. Patel steps forward, reaching into her purse. She pulls out a card. "Just in case you change your mind. He's a very sweet boy. He's just holed himself up with studies, what with being a doctor. Has a great big mansion on the north shore." Her eyes light up, selling her cousin to me.

"I'm just not looking for anyone at the moment, but maybe I'll think about it."

I shoot her an easy out that should allow me to leave this conversation and Cristian's proximity.

"What's this?" Cristian glances over us to read the card.

"Oh, it's my wife matchmaking again." Patel laughs.

"Cristian, I have a niece that you'd love." Mrs. Patel moves on from me to Cristian.

Perfect.

"Thanks for thinking of me, but I'm not looking for anything serious right now."

I can't help but wonder if that's actually true.

A puffed sound falls from Mrs. Patel's lips. "You're only getting older. You don't want to be chasing your grandkids around in a walker."

Cristian's head rears back.

"She's pretty. Just graduated from UC, smart as a cookie, but she's disappointed her parents by wanting to go to culinary school now." Again, she looks up to her husband and they share a look of what are you going to do.

"I wish her luck, but I'm going to take my chances on that whole walker thing and stay single a while longer." Cristian smiles and for some reason, he appeases Mrs. Patel to stop pushing. She's not giving him a business card or handing out her niece's phone number.

"I try. That's all I can do." Her hands come up in front of her in a placating gesture.

Patel wraps his arm around his wife's waist. "Let's get you home, Match dot com." He kisses the hairline of her scalp and a small piece of my icy exterior melts at the affection they share.

"See you both and if you're ever finding yourself alone on a Saturday night give me a ring." She winks.

Patel and Cristian shake hands before the couple ventures off into the darkness.

I turn around to head to the keg, but footsteps fall in line behind me and I know I'm not alone. Ignoring his presence, I walk into the woods where grown people are pretending they're hiding from the cops. Hello, half the force is probably here today.

"Bianco, what's up man?" Some guy approaches Cristian behind me. Not that I needed clarification that Officer Bianco was probably staring at my ass the entire walk over here.

"Not much," Cristian says.

A slapping of hands commences behind me. "Killer hat trick this past Thursday. I think we've got a shot this year."

Stop listening.

I step forward to the keg, waiting in line behind two women laughing about how they can't figure out the tapper, reminiscing about their college days and how they only drink from bottles now.

"Let me help." I approach, pumping and tilting their cups under the nozzle. A minute later they're saying thank you and complimenting me on my hat.

I forgot I was even wearing my favorite hat from a decade ago. Good thing my dad stores everything in marked boxes in the basement. He might be organized, but he's still kind of a hoarder.

The unfortunate part of helping the two women is that by the time I'm ready to fill my cup the keg needs pumping again. I place my cup down on the forest floor, ready to do just that when two strong corded muscular forearms come into my line of sight.

Cristian pumps and I'm not even going to ask why he's not wearing a jacket in the fall. He's probably one of those hot-blooded males who wears shorts the minute he hears bird's chirping after a long winter. I question those dumbasses every spring.

"Thank you," I mumble because it was kind of him to pump the keg, even if I never asked.

"You're welcome." He fills his own cup.

"Not on duty tonight, officer?" I insert sarcasm into my tone because being a bitch will make it easier for him to keep his distance.

"Well, Miss Flanagan, I'm off for two days if you're wondering."

I step away from the keg allowing the lingering guys who are talking about hockey a chance to fill their cups.

"That leaves me open for that date." He cocks an eyebrow.

My head falls back in defeat. "There is no date. You have a pass. Most guys would love the chance to get out of a date with the person who wins them at an auction."

He sips his beer. "I'm not most guys."

I sip my beer and don't respond. He's right. He's not most guys. Most guys don't look like he does. That or I've been hanging around the wrong places.

"Some might say that most women would love to go on a date with a police officer."

"I'm not most women."

He laughs. One that heats my insides and makes him even more attractive. I know I'm going to be visualizing him the next time I pull out my Unicorn Cock vibrator, but I'll deal like I always do.

"I agree," he says when he finishes laughing.

"Perfect. Then it's a deal. No date." I smile and turn on my heel heading toward the bonfire.

"Whoa." His hand gently grabs my arm.

I spin back around.

"You know that's not what I was saying. Come on, Vanessa. I need your dad off my back. One date. It's not going to kill anyone."

I purse my lips, trying to figure out how I'm going to get him to let this topic go. I've had one police officer dictating my entire life already, I don't need another.

"Just lie," I say with a shrug.

His strong shoulders sag a bit and he shoots me a look like 'give me a break.' His eyes are those of an innocent man who probably always does the right thing. I'm doing him a favor keeping him at arm's length.

"Fine," I say when the silence stretches out.

He smiles.

I hold a finger up into the air. "You do one thing tonight that you'd never normally do and I'll go out with you." I smirk. Let's see Mr. Squeaky Clean take me up on that offer. I'm picturing my victory already.

"What?" He screws his face up then sips his beer.

I cross my arms around my middle, waiting for him to say no way so that I can move on. "You heard me. One spontaneous thing. Here. Tonight."

"Like what?" he asks, his eyes scanning the area around us that I now realize is quickly emptying out. Half these people probably have babysitters to get home to.

I shrug. "That's for you to decide."

His forehead bunches. "What do you want me to do? Jump over the fire or some shit like that?"

"I'd prefer if you didn't end up in the emergency room, so

no, I don't expect you to jump over a roaring fire. That would ruin Maddie and Mauro's night."

A pissed off look crosses his face and he downs most of his beer.

"That's it, let's go, Cris. It's two against two and I need a guy." Luca, Cristian's little brother, twirls a soccer ball on his finger as he steps up to us. Lauren follows behind with a girl I don't recognize.

"What?" Cristian glares over at his brother. "I'm not playing soccer tonight in the pitch dark."

He has a point.

"Come on Cris. Lauren says she can score five goals on me." Luca glances over to Lauren who has a shit-eating grin on her face, and he rolls his eyes.

Cristian blows out a breath. Lauren saddles up to my side, kicking the soccer ball from Luca's hands. She does some fancy footwork then kicks the ball in the air before catching it. That girl has coordination I do not.

"The answer is no. Find Bentley, he's over there." He points toward the bonfire.

Luca must know his brother never does something he doesn't want to do because he barrels away from us without a word.

"What's going on over here?" Lauren asks, walking backward, twirling the soccer ball on one finger like Luca was moments ago.

"Nothing," I say.

"Lauren, what's the craziest thing I can do tonight?" Cristian hollers out and Lauren's feet stop, staring at me over his shoulder.

She knows this game. We play it often. Well, not since college when guys tend to think they can say hello and you'll be falling all over them. There's nothing wrong with making them work to impress you a little. It builds character. LOL.

Lauren being Lauren pretends to think about it. In the past, we've had guys shave their heads or their eyebrows, dress in girl's clothing, striptease with a pair of girl's panties on. God knows what Lauren's going to recommend.

"You're a smart boy, Bianco. Turn the tables," she says. "What's the worst thing you could do to Vanessa tonight?"

I flip her off. Nice friend I got there. Who wants her?

A devilish smile creeps onto Cristian's lips. "Anyone tell you, you're a fucking genius, Lauren?"

She laughs. "All the time. Tell your brother for me though."

Luca comes over, stealing the soccer ball from her hands, while a guy tripping over his own feet follows behind. The girl and guy standing on the sidelines watching Lauren and Luca argue about who goes first.

"So, Officer Bianco, what will it be?" I cock a hip and a brow.

"Maybe a date with you isn't worth the embarrassment?" He steps closer and I back up an inch, unease setting in as his demeanor grows more confident and sure.

I shrug. "That's fine. I'm happy to split ways now."

He takes another giant step forward and sips the remaining beer from his cup, tossing it down to the grass, his gaze intense and set on whatever he's about to do.

"What are you doing?" I ask, my voice weaker than I'd prefer.

We're chest to chest now because he's taken me by surprise and I forgot to flee with his approach. Okay and maybe his eyes mesmerized me. A little. Not much.

"I'm going to do the one thing I didn't think I'd do tonight." His voice has dropped an octave and we're alone in the darkness of the forest now where the warmth of the bonfire has disappeared. A cold chill runs across my cheeks until Cristian's hands land on either side of my face. "I'm going to kiss you."

His lips fall to mine. Did I say it was cold? It's not. It's warm. Cristian's mouth on mine steals the chill from my body. I should knee him in the balls or at least push him away, but I don't. Instead, my lips betray me and move in time with his. I wrap my arms around his neck and I rise to my tiptoes, kissing him back.

His arms cradle me flush against his body, his tongue exploring mine and under the canopy of the forest, away from any prying eyes, Cristian Bianco sets my body on fire.

I love breaking other people's rules, but I'm not sure about breaking my own.

CHAPTER THREE

Vanessa

"*I* thought you had plans tonight?" Lauren asks, taking her black bean veggie burger out of the microwave and walking over to the center island.

"I do." I grab a soda from the fridge and sit down on a breakfast stool across from her.

"A Coke and Pop Tart? Nice. You'll be full *and* bloated." My health nut roommate wraps up the burger in a tortilla with lettuce, salsa, and a dime-sized portion of sour cream. God forbid she enjoy her food at all.

"Well, it's a date with Officer Bianco." I shrug.

Lauren glances up from her plate, her eyes urging me to just call him by his name. I refuse.

"You finally said yes?" She moves to the fridge and pulls out a veggie tray of carrots and cauliflower she's already cut up.

Seriously, that's her dinner?

I crack off a piece of my Pop Tart. "I did."

"Now you're spoiling your appetite. I bet he has something amazing planned for you guys."

The smile on her face showcases how much she likes Cristian. Her and Maddie both go on and on about what a great guy he is. I don't refute that. I'm sure he'll make an excellent boyfriend or husband for anyone but me.

"It's worth spoiling my appetite. Hello, it's pumpkin spice?" I hold it up to her.

She cringes and shakes her head. "That shit is everywhere. The other day I saw pumpkin spice Oreos at the store. Why would anyone mess with an Oreo by adding pumpkin to it?"

I toss a piece of pumpkin spice goodness into my mouth, chew and swallow. "I agree with you on that one. Oreos need to stay Oreos. As far as everything else, pumpkin spice is the best." I gulp down some of my Coke.

Rounding the island, she sits on a stool next to me. "You're not even the least bit attracted to Cristian?" she asks before biting into her healthy dinner. She's still in her scrubs from her job as a physical therapist and I predict she'll be on the couch for the rest of the night.

"I'm not blind. Luckily, the glint from his badge does a good enough job of blinding me from his looks."

"You know not every police officer is like your dad?"

I chuckle. "Of course."

"And that you're typecasting Cristian?" She sips her Vitamin Water.

"Look, in my experience, police officers are either crooked or straight as an arrow. Cristian is the latter."

She blows out a breath. "You don't know that. You don't really know *him*. Why not give him a chance?"

"Good thing I live in Chicago with roughly a million men." I crumple up my napkin and toss it into the trash.

Lauren and I are similar. Normally we don't push the

other toward a specific man so I'm unsure why she's being kind of mom-like right now.

I can feel Lauren's gaze on me before I even turn back around to face her.

"It's been nice having you around at night lately. Did you... break up with someone?"

"No breakup, but I don't work nights anymore."

Her eyes widen. "Really? What were you doing exactly?"

This is Lauren at her best. Or actually her worst. She thinks she's sly, but I'm not about to accidentally tell her what I've been doing to earn money to start my own fashion line.

"Just earning some cash so I can get the samples I need completed."

"And you're good. You've got enough cash now?"

I nod, a smile creeping onto my lips.

When I decided to be a fashion major in college, I never thought it'd cost so much money to get clothes made. I can sew, but it's time and labor intensive. Besides, I'm better at designing. In order to get the samples I need made—and hopefully the clothes themselves after I can get them into some boutiques here in the city—I have to have production somewhere else.

"I did. And Rose and Ivy down on Chestnut has agreed to see my spring line."

Excitement fills me and I don't know why I didn't tell either of my best friends earlier. They've always encouraged me and had my back offering their own suggestions on how to make my dreams a reality. Maddie always said I should try to work for a design company and move up while Lauren thought I should open my own online store. But for me, it's always been my dream to have my clothing in boutiques. If I'm honest, at some point I want my line to be so in demand,

I'm featured during New York Fashion Week. But, baby steps.

"VAN!" she shouts, rising from her chair and wrapping her arms around my shoulders, swaying us back and forth. "We need to celebrate!"

"Let's celebrate after Rose and Ivy actually agree to buy some of my spring line." I pat her back since she's not releasing me.

"No. We celebrate everything. Not to mention I need a girl's night out. Maddie's never home now that she's with Mauro. The three us need this."

I laugh because it sounds more like Lauren needs a night out more than Maddie or me. Dragging her away from Mauro will be a struggle since they're in that whole new love infatuation phase right now.

"Deal. Let me get this date with Officer Bianco over with though."

She purses her lips but doesn't say anything, heading back to her plate of food.

"I'll message Maddie and we'll set a date."

The perma smile on her face says it all and erases some of the guilt I've felt the past few months. I know she was worried about what I was doing for the money. But that's all behind me now and no one will ever know.

"Oh, I'm so excited for you!" she says after she finishes swallowing.

The back door opens, and Maddie and Mauro walk in, laughing and holding hands. I'll admit, they are super cute together.

"Oh great, as if I needed a reminder that I'm a loser with no one," Lauren mumbles over her mouth full of veggie burger with an exaggerated eye roll that tells me she's joking.

Maddie breaks away from Mauro, but he stays one step

behind her. When Maddie stops at the breakfast bar, Mauro wraps his arms around her waist so she's flush to his chest.

"What about my brother, Luca?" Mauro asks, his hearing way too good for a man who has sirens blaring around him the majority of the time.

Lauren rolls her eyes. "I wasn't talking about a one and done."

Maddie's gaze veers to me. "Is that what you're wearing?" Her forehead crinkles and a line forms between her eyes.

I glance down at my ripped jeans and oversized t-shirt. Hey, I put on a necklace. "What's wrong with it?"

Mauro's hands rub along Maddie's hips and his mouth is dangerously close to her neck.

Hello? Do they not see us here?

"It's just that you usually wear a dress on a date." She leans into her boyfriend's strong chest.

I down the rest of my Coke and place the bottle on the counter. "I don't want him thinking this date means anything."

"And yet, you have on a full face of makeup and a gold necklace strategically dangling between your tits." Lauren's eyebrows raise.

I glare at her. "I have my own standards of how I look when I go out in public."

"I'm just happy you decided to go out with Cristian," Mauro says.

Lauren laughs, pushing her empty plate away from her and pulling one leg up so her foot is resting on the seat. "After she made him participate in the 'do something you'd never do' thing like she used to in college."

Mauro's hands still and his gaze finally moves off Maddie and over to me. "What did you make my brother do?"

"Vanessa would get hit on every five minutes. Especially at the frat parties," Maddie says.

"That's an exaggeration." I slide up on the counter, shaking my head.

Lauren and Maddie both look at me.

"No, it's not," Lauren says. "She was the sparkling diamond while Maddie and I were more the diamonds in the rough in our trio."

Mauro kisses his girlfriend's neck and clutches her closer to him. He whispers something in her ear, spurring a flush to overtake her creamy colored skin. She nuzzles her face into his and it's enough to make me want to run to the bathroom and revisit my Pop Tart and Coke.

"Anyway..." Lauren interrupts.

"Yes." Maddie straightens and re-joins the conversation. "She'd make them do something crazy to earn a date with her."

"One guy shaved off all the hair on his body," Lauren says.

Mauro's eyes widen. "Men are fucking stupid. What did my brother do then?"

Lauren looks at me, waiting for me to respond because she doesn't know what Cristian did either. No one does.

"He..." I let it hang, not really sure whether I want Mauro to hear this.

"He kissed her. I told him to turn the tables on her," Lauren says proudly.

Maddie raises her hand to Lauren for a high five.

Traitors.

And here I thought no one saw.

"He kissed you?" Mauro's tone is laced with confusion.

His do good, rule-following, stay inside the box brother, kissed a girl to get a date.

"Yeah." I shrug, trying to play it off like I'm unaffected, but the truth is that I've been trying to forget our kiss all week. And once this date is over, I should finally be able to do just that. We can go back to Officer Bianco and Miss Flanagan, burying that kiss six feet under. Under concrete that is.

"I'm impressed," Mauro says, sounding just that.

"It looked like one hot kiss." Lauren stands from the breakfast stool and throws her paper plate in the trash, picking up my empty bottle and waving it in front of my face. "I got it. No worries."

"Thanks." I tilt my head and wink.

"Your sweet flirtations don't work on me. I'm not Cristian."

The doorbell rings, but before I can hop off my stool, Lauren runs toward the front door.

"I hope she's nicer to him than she was when I first started seeing you," Mauro says to Maddie, taking the opportunity to twist her around and kiss her. I grant them the privacy they don't seem to care whether or not they have.

By the time I reach the foyer, Cristian is already inside and Lauren is asking him if he wants a drink.

"No time for drinks. I'm sure Cristian has reservations," I say, passing by Lauren and ready to head out the door.

Before I can get the hell out of this house, Cristian holds out a box to me.

Chocolates?

"I hope you're a pumpkin spice lover?" Cristian says, rocking back on his heels, his eyes holding not one ounce of timidness.

I open the white bakery box to find three Whoopie Pies, the delicious smell of cinnamon filling my nose.

Lauren coughs, pretending to gag.

"Cris!" Mauro's deep voice booms through the room, interrupting the moment.

"Hey guys," Cristian raises his hand in greeting. "I thought you guys would be at your place?"

"We're just picking up some of Maddie's things." Mauro's hands again venture along Maddie's body.

"Don't be banging upstairs, okay? You have your own place now, so I don't need to hear the two of you." Lauren rolls her eyes.

I get where she's coming from. Watching them so in love, it's hard not to want the same for yourself.

"Lauren," Maddie sighs although everyone in this room knows the two of them can't go more than fifteen minutes between kisses when they're in the same room.

"I'll wait until I get her up in the room. That's my only promise." Mauro smacks Maddie's ass as she rounds the staircase to head up.

"I'm going to The Little Coffee Shop." Lauren grabs her jacket and heads toward the door. "You two have fun and be sure to do something I would do." She winks at us and places her hand on Cristian's arm before sliding out the front door, leaving me alone with him.

"Thank you for these." I hold them up then place them on the foyer table.

"You didn't really scream a flower girl."

I grab my own jacket and Cristian takes it from my hands to hold open for me. I slide my arms through and pull my hair out from being tucked under the back collar.

"Ready?" he asks.

I nod and step in front of him. Once I lock Maddie and Mauro in the house, Cristian walks next to me down the short walkway to where his car is parked at the curb.

I hadn't thought about what Cristian would drive, but a little sporty Audi wasn't it. I assumed a Honda or Toyota. Something reliable and good on gas mileage.

"Nice car," I say as he opens the passenger door for me.

"Bet you were expecting a Prius?" He smiles and I'll admit

my insides might quiver a little at his brilliant white teeth on display and the boyish charm the smile adds to his face.

"Well, it fits..."

"Stereotyping, huh?"

I shrug.

He says nothing for a moment as he stands there, ready to shut my door. "You look beautiful tonight." His gaze flows up and down and his dark eyes practically turn molten as he takes in my body. I cross my legs to ease some of the building pressure pooling between my thighs. "Even more so in my car," he adds.

Since I can't seem to get a word out, he shuts the door.

As he winds around the front of the car, I take in his dark gelled hair, his stylish sweater, and designer jeans. When he slides in next to me, his cologne fills the space and I force myself not to close my eyes and bask in the scent.

Damn it, resisting him is going to be harder than I thought.

CHAPTER FOUR

Vanessa

*C*ristian parallel parks like a pro. Probably not impressive to anyone who actually has a driver's license, but the thought of squeezing a car between two other ones scares me to no end.

"What's this place?" I ask.

"It's called Farm to Table. It's new." He shuts off the car and turns to look at me, waiting for me to say something else.

I purposely don't.

He opens his door and I hem and haw in my mind whether I should just climb out myself, but while I'm thinking about it, he beats me to a decision and opens the door for me. He offers his hand, but I climb out without his assistance. I catch his small smirk thinking I'm purposely being difficult. Maybe I am. This date cannot go well. Nothing good could come of that.

"Is this a health food place?" I ask, happy I had that Pop Tart and Coke if all I'm going to be served is kale and greenery that looks better as a garnish then it does as my meal.

"No. It's just organic, grass-fed beef and locally sourced produce." He opens up the glass door for me to walk in ahead of me.

"So, steak is an option, then."

He follows me into the dimly lit restaurant that has a definite intimate feel. Not exactly what I expected based on the name of the place. Candlelight flicks against the dark stained wooden tables and cushioned fabric chairs. Overhead yellow lights are encased in chicken coop wire, giving it a flair of expensive but carrying through the farm theme.

"Bianco," Cristian tells the hostess, whose eyes take a leisurely stroll over his gorgeous face and lean, athletic body.

The invitation in her gaze has me grinding my molars, but only because it's so completely against girl code to be checking out another woman's date. Because really, what do I care? He's not mine. Maybe if I get her number for him, he'll stop using mine.

"We have the table ready for you." She takes two menus and steps away from the podium, waiting for me to follow.

As we head away from the main dining room, I'm wondering what kind of crappy seat she's leading us to.

"Cristian!" A female voice sounds from one of the tables and we glance over, seeing a woman raising her hand in a friendly wave.

Cristian stops, his hand landing on my hip to tell me to slow down, too. A zing of electricity shoots through my body from his touch. Bastard probably has static cling.

"Let me just say a quick hello," he says.

The hostess has stopped in front of a door, her impatience clear as she wonders why we're still not following her.

Cristian looks over at her. "Is it through there?"

"Yes," she says.

"Okay, we'll be right there. I just need to say hi to some friends. We'll find our way."

The woman seems unsure at first, but eventually steps away and heads back to the hostess station.

"Sorry about this," he murmurs, weaving us through the tables toward an eager blonde who's sliding out from her chair and I now realize looks vaguely familiar. "Chelsea," he says, kissing her on the cheek and then hugging her to him.

When he says her name, I realize that she's one of the women I met at the first responder's bachelor auction who got me into this whole date with Cristian in the first place.

"Whoa, look at you," Cristian gestures to her pregnant belly.

The other couple at the table, smile and look between the two of them.

A man stands up from behind Chelsea, towering over her. From his protective stance, I'd say he's the daddy, and since he looks familiar as well, I'm assuming I saw him at the auction, too.

"Yeah." The woman smiles and looks up at the man behind her.

Damn, it's Mauro and Maddie 2.0.

"You remember Dean." Chelsea signals between the two men.

Dean holds his arm out from behind his fiancée's—based on the sizable diamond on Chelsea's left hand.

"Good to see you again," Cristian shakes his hand. "Congratulations to you both on the baby."

"Thanks, man." Dean squeezes Chelsea's shoulder after he lets Cristian's hand drop.

"We're a little excited if you couldn't tell." Chelsea smiles and her eyes find mine behind Cristian. She gives me a knowing look and then asks Cristian, "Who's this?"

I appreciate her not mentioning the night of the bachelor

auction and so I roll with it, pretending that we're meeting for the first time.

Cristian steps back, his hand landing on the small of my back. Another electric shock races up my spine and I know I can't use the static excuse of again.

"This is my date, Vanessa."

Chelsea holds her stomach and grins at me. "Nice to meet you. I'm sure by now you've figured out what a great guy Cristian is."

I smile politely. I may not want to be with him, but I would never embarrass him in front of people he knows.

"Well, we should get going to our table." Cristian breaks the uncomfortable silence.

"Of course. I'm sure we'll pop by the deli at some point to show off our new addition." She stares back up at her fiancé.

"Hopefully I'll be there. Besides, I'm sure Mama will keep me updated, too." Cristian hugs her one last time and shakes Dean's hand. "Best wishes to you both."

"Thanks," Dean's deep voice says and his hand rests on his fiancée's hips.

"Nice to meet you, Vanessa." Chelsea shakes my hand and gives it a quick squeeze before Cristian's hand lands on the small of my back again, leading me away.

Thank God. How awkward.

I stop in front of the doors that seem to be leading into the back of the restaurant, unsure if this is where I'm supposed to go. Cristian's hand leaves my back and I exhale in relief, but a moment later his hand entwines with mine.

I take a deep breath, hoping to calm the nerves that are suddenly present. I don't want to have this reaction to him, but it seems I can't help it.

We walk down a small hallway that opens up to a smaller kitchen where a man in a white chef's coat is busy working. He looks up at the two of us and smiles. "Welcome." His graying hair peeks out from his black hat while he cuts up a carrot.

Christian smiles and nods, leading us to a small table on the other side.

Oh my God, did he get us the chef's table?

Cristian holds out my chair and I slide into it wishing I would've worn a dress. I mean, ripped jeans for the chef's table? I feel like an idiot.

A waiter walks in with two bottles of wine, holding them up for us to choose.

"You pick," Cristian nods to me, laying his napkin in his lap.

I have no idea what a good bottle of wine is. Knowing I prefer the sweetness of white, I pick that one and the waiter opens the bottle and pours it into our glasses.

Over the candlelight, Cristian picks up his glass, holding it out in front of me, in an offering to clink glasses. My trembling hand picks up my own glass, the wine sloshing inside.

"Thanks for having dinner with me," he says and a smile that makes my heart race and my palms clammy spreads across his face.

I clink my glass with his and take more than a little sip, placing it back down on the linen tablecloth.

"Excuse me. I'm just going to the bathroom." I slide my chair out and stand. Cristian stands and I place my napkin on the chair.

"I think it's…"

I leave him while he's still directing me—I'm on a mission. I head to the bathroom, but instead of locking myself in the stall, I study myself in the mirror.

Why did I think I could do this? Go on a date and not let hope sink in? I'm not looking for someone right now. Especially with trying to get my spring line together. Even if I was, a *police officer* would not be a wise choice. Not for me.

Still, I can't deny that he's attractive. My body practically purrs when he looks at me. But I cannot go there. That's when the idea comes to me because I need out of this date like a woman from a bad marriage.

I straighten my shirt, making sure my necklace dangles exactly where I want the waiter to be looking when I approach him. This will totally work and I'll never have to be alone with Cristian Bianco again.

Leaving the restroom, luck must be on my side because the waiter is about to walk through the doors with a basket of bread.

"Excuse me," I say, arching my back slightly.

Yes, I'm using my assets here. Don't judge.

"Did you need something, Ma'am." His eyes dip like I knew they would. He's way too young not to be enticed by a pair of full-sized Cs.

I dig into my pocket and hand a folded up twenty to him. "Spill a drink on me?"

He chuckles at first, confusion marring his features. "What?"

I glance around to make sure Cristian's friend isn't around. "Just spill a drink on me so I have an excuse to leave."

Now he full-on laughs, the baskets of bread shaking in his hand. "I've never..."

"Whatever. Just spill the drink on me. Okay?"

He purses his lips, his eyes scanning the immediate area, tucks the twenty in his front shirt pocket, and nods.

"Thank you."

I slide by him, going through the doors first. Sitting back down in front of Cristian, my stomach jumps again when he smiles at me.

With any luck, the torture I'm putting myself through will all be over soon.

CHAPTER FIVE

Cristian

I didn't reserve the chef's table to impress Vanessa. Well...okay, maybe a little bit. As much as I'm pushing the whole idea of a serious relationship with someone to the side, for the time being, I'm not going to drag her to a Hooters and down a few oyster shots to get her in the mood.

We sit at the table eating our salads and I watch as her gaze keeps flickering to the waiter. The fuck? The guy's okay. Tattoos which I internally roll my eyes at knowing every girl probably loves them. He's scrawny if you want my opinion. Probably never seen a weight room in his entire life.

I shake my head, sitting back in my chair and bringing the wine glass to my lips.

Now, I'm mentally picking on some guy because I was stupid enough to lay down a wad of cash on a girl I knew would be hard to get. Fuck me. This is exactly why I don't put myself out there.

Being a police officer, more numbers are tossed my way than Tom Brady. Okay, that's only because the average woman doesn't have access to Tom Brady. But I get plenty of action when and if I want it. Some turn into clingers, others just want to say they fucked a cop. None of them have piqued my interest since my ex and that ended years ago. Vanessa's the first one to make me want to put forth any effort in a long time.

"The wine is good." She smiles over the rim of her glass. "I really need more water though." She looks around for the waiter she's been eating up with her eyes all night. They might as well bring out a hose from the amount of water she's consumed since she returned from the bathroom.

I nod, raising my hand, catching the attention of the waiter who's at the chef's station, chatting about the next course. Yeah, there are seven and we're only on our second. Five more courses to endure her scoping out some other dude.

The waiter glances back to the chef and the two share a smirk. Even they can see this date for the shit show it is—a man spending an ungodly amount of money on a girl who has zero interest in him.

"Water?" he asks, approaching the table.

Vanessa raises her glass and as they're exchanging it, the glass slips from her grasp but the waiter catches it.

"Quick hands," I comment.

Vanessa forces a smile, holding her hand out for the glass, but the waiter places it on the table beside her plate. He leaves and the silence weighs down between us again.

"What do you do for a living?" I ask, forking another pile of lettuce and placing it in my mouth.

"Oh, just..." She stops talking abruptly, looking around. Grabbing her purse that's hanging on the back of the chair, she pulls out her phone and stares down at the screen for a second. "I'm sorry, all this water...I have to go to the bathroom again."

I nod, rising from my seat but she rushes out so fast I only get halfway up.

Fuck this. I know when to throw in the towel.

I pull out my phone, checking the Blackhawks score. She takes so fucking long that I stream the game as I finish eating my salad. Screw the gentlemanly act of waiting for her to return. She's made it clear that she wants nothing from me.

"Would you care for another bottle?" The waiter approaches, picking up the bottle of wine.

We already finished a bottle?

"No. Actually, we might cut this date short. My apologies."

The guy tucks the wine bottle under his arm and looks over his shoulder toward the door. If this guy asks for permission to ask Vanessa out, I am going to lose my shit.

"Listen, I hate to be the one to tell you this, but your date..."

Fuck me, seriously.

My gaze locks with his and I wait.

"She paid me twenty dollars to pour a drink on her." He cringes.

"Really?" I ask.

Is it pathetic that a small part of me is happy she hasn't been eye fucking the waiter all night but actually waiting for him to dump a drink on her?

He bites the inside of his cheek, glancing over his shoulder one more time. "And you spent all this money." He picks up my salad plate, eyeing Vanessa's which is still untouched.

An idea comes to my mind. "You know what? We're going to finish the dinner."

His eyes widen. "Why?" He immediately shakes his head. "Sorry. As you wish."

The guy probably thinks I'm an idiot, but truth is I already paid for this meal whether we eat the food or not. I'm going to enjoy it even if she doesn't. And yes, a small part of me kind of wants to torment her for embarrassing me.

Just then Vanessa steps into the small kitchen, placing her phone face down on the table while she slides into her chair and spreads the napkin on her lap.

"Next course is coming, if you want to finish up your salad," I say.

She removes her fork from resting on the edge of the plate. "No, I actually didn't like the salad dressing," she almost whispers.

"You never tried it."

Her face reddens, her gaze falling to her plate.

"I'm sorry, Cristian, I just think maybe we should cut this evening short."

I blow out a breath. "Listen, Vanessa. I get it. You don't want to date me. Trust me, you're not breaking my heart. I thought you could tolerate one dinner for the simple fact that your dad has been up my ass about taking you out on the date you won. And I know that yes, Maddie bid on me on your behalf. But I've already paid for this night and it wasn't exactly cheap. So, whatever you're thinking this is, let's just enjoy this dinner as acquaintances."

She leans back in her chair, a slow smile forming on her lips. "You don't want to date me?"

"Why would I ever want to date my boss's daughter? I don't have a death wish."

She tilts her head from side to side, her eyes lighting up like everything is clicking together. "I thought that since you were calling..."

I bring my drink to my lips and take a sip before responding. "Sorry to disappoint, but I want SWAT and I need your dad to write me up a hell of a reference to get it. If that means following through on a date with you, then that's what I'll do."

I purposely leave out the fact that, yeah, I am attracted to her and if things were different she might be someone I'd want to date. She intrigues me.

"Oh." Her voice is quiet now.

Did she really think I need to hound a woman for a date?

She picks up her fork. "Then yeah, let's have dinner."

Surprisingly, Vanessa isn't bad company when she's not trying to blow you off. She has a degree in fashion which doesn't surprise me—some of the outfits I've seen her wear at times look like they came from the costume department of the Zoolander movie. I prefer her look tonight. Casual and put together, yet still beautiful.

We talk about the differences of my big Italian family versus her small one that consists of her dad and a grandma she rarely sees. When the subject of her mom's passing comes up and wetness coats her eyes, my heart pricks. Of course, me with my great sense of timing, I ask right before I open the passenger door to drive her home.

"I'm sorry," I say from the driver's seat, apologetic for broaching a subject that is still so painful for her.

Word around the district is that the Commander has been a widow since Vanessa was young and that he never dated or remarried because he had a daughter to raise.

"It's fine. Probably shouldn't have had that second bottle of wine. Alcohol makes me emotional." The shakiness in her voice layers more guilt on my shoulders. "It was a long time ago." Her gaze finds mine through the darkness of the car interior. "Her death was long and drawn out and while there are pluses and minuses to having time to say goodbye, it was difficult to watch." She blinks rapidly a couple of times and then waves me away with her hand. "You probably know all this. Gossip and police officers aren't exactly like oil and water."

I chuckle because she's not wrong. "What else can we do when we spend eight hours in a patrol car? Though I do have the highest level of Candy Crush at my station." She gives me a small smile and I drive out of the parking lot only to stop behind a long line of cars that tells me it's going to take some time before we get back to her place. I shouldn't expect anything less. It's Friday night—everyone from the burbs descends on the city.

"I suck at phone games," she says.

Speaking of phones, hers lights up the car from where it sits on her lap, but she quickly silences it and flips it over.

"Are you better at other types of games? I heard Maddie and Mauro are becoming regulars at Dice and Spins?"

She laughs even harder at my mention of the board game café my brother has become a recent fan of. "Maddie loves that place, so I'm glad Mauro has found a love for that place, too."

"Have you been to their house lately?" I ask. I was there last night helping Mauro install a fire pit in the back. I still can't believe how they've transformed that dump into such a nice home.

"I haven't had the time, but I told Maddie I'd come by this week."

"Mauro framed Maddie's first Boggle sheet."

"He didn't?" she asks with a laugh, finding it as humorous as I do.

"Yep," I say, signaling and changing lanes so I can get off the main drag and use some of the side streets. Sometimes it pays to know the city so well. "Put it up right in their dining room. I told him to save that sappy shit for the bedroom."

"And what did he say?"

I shrug. "Said he wants it out there for everyone to see how smart his girl is."

I glance over to see Vanessa smiling wide. "I am really happy for the two of them." There's a hint of melancholy in her tone I've never heard from her before.

"Me, too but he'll probably be Mama's favorite soon."

"Why?"

"Because he'll give her her first grandchild."

She reaches out and grips my right forearm. "What?"

Thankfully I'm able to keep us on the road. I'm doubly thankful that I'm able to pretend the feel of her hand on my body didn't have me wanting to reach out for more.

"Maddie's pregnant?" she practically screams.

"NO!" I rush out. "I'm just saying, I'm sure whenever they do marry it won't be long."

"Phew." She lets her hand drop and leans back against her seat again. I know I've been preoccupied lately, but I couldn't have missed that."

"What have you been up to?" I turn down her street, finding that I don't really want the night to end. Our conversation has been flowing nicely since I told her she didn't have to worry about me wanting anything more to happen between us. I've enjoyed being able to talk about people we mutually know or my family. When I first start dating someone, I tend to keep that area of my life closed off. Maintaining privacy is rule 101 when you're a police officer. All social media accounts are private and I investigate anyone that friend requests me before accepting.

"I was just working nights and Lauren and Maddie work

during the day. Different shifts didn't leave a lot of time to be together."

I nod in understanding. When I was night shift as a rookie, it sucked. I was dragging ass every day and missed out on a lot of my family and friend's events. Not like you can drink a beer at a bar-b-que when you have to report to work at eleven at night.

"I get that." I slow down as I approach her house.

I like this area of the city. Vanessa lives on a residential street with mostly houses whereas Mauro and I share an apartment on a busy street where it's hell to find parking.

Shit, I still can't get used to that. After this month, it's *my* apartment and I haven't even decided what I'm going to do about a roommate. Luca keeps pestering me about it. Sharing the rent would be nice but dealing with his mess and his douchebag friends would not.

"Oh my God." Vanessa sits up straight in her seat, her hand on the window as though she's seeing something she can't believe.

"What?"

I pass a black town car parked two houses down from her place, but because every house on her block has garages in the back, I have no problem finding a parking spot right in front of her house.

"No. Um..."

"Vanessa, are you okay?"

Little beads of sweat have formed along her hairline, her gaze darting behind us and then over to the house. Her eyes are wide and panicked. Even if I wasn't a police officer, based on her demeanor and her body language, I'd still know something is wrong.

"Can you put the car in drive? Just go." She points in front of us and motions me forward with her hand.

I don't flee from fear, I search it out until there's nothing left to fear. If there's something or someone here that worries her, I'll deal with it.

So instead of doing as she asks, I turn off the ignition.

"What are you doing? NO!"

My hand finds the door handle and I'm about to open the door when Vanessa turns the key in the ignition and tries to throw my car into drive. Leaving me no choice, I take my foot from the brake and take over before we end up through someone's front window.

"What the hell?" I steer us away from her house and glance over at her.

"I'm sorry. It's just some jerk who hasn't been able to handle the word no." She grabs her phone and starts hammering out a message to someone.

I slam on the brakes. "Let me clear up any confusion on his part."

"No, just keep driving." She lets out a relieved breath when I put my foot back on the gas and I turn off the street, back to Irving Park. "It's fine, but...can I hang at your house?"

"Um..." That was not what I was expecting.

"Just for a few hours. I'm sure he's going out with his friends and I can Uber back to my house later."

What kinda man does she take me for?

"Number one, I really wish you'd let me handle this right now. Number two, you can stay at my house for as long as you want. Number three, I'll be driving you home."

"Number one, you're not my boyfriend, so it's not your place to handle my private life. Number two, I won't overstay my welcome into tomorrow morning. Number three, I'll have Maddie pick me up. Lauren is out with some friends and is probably spending the night there since they live closer to Rush Street."

She relaxes back into the seat seeming to be more at ease

now that she's told me how it's going to be and picks up her vibrating phone.

I shake my head over the fact she's coming back to my apartment on her own suggestion. This isn't how I thought tonight would go. I'm starting to realize that Vanessa is full of surprises.

CHAPTER SIX

Vanessa

Cristian's apartment is like the man himself—all man, dark and put together. I take in the dark wood floors, the black appliances, and granite countertops. There are no pictures of people on the wall or picture frames adorning the shelves. It's all concrete and steel embellishments with no knickknacks and nothing is out of place. In fact, I'd think it was just a furnished apartment if I didn't know he lived here.

He tosses his keys into a brown leather bowl on the table in the front room, toes out of his shoes and leaves them neatly next to the table.

Jesus, just like my father.

"Are you thirsty?" he asks, making his way into the kitchen.

Thankfully, he let the whole lie about a stalker ex-boyfriend go without pressing me on it. I can't tell him the truth of who sits in that town car. I thought I'd crossed all my t's and dotted my i's, but the fact there are five new voicemails on my phone and the car was waiting for me says I missed something.

I'm not ready to go back to that life right now. So, instead of listening to my messages, I leave my phone in my purse, slip out of my boots, and head toward Cristian's comfy dark grey couch.

"Where did you get this?" My voice is groggy as my ass sinks into the cushions. It swallows me up in the best way possible. Tucking my feet under me, I lean on the armrest for support, when what I really want to do is lay flat across it.

"Pretty great, right?" He rounds the back of the couch with two bottles of water.

I guess neither one of us will be drinking anymore tonight. Probably a good decision so I don't do something I'd regret. There's no future for the two of us but resisting his molten eyes and killer body is easier said than done.

"Took me forever to find it. Mauro bitched non-stop for a month while we waited for it to be delivered but it was worth every day of his moaning."

He opens the water bottle, securing the cap before handing it over to me.

Hmm. Thoughtful.

"Thanks," I say.

Sitting down on the other end of the couch, he sets down a coaster and slides another across the table to rest in front of me. It's a clear hint.

"Can we talk about the guy in the town car?" he asks, not bothering to press the power button on the remote resting in his hand.

Shit.

Cristian is a police officer, and a good one at that, which means he won't rest until this case is closed in his mind.

"I'd rather not." I sip my water, staring at the black television.

"I can't let you go home tonight knowing that some creep is stalking you." I glance over at him, his gaze is trained on me and for the first time, I'm getting an idea of what it must be like when Cristian the police officer pulls you over.

"I sent him a text and told him my roommate was going to call the police if he didn't leave. He really is just an innocent guy with a bruised ego. He apologized."

All lies. I'm literally spitting lie after lie at him to get him to drop this. But I lived most of my life with a cop and I know it's probably going to take more than this to assuage his concern.

"Really?" he asks with a raised brow.

"Yeah." I sip my water again and the chill of the liquid running down my throat does nothing to cool the feeling of a hot poker in my stomach from being deceitful.

Don't get me wrong. I'm an excellent liar. You have to be when your dad is a police officer, but it doesn't mean I enjoy it. I'm just doing what's necessary.

"Your voice...you were scared," he pushes.

There are those cop instincts. Where a normal guy would have taken me for being spastic, he obviously heard the fear that had me in its grip.

"Maybe, but you know us women, drama llamas."

I hate that I just went there, but desperate times and all that. Hopefully my independent female card won't be revoked for that comment.

He shrugs and I can't tell if he's letting it go.

"Please don't tell my dad, though. He'll have one of you guys following me everywhere I go."

He chuckles lightly, placing his water on the coaster. "No worries on that front."

"Thanks."

He clicks power on the remote and turns his head to meet my gaze. I find myself stuck in the tractor beam that is his dark mocha eyes and my breath grows shallow, my skin heating when his eyes dip to my lips for a second.

"You're welcome," he says in a soft voice.

The television flickers on, sound blaring through the apartment.

"Fucking Luca." The volume bar shows on the television as Cristian lowers it down to a non-nursing home level.

"Why did you give him a key?" I ask.

"Because he's my brother."

He says it like it's the obvious answer and I suppose to someone who grew up with three brothers so close to his age it may be.

"Anything specific you want to watch?" he asks, flipping through the channels. He tosses the remote at me, leaving it on a Kate Hudson movie. Probably because he thinks she's hot.

We sit in silence as the movie plays, every once in a while, our laughter cuts through the uncomfortable vibe. I glance at the clock on his cable box figuring I have about two more hours before the town car will leave.

Bill would never miss starting time.

———

The girl in the movie we're watching is kissing her best friend's guy. That's not true friendship. Does he think I'm the kind of girl who wants to watch a movie where a girl steals her best friend's guy? I'm a ride or die bitch. Not to mention, if I enjoyed roses and poems and romantic gestures, I'd have married my chemistry lab partner freshman year. Give me a thriller or suspense movie and I'm down, but I've managed to sit through most of this movie.

The tension between us is palpable at this point and I feel like I'm crawling out of my skin. I'm hyper-aware of the sound of him swallowing every time he takes a drink of water or the way he's been tapping the index finger on his right hand against the leather seat for the past several minutes. Every time he shifts in his seat I wonder if he's going to shift closer to me and I'm inevitably disappointed when he doesn't.

Deciding to throw self-preservation to the wind, I slide a little closer, leaving half a couch cushion between us. Cristian's gaze shifts to mine and back to the television. He's been nothing but a gentleman since he arrived at my door tonight. What I wouldn't do to see another side of him.

Refusing to let this night be a complete suckfest while I'm spending it with a guy who could model on the cover of a Men's Fitness magazine, I make a bold move. I fling one leg over his lap, sliding forward until my core is pressed to his middle. It isn't subtle, but I've never been a subtle girl.

Surprisingly, Mr. Noble's hands grip my hips and instead of pushing me off, he slides those hands up my back until his fingers are threaded through my hair and he's guiding my head toward his.

I'm not gonna lie, the move is sexy as hell and a total panty melter. Where does a nice guy who seems to always want to do the right thing learn that technique? Scratch that, I don't want to know. I might not be looking to be Mrs. Cristian Bianco someday, but I don't need to visualize him with another woman minutes before I let him steal home base.

Our lips brush and Cristian's tongue runs along the seam of my lips and I open eagerly for him, remembering the thrill of our first kiss in the forest. The slide of his tongue along mine gives birth to a million butterflies in my stomach, fluttering their wings so rapidly that I lose myself for a moment.

Damn, he's a good kisser. He's steady and firm, never keeping the same rhythm long enough to get bored. His hands don't venture out of my hair, but somehow, I'm more aroused than if he was feeling me up. He's not demanding like some guys who yank at my strands and put my head where they want it. He's not shy and timid like the guys who let me control the kiss. He's not pecking at me like a hummingbird searching for nectar. He's slow and steady and thoughtful and I've never felt more desired by any man.

He closes the kiss and a whimper I didn't intend leaks out making me appear desperate. Instead of pulling away or pushing me off his lap, his hands wrap around my face until they're holding my cheeks.

"I think you know I want you, but it's our first date." His eyes are heavy with gold flecks in his dark brown irises.

"I'm not saving myself for marriage."

His lips tip up into a grin.

He thinks I'm funny. I don't know if any guy has ever found humor in my ever-present sarcasm. It's sort of my state of being at this point. A warm feeling I won't acknowledge seeps into my chest.

"I know that, but so far our kiss was the only time I really felt like we were on this date together."

My fingers creep down to the hem of my t-shirt and lift. His gaze dips down to watch.

"Work has been distracting lately, I'm sorry, but I'm enjoying this part the best so far." I pull the cotton fabric over my head and Cristian's chest heaves with a deep breath as he watches the swell of my breasts rise and fall from my own erratic breathing.

"You're so beautiful," he whispers, running his knuckles over the crest of my breasts.

The light brush of his skin on me feels like it leaves a fire in its wake and all I want is more. More of him. More of the two of us together.

Pulling me closer, he sprinkles kisses along the swell of my breasts while he unclasps my bra, releasing me and tosses the scrap of fabric to the side. He stares at me like I'm the gates of Heaven after a lifelong stint in purgatory.

"If I was a better man..." he mumbles.

"I don't want you to be a better man tonight." I lean in farther, my teeth latching onto his earlobe as his hands cup my breasts, thumbs brushing over my nipples. "Lose yourself with me," I whisper, closing my eyes at the sensation building between my legs.

He wastes no time pinching my nipples and surprised, I rock back before finding his lips for another out of this world kiss. All the worry and fear that's been a constant in my life for months evaporates and the only question left in my mind is what Cristian Bianco will do to me next.

CHAPTER SEVEN

Cristian

*M*y dick is at full salute, ready to make an introduction. Of course it is, she fucking straddled me.

Out of nowhere.

One minute I'm watching a love scene where the couple is making out on a rooftop and the next thing I know, Vanessa's on top of me and the flowery scent of her shampoo surrounds us.

I could've pushed her off, but hello, I'm a single man and she's a hotter-than-hell female. You do the math.

Our tongues slide along one another's and instead of fighting me for control like I thought she would, she's letting me take the lead and it makes me like her even more.

Don't get me wrong, she's not a passive non-participant. Her fingers push through my hair, gripping the strands and holding my face to hers. All the blood rushes to my dick when she slides forward more, her hot center pressing on my hard length as I cup her ample breasts, tweaking her nipples between my finger and thumb.

Damn, she feels better than anyone who's come before her and we're not even to the good stuff yet. A vision of her without jeans on, her wet panties running along my bare dick implants itself in my mind.

Stop thinking. I could come in my pants from the thought alone.

Rolling her over, I press her back to the couch, nudging my hips between her legs, continuing to kiss and dry hump her like a horny teenager whose parents are asleep upstairs. Her moans tell me she doesn't mind and the sound is like the starting whistle to my over-eager libido.

My lips crave the feel of her skin. Moving my lips off of hers, I sprinkle soft open-mouthed kisses along her jaw and across her collarbone. "You're so soft," I murmur against her heated skin.

Her hips rise off the couch, and I grind my thigh into her center as she wraps herself around me. I knew waiting a month for this couch was worth it. It's big enough and deep enough for shit like this.

"Strip me," the soft plea leaves her swollen pink lips.

Hey, I'm a police officer—I know an order when I hear one. Her gold necklace falls across her neck, laying on the cushion. I lean back, my gaze devouring the swell of her breasts.

I rasp my knuckles along her side. She squirms, her eyes fluttering shut with a sigh, then I take the delicate chain off and place it on the coffee table.

Does she know how beautiful she is? How many times have I heard the guys at the station talk about her? I close my eyes, pushing their vulgar comments out of my mind because it's inducing a rage inside of me that wants to stamp her with my badge number.

"Please, Cristian." Another soft plea leaves her lips and I'm torn. I've never really been a one and done kind of guy and something tells me one time with Vanessa will not be enough. But my dick is screaming at me to get on with this— we don't need to romance her, she's not looking for Prince Charming, she's looking for a dick that will get her off and you have said dick.

I need to get out of my own fucking head.

My hand rests on the button of her jeans. I manipulate the button open and unzip the zipper, diving my hand down the front of her pants. Soaked silk panties greet me and my lips fall to her rising and falling stomach.

I drag the denim down her legs, dropping them to the floor before nestling between her thighs once again.

"Take off your shirt." She pulls at the button-down I'm wearing.

Our eyes meet over her body, an impatience in her tight lips that says she's not looking for foreplay.

What kind of woman doesn't want foreplay?

That's one of my strengths.

Following her lead, I sit back up on the couch, my hands moving to the buttons on my shirt, but she rises up to her knees, starting on the bottom set of buttons while I work my way down. We meet in the middle and she slides the fabric down over my shoulders.

"Shit, Bianco. You're fucking ripped." Her gaze takes me in, her hands explore my chest and my cock is practically throbbing in my pants.

Suddenly all the grueling training, low sugar, vegetable everything is worth it. Vanessa Flanagan drooling over my physique was worth every missed lasagna and spaghetti meal.

Her fingers dip over one ab to the next. "I can't believe you've been hiding this."

She's straddling me again and I can't deny that I want her to free me from the barrier of my pants.

"You haven't seemed interested." I cock an eyebrow at her.

"I'm interested now."

She slides back on my legs, her fingers freeing me from my pants.

My dick springs up happy to finally be invited to the party. Vanessa takes no time palming my length, cum beading at the tip quicker than I'd like. Vanessa doesn't seem to mind as she slides her thumb over it, coating my tip.

"Bianco," she whispers.

"Yeah," I say softly, taking each breast in my hands and running my thumbs over her peaked nipples. Utter perfection.

She slides closer and her wetness coats my dick. "I really need you to fuck me now." Her teeth latch onto my earlobe and she tugs.

I could've taken my time with her all night. She denied me from going down on her, now she's rushing me away from enjoying her tits.

Vanessa's attitude would be a breath of fresh air to any male out there, but still, I find myself wanting more.

Still, the lady shall get what the lady wants.

I stand up, my jeans falling to the floor. Vanessa's long legs wind around my waist. See, I knew they'd look good there.

I step out of my boxers and jeans and almost drop her once. Thank God for the push-ups I do every morning.

Carrying her down the hall only because that's where my condoms are, she kisses my shoulders, my neck, my lips. Her wetness increases and my balls tighten from my dick sliding through her folds like a damn slip and slide.

We enter my bedroom and I sit down on the bed. Vanessa doesn't get off me. Grabbing a condom from the drawer,

Vanessa snatches it from my hand, rips it open and slides it down my shaft.

Fuck she's so hot.

Inching up while we still sit on the edge of my bed, she sinks down on top of me, and I groan and try to think of anything other than the vise-like grip she has around my cock.

A low growling moan escapes her lips and she arches her back and places her hands on my thighs.

I pump my hips into her. It's a sweet form of torture being inside her. She rides me slowly, pulling in and out and circling her hips. Both our eyes are locked on where we connect and I'm still in mild shock that Vanessa is on top of me right now, having her way with me.

I wrap my arms around her, pulling her to my chest. Slow and steady just isn't doing it for me anymore. I stand up, walk two feet to pin her against the wall and grind into her depths.

Fuck, now I'm in trouble.

The slickness between us is the only noise in the room other than our labored breaths.

I'm close and I hope to hell she is, too.

My lips crash against hers and her heels dig into my ass, gaining leverage to slide up and down on me. I love it that she's an equal partner in the task of getting one another off. Her hands wrap around my neck, holding my head to hers, our tongues spearing into one another's mouth. We're both frantic in our movements and sweat drips between our bodies.

"Fuck, Bianco, I'm coming!" Her walls tighten around my dick so hard she might actually squeeze the cum out of me.

Instead of slowing down, I keep it going, my release only seconds away.

Her orgasm hits first and her head flies back against the wall, her eyelids droopy and sated.

I pull back to look at her. She's the most beautiful thing I've ever seen. Right now the thought of seeing her like this in the future and well, the drip of sweat that just fell between her tits has me coming. A few more jerks and I come with a loud groan, nestled into her neck.

I swing us around and we fall to the bed collapsing on the soft comforter. I strip off the condom, tie a knot and dump it in the trashcan beside my bed.

This is not where I thought this night was headed.

I can't believe I just slept with the Commander's daughter.

CHAPTER EIGHT

Cristian

$\mathcal{V}$anessa lays sated in my bed, not reaching for the comforter to conceal herself. She's comfortable in her own skin.

Damn. There's something so sexy about that.

Turn off the lights and I'll pass out now.

Our breathing is still working to find an even rhythm when she sits up and looks down at me. "Take me home?" she asks, rolling to the side of the bed then standing.

And there you have it, folks. The true mark of a one-time fling. She can't even stick around for round two.

No way the best sex of my life is her worst.

I sit up, resting my elbows on my thighs and nod.

She heads out of my room, her delectable ass both a sweet goodbye and a kick in the ass reminder that I won't be seeing it again.

Fuck, maybe I should've taken my time, because I already want her again. Well, my dick wants her again.

Raising from the bed, I follow her down the hall. She's

rounding into the family room when I hear a key insert into the door.

I'm gonna kill Luca.

"Cristian?" Vanessa's eyes are wide and her tone is panicked.

I run, just as the door starts to open a bit, but I slam it shut right before I can see who it is.

"What the fuck?" a male voice says. I don't know if it's Mauro or Luca, but it's one of my brothers.

I secure the latch so he can't get in.

"Get dressed," I whisper-yell to Vanessa as I race down the hall to the bedroom to grab my own clothes. I reach down and grab something off the floor, quickly stepping into them.

"Yeah, um... those are mine." Vanessa stands in the doorway half-dressed and pointing at me.

I look down to see I'm stepping into her pink silk panties.

Great last impression.

"Shit, yeah." I slide them off and hand them to her.

"Was that a sly way of trying to keep my panties?" She giggles, putting them on herself and then looking around for her jeans.

I'm shrugging into my shirt when I spot them.

Bang, Bang.

"Let me the fuck in!"

It's Mauro. That's clear now. Luca would've climbed the outdoor fire staircase already.

"Give me a damn minute!" I yell back down the hall.

I toss Vanessa her jeans and button up my own shirt in an attempt to make it look like we didn't just roll out of bed, though I guarantee Mauro's going to know exactly what went down here.

The banging starts up again and stops abruptly. Now all I

can hear is Maddie fighting with Mauro about giving me some privacy. Great, she's here, too.

I wait for Vanessa to finish dressing but even so, her hair screams that she's been well and thoroughly fucked, which sadly gives me a caveman feeling of pride in my chest.

I point to her hair, wordlessly, and she starts finger combing it.

"I'm good," she says, out of breath when she's done.

I leave the bedroom and walk over to the door unlatching it, turning the knob to let them in.

"About fucking time." Mauro's eyes are murderous as he steps in and then impatiently looks over his shoulder at Maddie.

"Yes, I'm Mauro's girlfriend." I glance out in the hall to find Maddie talking to Mrs. Johnson from across the hall.

She tries to put her hand out in greeting, but Mrs. Johnson won't let that cat out of her arms.

"You woke up Mr. Whiskers. I'll never get him back to sleep," the old woman says.

"Oh, we're sorry." Maddie cringes, looking back to us. She holds her hands out. "Maybe I could."

"Don't do it," Mauro mumbles under his breath.

The cat hisses and shows her all of his teeth, making Maddie jump back two feet.

"He doesn't like women," Mrs. Johnson says and it's clear she doesn't have her fake teeth in.

"Oh, only you I suppose."

Seriously, leave it to Maddie to try to sweet talk the meanest lady in Chicago.

"Madison," Mauro's impatience shines through in his tone.

She doesn't even look back, holding up her finger. "We're sorry, Mrs. Johnson, it won't happen again."

"Says you. They have parties every night there and that one brings girls around giggling in the hallway at 3 am."

She points to Mauro and Maddie glares back like she's going to kill him.

Mauro holds his hands up in the air. "I've been with you every night."

He has a point. I'm not even sure who she's talking about. The hell if it's me. I wish it was. It's probably Luca, and he doesn't even live here.

"Well, you know single men," Maddie says but leans in closer like Mauro and I can't hear her. "It wasn't the big one, right?" she asks, pointing between my brother and me.

"Mad," Mauro says like 'what the fuck you don't believe me.'

Mrs. Johnson appraises us, squinting her eyes. "No, not the big one."

"Mauro is not the big one!" He might have one inch on me, but I guarantee I'd beat him in a foot race.

Mauro's hand clasps my shoulder. "My girlfriend's smart. She knows I'm bigger." He winks, his sour mood lightening.

"Cristian," Vanessa says from behind me and without looking I can hear that she's irritated.

Mauro's eyes widen, shifting to her, back to me, back to her, and then finally meets my gaze again with a smirk on his lips.

"Mad," he says again to urge her into the apartment.

She smiles sweetly over to him and continues to listen to Mrs. Johnson talk about her dead husband. I guess I never thought about her being married. Kind of didn't think anyone could stand her enough to want to put a ring on it.

"I better get going. Nice talking to you and I promise to tell Cristian to stop bringing home those giggly girls. They're not the type his mom would want him to settle down with." Maddie reaches forward and touches her arm because

Maddie's a toucher and surprisingly Mrs. Johnson smiles and Mr. Whiskers doesn't attack her.

"Nice meeting you, Maddie. Good luck with the house."

What the hell? The old witch hates us, but Maddie spends five minutes with her and she's smiling, gums and all.

"Bye Mrs. Johnson," I say, waving.

She narrows her eyes and shuts the door, five locks clicking into place.

"I don't understand why you guys don't like her?" Maddie walks by both Mauro and me into the apartment.

She's in a pair of fleece M&M pants with a shirt that says, 'Always kiss your firefighter goodnight,' courtesy of my ma I'm sure.

"Oh." Maddie stops short, and Mauro runs smack into her.

Steadying himself by placing his hands on her hips, he steps to the side.

"Hey Vanessa," he says, walking down the hall toward his bedroom.

"Van, what are you doing here?" Maddie looks between the two of us, waiting for one of us to answer.

Vanessa smiles and shoves her hands in her back pockets, effectively pushing her tits out. Oh, was I the only one who noticed that?

"We were just watching a movie," Vanessa says.

"Come on, Mad!" Mauro yells from his room.

A blind person could tell that something more happened here than movie watching. Thankfully, it's Maddie and not Lauren walking into this scene. Maddie's polite enough to not add drama to the tense situation by calling us out.

"Don't you guys have a house?" I ask her.

Vanessa shoots me an impatient look.

"Something's wrong with the heater. His apartment is

closer and he's working in the morning. So here we are." She shrugs both shoulders.

"MAD!" Mauro screams.

"Relax, you're going to piss off Mrs. Johnson," she yells back down the hall. She looks between both of us and lowers her voice. "I think he's upset he couldn't fix it."

"Stop talking about me like I can't hear you!" he hollers and Vanessa giggles.

"He really does have good hearing," she says directly to Vanessa, so I assume this is something they've discussed before. "I told you," she mouths wordlessly to her friend. "I love him though, and he's excellent in bed," she says in a loud voice this time.

"Get in my bed and I'll remind you how excellent again," Mauro yells.

"He's too much." Vanessa giggles again.

"Yes, I am, Vanessa!"

Maddie rolls her eyes. "Anyway, I guess I'll leave you guys to the...movie was it?"

"Yeah, you know that one where the girl steals her friend's boyfriend." Vanessa is trying to explain the movie we started watching like Maddie believes the story. "The one with Kate Hudson."

"Oh yeah, I love that one. It has the guy from The Office in it, too, right?" Maddie shows no sign of joining Mauro.

"I'm taking Vanessa home now," I chime in to end this awkward situation.

"Okay. Well, I better get to bed." Maddie starts walking backward down the hall.

"Yes, you should. Your stud of a boyfriend is waiting on you, naked if it were my guess," I say.

Maddie's face turns bright red. "He was only joking."

"No, I'm not," Mauro calls out.

"He is," she insists and I raise my eyebrows.

Another key in the door sounds from the lock, freezing Maddie in her steps before she reaches the bedroom.

Vanessa blows out an exasperated breath and looks up at the ceiling.

"We're closed, asshole!" I yell because there's only one other person it could be at this time of night.

"Funny, jackass," Luca walks in like he owns the place and the only good thing about it is that he's alone. "What's going on here?" He takes in the scene, breaks the distance across the family room floor, ignoring myself and Maddie. "I'm Luca," he says, holding out his hand to Vanessa.

"Vanessa," she smiles, a little too wide for my liking.

"Luca's my little brother," I fill in, putting a heavy enunciation on little.

"Younger actually," he says.

"No, little."

"Fuck you. You're a quarter inch taller." Luca shifts his gaze away from Vanessa and heads to the fridge.

"I'm the tallest in case anyone was wondering," Mauro calls out. "Mad, the big guy is getting sleepy."

Luca cracks open a soda that was left over from Mauro, for which I'm thankful. The soda's been teasing me in there all week.

"Luca's here," Maddie says.

A long drawn out groan sounds from down the hall.

"He's getting restless in there." I point to Mauro's old bedroom.

Maddie shrugs.

"I thought you two were cohabitating in your love nest?" Luca props himself up on the breakfast bar, showing no sign of leaving.

"Don't *you* have your own place?" Maddie asks with a sweet smile.

Luca winks and tips his soda can at her. "The bar was a

bust. Figured I'd take my chances of Cristian being up and not jerking off."

Vanessa's gaze searches mine out and I try to fight back a smile.

"Oh no worries there, we walked in on him and Vanessa banging," Mauro shouts from the bedroom.

A huge grin overtakes Luca's face and he looks between Vanessa and me.

"Why don't you just come out here and join the conversation?" Maddie calls out to Mauro.

"Because I'm waiting to fuck my girlfriend!"

Maddie giggles.

"I thought when you settled down you made love, not fuck?" Luca asks her and the commitment-phobe actually looks like his question is serious.

Maddie narrows her eyes and shakes her head at him.

"You need to leave," I say. "Maddie and Mauro are going to bed and I'm taking Vanessa home."

Luca doesn't move. "Is Uber shut down?"

All three of us stare at him in confusion.

He shrugs. "Why do you need to drive her home? Isn't that why Uber was invented?"

"You're such an idiot." I shake my head at him.

"No wonder Lauren won't go out with you." Vanessa gives Maddie a hug before meeting me by the door where I grab my keys.

"That's not why she won't go out with me," Luca says.

All three of us rest our eyes on him questioning his comment.

He hops down like he didn't leave us hanging. "I'll take Vanessa home."

"No." My response is instant.

"Great, it will save Cristian a trip." Vanessa leaves my side for my brother's.

Not gonna lie. That was like a sucker punch to my ego.

"Why would you take Vanessa home?" Maddie asks, the skepticism in her tone matching my thinking.

"I'll fucking take her home if it gets you in my bed faster," Mauro chimes in.

I'm surprised he's still awake.

"No need, Mauro. Go in there and screw your boyfriend before he has to rely on his hand." Vanessa points to Maddie. "Luca can take me home and try to have a run-in with Lauren."

"What?" Luca looks back at her like she's got five heads. "I'll be dropping you off at the curb so I don't have to see Hunt."

We all know different, but no one says anything about the love/hate thing they have going on.

"Cristian you take her," Maddie urges.

I step forward but Vanessa places her hand on my chest and it's with a very different feeling to it than half an hour ago.

"I'm a big girl, Maddie."

"Maybe I should go with you." Maddie moves to the door, sliding on her shoes.

"No, you shouldn't babe."

Maddie holds up her finger. "Hold on one second."

She only gets halfway down the hall when Mauro walks out of his bedroom in his boxer briefs, wrapping his arms around Maddie and dragging her into his room. She giggles and then says something to him I can't hear.

"Let's go." I swing the keys around my finger.

"Cristian, you stay here. It's fine," Vanessa says. "If you want I'll text you when I get inside my place."

"How am I the one getting screwed in this situation?" Mauro asks as he re-enters the hall, throwing up his arms as

Maddie kisses him bye and heads in the opposite direction of his bed.

"Mad, no," Vanessa groans.

"It's fine. He's got an early shift tomorrow and needs his sleep. And I get a little alone time with you." She swings her arm through Vanessa's.

At least Vanessa won't be alone with Luca.

"I can't sleep without you," Mauro whines.

"You do it every third day," Maddie blows him a kiss.

"I hate both you fuckers. I was a happy kid until Ma said she had a baby in her belly." He flips them off and disappears into his room. "Love you, babe. I'll send a guy over to the house tomorrow for the heater," he calls out before shutting his door.

"Come on Luca, we'll wait for Vanessa outside," Maddie says. "But keep your voice down. Mrs. Johnson's already complained tonight."

Luca opens the door.

"You better guard my girl with your life, Luca," Mauro yells through his bedroom door.

Luca shakes his head not even entertaining a response to our brother.

When Maddie and Luca are out the door, Vanessa doesn't let the door shut all the way. She glances at Mauro's bedroom door.

"Thanks for dinner, Cristian. This was nice." She smiles.

"You're welcome."

Before I can say anything else, she's out the door with no goodnight kiss, no discussion of a second date, nothing. I guess this is how adults do a one and done.

I'll be honest—I'm not a fan.

CHAPTER NINE

Vanessa

"So you're doing the nasty with my brother?" Luca asks as we settle into his car—a lime green Dodge Charger that screams 'look at me.'

I let Maddie have the front because I need to process everything that happened tonight and sitting next to another Bianco isn't going to make that any easier.

"Yes, for some time now." Maddie laughs.

"Yeah, nope. Not talking about you." His eyes find mine through the rearview mirror. "I was talking to the one with just fucked hair."

I squint my eyes in displeasure. Luca's a show off right down to this ridiculous car. I mean we live in Chicago. He's probably one of those guys who has their winter car and their summer car.

"That's none of your business," Maddie whispers to him as if I can't hear her.

She's known Luca since they went to high school together. Hence the whole Lauren and Luca love/hate relationship.

After tonight I see exactly why she doesn't want to date him. I wouldn't either.

"He's my brother," Luca says as he pulls out onto the street. "I think it's only fair that I ask what her intentions are." He chuckles to himself.

Maddie shoots me apologetic look over her shoulder. Maybe it's a good thing she came tonight.

"We had a date. Now it's over," I say.

"Shit. No way my brother is that douchey in bed. Is he selfish? Didn't he muff dive first?"

"LUCA!" Maddie punches him in the shoulder.

Luca only laughs and turns onto another street. "What? It's a legit question. Trust me, Mauro would want to know if Cristian's giving us a bad name out there."

"First of all, all Mauro should be concerning himself with is if I" —she points to herself— "am feeling neglected which is none of your business, but for the record, I'm pretty sure your brother is a much more giving lover than yourself."

Luca tries to interject, but Maddie cuts him off.

"Second, nothing about Cristian screams selfish. I'm sure he performed oral sex before doing the deed."

I definitely would have remembered if his face had been between my thighs. A girl doesn't forget something like that. Truth is that we were both so desperate for each other that there wasn't any time for that. As I sink into the memories of tonight, I'm focused on the feel of his callused palms running the length of my body. His lips and tongue and how they felt on my skin. How I struggled to keep my eyes open because I've never felt so worshiped. The memory of the way he drove into me with my back pressed against the wall, has me clenching my thighs.

Damn, maybe I should've stayed the night. What would have been the big deal? One time versus one night.

"You make it sound like a science experiment. Come on

Maddie, I'd put money on the fact that you're a dirty talker. Just say the word cock for me."

"You should be happy your brother isn't in this car with us." Maddie shakes her head.

"I'm not scared of Mauro."

"Why don't we talk about the sky?" I interject, wanting to talk about anything other than sex with these two. "Look at the clouds up there." I look up out of the sunroof.

"Maybe you are right for Cris if you'd rather talk about the stars and moon instead of fucking."

Luca turns down our street. Thank God the town car isn't there. I haven't even listened to the messages yet.

"As enlightening as this drive has been, I think I can speak for both of us when I say that we're happy it's over. Enjoy the rest of your night, Luca." Maddie opens up the car door and I eagerly wait for her to climb out and fold the seat forward for me.

Maddie's shuts the door. "Oh shit. Kill the lights, Luca."

"I know I said I wasn't scared of Mauro, but I'm pretty sure if I stole his girl away from him he'd rip me apart limb by limb."

Maddie gives him her classic 'what the fuck is wrong with you' look.

"No. Look." She points out the window to our place a couple houses down, where Lauren and some guy are standing by the door, talking awfully close. "She must have had a date."

"She told me she was going out with friends," I whisper, inching up from the backseat to get a better view to shamelessly spy on my best friend.

"Who's that douche canoe?" Luca kills the lights and for the first time since we got in the car, he's quiet.

"I don't know. Do you know him, Vanessa?" Maddie asks.

"No, but he's hot. Good catch."

"I'm a good catch," Luca snips. "Look at his fucking outfit. Could his pants be any tighter?"

"Sounds like someone might be jealous," I sing-song which earns me Luca's annoyed glare over his shoulder.

"Why would I be jealous? I hate Hunt."

"The fact you can't even say her first name says you don't," I say.

Maddie snickers in the front seat.

"Hey, you're practically my sister-in-law, you should have my back. Family always comes first." He nudges her with his shoulder.

"No ring on this finger." She holds up her left hand. "Not to mention, real friends *are* family." She puts her palm up and I smack it because she's right.

"Hate to break it to you, but friends ends with end and family ends with i.l.y.," Luca says.

Maddie takes her eyes off our front door and we both stare at him with an expression I'm thinking will always be reserved for him. One that suggests he's really not saying that.

"I.l.y. stands for I love you. So, you're family and therefore have to be on my side," he says matter-of-factly.

Maddie laughs, buckling over in the seat, slapping the interior of the car. "I swear you're still able to surprise me."

"Look!" I point to the window.

The guy is bending forward, Lauren gradually inching toward him. They're going to kiss. I haven't seen her with a guy in months so either she's been hiding this one or this is their first date. His hand reaches up and cups her cheek, the shine of the porch light glinting off his blond hair.

"Aw." Maddie, the girl who can't get enough romance in her life, rests her head on the back of her seat. I'm sure she's got those love-sick eyes going like she does when Mauro enters a room.

"It's sweet and I feel horrible watching this, but it's perfection. It's nighttime with a slight chill, the darkened street with one light above them. It's like a movie where the guy drops the girl off at the door. So romantic." Even I'm eating up Maddie's words as she sets the scene that's right in front of us.

"Here it comes." I sit up straighter in my seat. The guy's hand slides into her hair and he tilts his head down.

HONK!

I jump.

Maddie jumps.

"What the?" I ask.

"My hand slipped." Luca's cheeks are flushed. He shrugs.

All six of our eyes shift to the couple we were just admiring. They've backed away from each other now. Lauren spots us or at least the car. Does she know what car Luca drives?

"I think we should get out so she knows it's us," I say.

Maddie fumbles for the door handle. "Yeah." She opens the door. "Thanks for the ride, Luca." She kisses his cheek and climbs out.

"Tell Hunt I'm sorry for fucking up her goodnight kiss," he says.

"Are you really sorry?" I raise both my eyebrows and climb out of the car.

Luca says nothing. Maddie's already halfway up the sidewalk where a relieved Lauren turns her attention away from her date to her.

"Don't worry big guy, your secret is safe with me," I whisper.

"Whatever you're thinking, you're wrong."

I wink. "Am I though?"

I shut the door but Luca's springs open. His gaze isn't on me though, but rather on Lauren. The energy in the dark night intensifies as the two of them stare at one another.

Oh, I am so right on this.

"You're the moron who honked his horn?" Lauren puts both hands on her hips.

"Sorry Hunt, hand slipped."

Luca's usual cocky smirk appears and he's transformed into a different man than who I saw just minutes ago—the man who realized I might've figured out his biggest secret and told the world. But I don't roll like that. One day he'll have to man up and fight for what he wants.

Maddie might be about hearts and flowers—and M&Ms —but fighting for the other person, that's romance to me.

"Yeah right." Lauren turns to her date and soon he's walking away from the house while Maddie is headed inside.

I file up the stairs, passing Lauren's now confused date. "You should go give Luca a piece of your mind," I murmur to Lauren as I pass and join Maddie in the house.

"I can do it from right here." Her gaze is glued to the youngest Bianco brother who's still standing in the opening of his car door.

"Night, Hunt," he calls out.

We all get inside and either everyone is too worked up to talk, or we're all figuring out what to do now. Maddie ends up sleeping with Lauren since her bed is at their new house. I end up sleeping alone, tossing and turning the entire night trying to push away the memories of Cristian's heated gaze while he slammed into me.

He's not at all what I expected. I knew he'd be able to get me off, but I never thought he'd make me want him again.

As long as I stay away from him, I should be in the clear.

CHAPTER TEN

Vanessa

*L*auren jumps on my bed. "It's Cheapster Day. Get up lazy!" She continues to hop up and down, her legs weaving around my body. Thank goodness she's athletic.

Cheapster Challenge is something we made up back in our college days. We all head out to Nordstrom Rack and find the lowest priced item we can that's the most fashionable and whoever wins gets a frozen yogurt. We haven't had a challenge in forever since Maddie had the house and I was busy trying to earn some cash. I couldn't really spare twenty or fifty dollars on this challenge. But with all that behind me now, I can't wait to spend a little time with my girls.

I can tell by Lauren's excitement that she missed me as much as I missed them. It sucked lying to them but now it's over and I can actually enjoy starting my life after college.

"Get off my bed please," I whine because although I'm excited, ten more minutes of sleep would be nice.

"Come on. Mauro's on shift and Maddie promised to bring him some lunch after."

I sit up in my bed. "Why is Mauro interrupting our day?" I wipe the sleep from my eyes, fixing my ponytail.

"Because she's in love. Can we really complain though? She's taking us to a firehouse." Lauren collapses on the bed and her eyes do a flutter.

"Then I guess I need to look extra good," I joke because honestly, I don't need a boyfriend, just someone to fill my nights every now and again. With the new line I need to get ready, I won't have time for anything else.

She propels herself off the bed, leaving my room, and I hear her bothering Maddie a second later, quizzing her on Mauro's fireman friends. I guess the guy who was dropping her off last night was worth a kiss but not a second date.

I grab my phone from my nightstand, pressing the button to see that my dad sent me a message last night at one in the morning.

Dad: *Hey, sweetie. How about dinner tonight? Meet me at the station at five?*
Me: *Sure, Daddy.*

Immediately the three dots appear. Sometimes I think he has some special notification when I text him. I tell myself that because the thought that I'm one of his only contacts and that's how he knows it's me, pains me.

Dad: *Great. I can't wait to hear how your training is going. I was hoping we could both run it this year.*

By it, he means the charity 5k that we've done every year since I was born. Yes, every year. Stan's Donut Run raises money for the Greater Chicago Food Depository, something that was near and dear to my mom's heart. The bonus is that they have donut stations throughout the race and if you're the fastest you receive a year's worth of donuts. I'll never be first, but a girl can dream.

Problem is, I haven't trained for the past two years. I've walked, letting my dad continue the run, and he's been upset. He wants us to cross the line together. Which means I need to hustle because he really doesn't ask for much. Well, other than every spare minute, but he's a widow and I'm all he has around here.

I blow out a long breath, knowing the only solution is to get my ass in gear as I scroll through my calendar, finding that the race is in two weeks—right before Thanksgiving. I stare at my running shoes in my closet, shake my head and hop in the shower. Why do something I can put off until tomorrow?

———

An hour later, the three of us enter Nordstrom Rack.

"See you in thirty." Lauren's wearing her game face as she heads off, weaving through the clothes. God, she is so competitive.

"She'll play dirty, watch your back," I say to Maddie who is already veering toward the accessories.

Not a bad play. She's nailed us plenty with makeup palettes in the past, but I see her pause and look at the jewelry. No way she's thinking that she'll beat us on that.

As for me? I zero in on the shoe department.

I head to the clearance area because I'm secretly hoping that the lucky shopper urban myth is true and I'll find something for a penny. Didn't you know? When employees are scanning and tagging items, if an item has been on clearance for a long time and they're getting ready to ship it to the warehouse, they mark the item down to a penny. If you get it before an employee takes it off the rack, they'll honor the price. This has never happened to me, but you never know.

Heading to the tens because yes, I'm five eight and if I had those cute size six and a half feet like Lauren, I'd topple over. I find a pair of Hunter rain boots. They'd be more of a find if it was spring, but then again that's the reason they're on clearance. Plus, I'm not exactly loving the pink and blue flower design.

Scrapping that idea, I continue down the shoe aisle but quickly come to the end finding nothing.

As I head out of the abyss of shoes and into the main area, I spot Lauren rummaging through dresses. Yes, we have thirty minutes, but the girl is acting like there are swarms of women around vying for bridal gowns.

I don't spot Maddie and I highly suspect she's off on the phone with Mauro in some corner. If he's not on a call. They really are cute together. I wonder if I'll ever find that or better yet if I even *want* to find what they have. That would involve being vulnerable and an investment of the heart. The heart is fragile and I'm not sure I'm ready to risk mine.

"Stop spying." Lauren jumps out in front of me.

"Relax you little monkey."

She heads off to the fitting room so I mosey on over to the clothing department, knowing I'm probably not going to find anything marked down low enough.

"Done." Maddie surprises me, her bag clasped in her hands.

"Rules are you wait outside," I tell her, pointing my finger at the door.

"I had them double bag it so you can't see, plus what does it matter since I already bought my item?" She puts on that innocent 'trust me' face I always seem to fall for.

"True, I suppose."

"No shoes huh?" She's familiar with my M.O.

"Nothing."

As much as I want to be with my friends, shopping isn't doing it for me. I'm not competitive like Lauren who's probably stripping down like Zac Efron is naked and ready for her back there. I shop because I love fashion and putting different looks together.

"Maybe you should try home goods?" Maddie suggests.

I nod, knowing it might be my best option at this point.

"So, have you talked to Cristian?" she asks, following me over.

"No."

He hasn't even called me which, if I'm honest, surprised me. I thought he'd try at least one attempt. I mean the sex was worth at least one call for a try at round two, right?

Though I didn't call him either.

"I know he's been training hard," she says.

"Training?"

We end up at the home goods area, neither one of us investing much energy in searching through the clearance bin.

She picks up a picture frame. "He's a Spartan racer." She gingerly places the picture frame down in the pile where the glass will likely break soon.

"Spartan racer?" What the hell does that mean? I grab a cute mug with the saying, 'This might be vodka.' This won't win me the challenge, but I like the sentiment. "I think I should go to handbags."

We start in the direction of the handbags which is the opposite direction of home goods so we have to pass Lauren in the clothing area, who is trying on a tank top over the top of her clothes.

"That's not feasible. It's November in Chicago. No one is

wearing tank tops." Maddie glances at her watch. "Oh, and you have ten minutes."

Lauren does the whole two fingers pointing to her eyes and then two fingers at us. Like we're scared of her. Well, most of the time we're not scared of her.

Maddie and I giggle and head to the clearance bin in the back of the high-end purse department. My hand grazes across a Marc Jacobs bag as we pass. One day I'll be able to afford you. One day.

"It's an obstacle race thingy." Maddie puts a purse over her shoulder, pretending to model it.

"Cute," I remark at the small black purse that would go great with a date night dress. "Obstacles? I don't get it."

She puts the purse back in the bin, inspecting another. Meanwhile, the clock is ticking and I have nothing to purchase. "It's a race. Like running and I think he has teammates or something. I don't really know, but Mauro keeps making sure I'm available Sunday to go watch him."

"Huh." I move over to wallets.

"Lauren probably knows what they are."

"I know what?" Lauren walks over with a Nordstrom Rack bag in her hands, which means I'm the odd girl out. I swipe a small coin purse knowing I'll be buying someone's Froyo in five minutes.

"The Spartan thing that Cristian does," Maddie says.

Bypassing them I head to the register because I only have a few minutes before I have to forfeit. I don't really care about the challenge today, but I'm not about to lay down and admit defeat.

"I didn't know he was a Spartan." The admiration in her tone piques my interest.

It shouldn't since I'm the one giving him the cold shoulder.

"That's what Mauro said. We're going to his race on Sunday. Want to come?"

"Will asshat be there?" Lauren asks.

"I don't know. I'm assuming yes, but maybe he has to work."

"I'm still pissed at him. I just know that Klein would have been a good kisser. He had minty breath and everything. Luca screwed it up for me on purpose."

I keep my gaze focused ahead, not wanting to give away that Luca Bianco is hiding some affectionate feelings under his dislike for Lauren, I just know it.

"You should come, too, Van," Lauren says.

I know they just did some kind of elbow knocking, 'you ask, no you ask' thing behind me. Lauren's more outspoken and pushy so she's the one who did the asking. I'm not sure why they're both so invested in the idea of Cristian and I being a thing.

"He'll be all muddy and sweaty and muscly," Lauren says in a sing-song voice.

"That doesn't sound appealing," I lie and move forward to the cash register.

Not that I have to worry—neither one of them is looking at their watches—they're too concerned about my love life.

"Then it shouldn't be a problem for you to come." Lauren saddles up to my side as Maddie takes a phone call by the door.

"I don't know, I have plans."

The cashier scans the change purse and asks if I'd like a bag.

"That was Mauro," Maddie says, joining us with a smile on her face. "He said we can all go down together, and head over to his mom's house after for Sunday dinner."

"I'm out!" Lauren throws her hands in the air and walks away.

"Come on, it'll be fun." Maddie follows Lauren out of the store as I hand the cashier my credit card.

I need to figure a reason to get out of this and fast. Cristian all sweaty and dirty with his ripped muscles on display for all to see? I might as well run the Spartan race myself if I want to subject myself to that level of torture.

CHAPTER ELEVEN

Cristian

"How many miles did you do yesterday?" Tara, another Spartan, asks me while we're signing in for the race.

"I did five."

"Show off. I took a rest." She pushes me playfully, making me lose my balance for a second.

Tara is a flirt and I'm not the only guy whose attention she tries to grab. I'm fairly sure it only takes a six pack and a set of balls to score her high pitched voice and light touches.

"Anyone coming to watch?" she asks.

"My family is coming. Well, my brothers and..." I fail to mention Mauro saying Maddie told him Vanessa and Lauren might show and how Ma is preparing some big meal for afterward.

Ma won't be at the race because there's mud everywhere and it's in the middle of nowhere, but she'll praise me whether I come in first or last. She's the best.

"Oh, family. I thought maybe a girlfriend."

Do women really think the male species is stupid? I get where's she's going with this.

"No girlfriend." I unzip my sweatshirt.

"Oh, I would've thought—"

"CRIS!" Luca is a lifesaver. Today at least.

I glance over to find him walking up the path.

"Sorry, I need to go say hi to my brother. Good luck today, Tara." I wave, already increasing the distance between us.

Her eyes take Luca in and the small smile on her lips says he could be her next victim. I'm used to women looking from me to my brothers and vice versa.

"What's up?" We do a fist bump and I take in his shorts and t-shirt with a hoodie over the top. He's wearing his gym shoes and his Bulls hat.

"What's up? You're about to make me look weak." He laughs.

When I started Spartan races, my brothers were the first ones I asked to train with me. Neither of them found any interest in it. Mauro is more of a weights guy and Luca is still thriving on his fast metabolism and boxing when he has time. Other than the three of us playing recreational hockey and softball, our interests lie in different areas.

"Sorry about the other night," his voice is more serious now.

"What did you do?" The corner of my lips turns up waiting to hear what mess he's gotten himself into now.

"The way I volunteered to take Vanessa home. I shouldn't have..."

I shake my head. It's been a little over a week and I've talked myself out of making a fool of myself over that girl a few times by now. I've had to settle for beating off to the memory of sinking inside of her. I've never been so in the moment with someone before.

"Don't sweat it. I'm over her." I wave him off.

He cocks an eyebrow and his lips tip up in a sly grin.

"Really I am. I'm not gonna chase some girl who's made it clear that she doesn't want me."

"But the sex? Hot?" He waggles his eyebrows.

I'm not a kiss and tell guy and I'm certainly not going to start now when she might be arriving in ten minutes time.

"None of your business."

He slaps me on the shoulder, harder than usual. "Of course it was, she's gorgeous and you got the whole taboo thing going with her dad being your boss. I bet it was smokin'."

There you have it. My brother, ladies and gentlemen.

"I better go stretch. Thanks for coming."

"So you're not pissed?" he asks before I have a chance to escape.

I shake my head "No. I might not be looking for the mother of my future children, but I'm not chasing a fuck buddy."

He nods in understanding although I'm not sure he's ever had that problem in his entire life.

"See you at the finish line," I say.

"We'll be waiting." Luca shoves his hands in the pockets of his shorts, looking over his shoulder.

I jog back over to the race and start stretching, convincing myself once again that Vanessa isn't worth my time and will only bring trouble into my life. But even I'm not naïve enough to think that it could all fly out the window the moment I see her again.

———

It took about a millisecond before the words I told Luca crumbled after seeing Vanessa walk up. She's her usual fashionable self in tall rain boots, dark jeans that hug her hips, and a too short fleece cover. Her hair looks adorable in braids on either side of her head. As much as I try to deny it to myself, she's gorgeous dressed up, dressed down, naked, pretty much any which way.

"Are those your brother's girlfriends?" Tara asks, stretching her leg out next to me.

My buddy, Ian, jabs me in the back. His own secret code for here she goes again. Ian didn't have a girlfriend when we started, and he was the star in Tara's eye until his now-girlfriend tackled him after a win last year and kissed him. It's now his Instagram pic.

"One is. Mauro, the one with the firefighter jacket, is my older brother and his girlfriend is the brunette with the ponytail. The other two women are her best friends."

Tara looks them over trying to act sly, but I see her lips tip down. All three of the women are knockouts. Not that Tara isn't. She's got that cute girl-next-door look, with her dark hair and dark eyes. Unfortunately, I love light hair and light eyes. All the way back to my first girlfriend in the second grade.

"Nice of them to come." She bends over, turning her body so her ass is in my face. She's got a nice ass. Not as nice as Vanessa's, but she is a Spartan after all. You don't train that hard and not get rewarded with a great ass.

"Yeah. You have anyone here?" I ask.

"Maybe a boyfriend?" Ian chimes in, already snickering.

Not cool of him, but she is constantly asking us about our relationship status.

"No. I decided it's just easier if I come by myself. Nobody in my family really understands and..." Her words trail off as the announcement comes over the speakers that the race is about to start.

I get what Tara is saying without her even finishing. There's a shit-ton more pressure on my shoulders with my family in the stands. But I appreciate the support.

All the participants congregate by the starting area, waiting for the signal.

Ian elbows me. "Let's make this interesting."

I'm already determined to win in front of my family and Vanessa, so if I get a little something extra out of it than why the hell not. "What did you have in mind?"

"I have this parking ticket..."

"Yeah, nice try."

He laughs. "If I win, you agree to go to Colorado."

Ian loves Spartan so much he wants to travel the world to do the races, but I have my job and I have hockey and my family.

"If I win you stop asking me." I hold out my hand.

"Sure." He shrugs.

I don't really believe he's telling me the truth. I shoot him an expression that suggests I know he's full of shit.

"Fine, I have two tickets to see Kevin Hart when he's in town. They're yours if you beat me."

I hold my hand out. "Deal."

He holds my hand in his grip. "No backing out if you lose. You go to Colorado and be my partner."

I tighten my grip and nod. "I don't back out on bets, but I hope you got good seats for Kevin Hart. I'm not a nosebleed kind of guy."

Ian laughs, releasing my hand and readying himself to start.

"What's so funny?" Tara asks us.

"Just a friendly bet."

The announcer comes over the loudspeaker telling us to get in our ready positions. I push all pressure of the bet aside.

There's only one reason I want to win this race and that's the satisfaction of showing Vanessa exactly what she's missing out on.

CHAPTER TWELVE

Vanessa

*I*t took all of five minutes for me to realize the *real* reason Maddie dragged me here. Less than that if I'm truthful, but when it comes to Cristian Bianco, I prefer to lie. It's safer.

Watching Cristian sprint across the starting line, hop over a wall with what looks like little effort and race into the forest was hot. Like crossing my legs to tame the tingling between my thighs hot. He's wearing shorts and those compression pants along with a tight sleeveless shirt that showcases his strong biceps.

"Did you see that first guy?" some girl in front of us says to her friend.

Lauren jabs her elbow into my ribs. I scowl and rub my side. She shifts her gaze from me to the girls in front of us.

"That's Cristian. Ian wants to partner up with him."

"I don't blame him. He needs to be snatched up before someone else steals him away." The redhead paws at her friend with her five inch long nails.

"Maybe I should set you up?" the other girl suggests.

"There's no maybe about it. You've been holding out on me."

Lauren jabs me again. For the love of all that is holy.

"I'd prefer not to have a bruise there," I whisper to Lauren.

"Okay, I'll talk to Ian. From what I know, he's a great guy. Chicago police officer." The girl waggles her eyebrows at her friend.

The friend's eyes widen and she holds out her wrists. "Cuff me. Order me to do naughty things."

Ugh. I stick my finger down my throat. Lauren laughs, but her face still holds that smug expression that says I'd better hurry up and claim him.

"You're so bad," the friend says.

"It's impossible to behave around men like that. He could frisk me any time," the redhead continues.

I roll my eyes.

"I'm not sure Cristian is like that. I mean he's not really the one-night stand kind of guy."

"All men are the one-night stand kind of guys," the she-lion insists.

I tend to agree with her even if I don't like her.

"Not Ian. He wanted a relationship right from the start," the friend says with pride.

"That's because Ian knew he was trading up with you."

Lauren snickers next to me and when the girl turns around, she hits Maddie in the arm.

"What?" Maddie's head twists away from Mauro.

The girl turns back around thinking Lauren's snicker was to our other friend. I shoot her a friendly smile and all is back to normal in the bleachers.

"I don't get it, we can't see shit." Lauren stands, peering into the woods like she has binoculars or something.

"He'll come through there and we can go to see him at those six obstacles," Luca volunteers the information.

Lauren ignores him, but grabs my arm, prying me from the seats and walking down the stairway. "We're getting closer," she says to Maddie and the guys.

"Um, wait for me." Maddie follows us.

The three of us head down, and I can hear the guys footsteps descend after us.

"Well, hello there," the redhead drawls behind us, probably scoping out the other two Bianco brothers.

Maddie swings her arm through Mauro's, but Mauro quickly places his arm around her shoulders and gives her a kiss on the temple, murmuring something that makes her blush. This is now a regular occurrence with the two of them I try my best to ignore.

"Why are we going over here? I was fine on the bleachers," I whine, slowing my pace.

"I can't listen to that girl anymore and I swear I'll knee Cristian in the nuts if he goes out with her. Plus, we're here to watch him race. This is where it's going to get good and I want a front row seat."

"Want me to prop you up on my shoulders so you can see, Hunt?" Luca's egotistical tone holds more than enough sarcasm to annoy Lauren.

"Yeah right. You're not getting your head between my thighs—ever." She stands in front of the rope. "Asshole," she mumbles but surprisingly she doesn't go after him any further. Maybe she doesn't want to ruin Cristian's day.

It takes twenty more minutes before Cristian and another guy emerge from the woods. Cristian is caked in mud, some dry, some wet, sweat pouring off his face, but despite that, I have a hard time not picturing the two of us rolling around in the mud together and getting our own kind of dirty.

Damn it, I'm screwed.

He gets to a throwing arrow station, picks up the long stick and flings it right into the red bullseye. The other guy quickly gets his in although his is just outside the target area.

"GO IAN!" a girl screams in my ear from right next to me.

The girl from the bleachers and her friend have joined us at the rope line now.

So, that's Ian. I look him over. Her friend is right, he looks like he'd be an expert in the missionary style in bed.

Cristian gets out first, on to some other task that involves pulling a rope.

"GO CRIS!" Lauren screams. "KICK HIS ASS."

"I think it's more about beating your individual time and stuff," Mauro offers.

"Bullshit. No such thing." Lauren doesn't even spare him a glance, her hands wrapped around the rope, inching as far over as she can.

"Ma'am," some high school boy tries to tell her to step back.

Yeah, that's not going to happen.

"Come on CRIS!" Luca joins in as Cristian starts to look fatigued. He's edging Ian out who has nowhere near the guns as Cristian.

"I get why he doesn't wear sleeves, he'd rip his shirt." Lauren knocks me with her elbow for the third time and I'm about to do it back twice as hard.

"You're lucky it's not bikini season," I mumble.

She has no expression on her face, like she doesn't understand her own strength and that I'll be sporting a bruise for the next week.

Cristian jogs by us, giving Lauren and Luca a high five.

"Go, Cris, you got this guy!" Mauro yells and Maddie claps.

The girl I noticed all up on Cristian earlier sprints out of nowhere and I wonder where she's been this entire time. I saw her flirting with Cristian as she pulled her hair back before the race and I can tell she likes him.

Falling to the ground, they start sliding through more mud with wires above them. The girl holds an advantage because of how little she is.

"I could take that girl," Lauren says next to me.

"She slithers like a snake," Luca adds, and Lauren rolls her eyes not granting him her attention, which I think he might be after.

"GO CRIS!" Lauren screams and I press my fingers to my ear with the hopes she didn't do any permanent damage. "DIG HARDER!"

"He'll never let you come again," Mauro says to Lauren who is about a second away from hopping the rope.

"You guys know Cristian?" The girl from the bleachers finally realizes Lauren's been screaming his name for the past ten minutes. Brilliant, that one.

"Yeah, these are his brothers." Leave it to Maddie to be the nice one.

The girl takes in Mauro and Luca, obviously enjoying the view. I can't really blame her. Add in Cristian and it's an Italian trifecta.

"Oh, I'm Ian's girlfriend."

The two guys smile politely, clearly not knowing who Ian is.

"Mauro." He stretches his arm past Maddie to offer his hand. "This is my girlfriend, Madison."

The girl shakes both of their hands.

"These are my friends, Vanessa." She touches my arm because Maddie is affectionate. "The loud one is Lauren."

"I'm Luca."

After all hands are shaken, a pained scream echoes through the air.

Luca's attention moves right to the scene past the mud pit, about fifty feet from the finish line. The girl from earlier is howling in pain, gripping her ankle and mindlessly swaying back and forth.

"I bet she rolled it," I say.

"That's more than a roll," Lauren corrects. "Cris is going to stop." Lauren almost sounds disappointed in him.

"Definitely," Luca agrees and the two of them look at one another as surprised as the rest of us they just agreed on something.

Sure enough, Ian stops briefly to check on the girl, but once Cristian falls to his knees, trying to help, Ian jumps up and runs to the finish line.

"There's my man," the girl next to us says. "I knew he'd be first."

I try not to sneer. Really, I do, but if that was my boyfriend who just sprinted past someone who was injured without even trying to help, I'd question what kind of person he was.

With only a few people in sight still crawling through the mud, Cristian picks up the girl because she's probably a hundred and ten pounds counting all the mud caked on her. She holds on to his neck and he runs, carrying her over the finish line.

I suppress the dreamy sigh that wants to escape my lips. He drops her and motions for Luca.

"Gotta go be a hero. Try not to miss me, Hunt." Luca saunters past us.

I have to say, I like Luca. Not sure what it is about him, but I like the way he challenges Lauren.

She doesn't answer, her disappointment that Cris didn't capture first place evident in all her features.

"Should you go?" Maddie's cheek rests on Mauro's chest and she stares up at him.

His arms tighten around her. "Nah, those two got it covered." He kisses her lips because hey, it's probably been like a whole minute since their lips have touched.

The four of us watch as the girl leans on Cristian's chest while Luca looks over the ankle. Another howl of pain leaves her lips and she stares up at Cristian as if he can make it stop.

"Don't they have a medical team?" I ask.

Maddie's sly grin says she's getting the wrong idea. "You two seem really interested in the girl or is it..."

Lauren rolls her eyes. "I'm still pissed at Cristian. I mean seriously. He came in second when he could've totally taken that guy."

"Yeah, okay," Ian's girlfriend says like Lauren's smoking crack.

"He so would have. And at least he stopped to help that poor girl." Lauren steps in front of me.

As much as I want to back her on Cristian's behalf, I can't. It would only display my weakness where he's concerned and the last thing I need is to encourage my friends in that regard.

"Let's just go congratulate him. He did an admirable thing," I say.

Lauren eyes the girl, but I pull on her arm to follow me.

Thankfully by the time we hit the scene, the medical team has the girl on a stretcher and are carrying her away. Where were they earlier?

Luca stands, wiping his hands down his shorts and fist bumps Cristian. "You totally had that guy."

Before any of us can approach him, or he even has time to respond to Luca, that Ian guy smacks him on the back. "I'll set up a Kayak for flights to Colorado." He winks and I'd like to punch him in the gut, but he's walking away already.

"Colorado?" Luca asks.

Cristian waves off the question. "Just a bet. Guess I'm competing with him in Colorado now."

"I don't think it should count. That ass didn't even stop to help that girl." Lauren steps up, placing her hand on Cristian's back. "Congratulations on second place. Usually I don't endorse anything besides first, but you were clearly the better competitor." Her eyes seek out Ian who is now in a hug with his girlfriend.

"Thanks, Lauren." His gaze finds mine, slowly running down my body and back up. "Hey, Vanessa."

Suddenly, it's so hot out here that I want to strip off my jacket.

"Hi. Good job out there." I thumb toward the course like an idiot.

My body's doing that low-level hum like it always does in his presence.

"Thanks. Thought I had him."

"You did." Mauro barrels into the group, Maddie in tow.

He does a whole slap of the hands lean in for a hug thing that guys do. "Had to go and be all noble, didn't you?" Mauro laughs. "Luca would've run right past her."

"Whoa, whoa, whoa...who was the one looking at her ankle? Mr. Do-Not-Disturb-when his-girlfriend-is-around."

Mauro smiles over at Maddie. "Jealous?" he asks, his eyebrows raising.

"Never," Luca scoffs.

"Let's go to the house. Ma was complaining about a headache last night. She'll need help today." Mauro entwines his hand with Maddie's and they walk off.

"Assholes. There's a medal ceremony," Cristian says.

"I don't think I can see that jerk get first place. I might toss my coffee over his head," Lauren says even though she isn't actually holding a drink.

Cristian swings his arm around her shoulders. "You're a great little cheerleader. You're welcome anytime."

She smiles. "You have me thinking I want to be a Spartan."

"Great." Luca rolls his eyes.

"What? Afraid it's another thing I'll be better at than you?" she asks.

"Try it. I bet you can't even get over that wall." Luca points to the first obstacle Cristian had to do, crossing his arms and raising his eyebrows.

"Watch my ass get over that in one attempt." She runs off toward the wall. Of course she does. She isn't even in athletic wear. She's wearing jeans and a sweater with cute rain boots.

"Yeah, watch her ass, Luca," I say through a chuckle.

Cristian laughs, stepping back from his brother so we're right next to one another.

Lauren does just as she said she would which is more than impressive. "Let's go, Bianco." She raises her hands as she comes back around from the other side of the wall.

"You're so screwed," Cristian says to Luca who isn't really paying attention because he's already heading toward the wall and Lauren. Exactly where he wants to be.

Me, on the other hand, am exactly where I shouldn't be— alone with Cristian.

"Thanks for coming," he breaks the awkward silence first.

"It was fun. I'm glad I came."

We both turn toward one another. My body is more aware of his proximity now that I've slept with him and know what's under his mud-caked clothes.

"You been good?" he asks. "That guy hasn't bothered you anymore?"

I shake my head. "Nope."

After I returned Bill's calls and made it clear I would *not* be going back to work with him, I haven't heard from him again, thank goodness.

"Good."

I nod. "Well, I should get going. Lunch with my dad. Congrats again."

"You're not coming to my parents'?" A crease mars his forehead.

"No. My dad wants to introduce me to his girlfriend. Should be horrible." A hollow laugh escapes my throat.

I've wanted my dad to get a girlfriend for years, but now that it's happened and I have to face seeing him with someone other than my mother, I'm finding it more difficult than I expected.

"Vicki came by the station a few weeks ago. She made a bunch of cookies to drop off. She seems really nice. I'm sure you'll like her."

I nod and plaster a fake smile on my face. I'm a good liar, the last few months have proved that, but somehow Cristian sees through it.

He reaches out and places his hand on my arm. "Do you want some company? Just someone to be on your side of the table?"

I should decline his offer, but my gaze meets his, and for some reason, the answer that comes out of my mouth is, "That would be great."

CHAPTER THIRTEEN

Vanessa

*C*ristian parks along the curb and I walk down the steps in the front of the house prepared to tell him to leave. His family wants to celebrate his achievement and he should be with them. He has no reason to be here for me.

He rounds the front of the car, much cleaner than I last saw him. He looks model worthy in a pair of dark jeans and a button-down shirt. His hair that was matted with mud is now clean and gelled.

"Am I dressed okay?" he asks, taking in the conservative dress I'm wearing.

"You look perfect."

Since I was an asshole on our date and wore ripped jeans, this dress is to somehow make up for that fact. Especially since he's offering to have lunch with me and my dad.

"You look gorgeous. As always." He opens up the passenger door and I slide into his Audi.

It's spotless on the inside and smells of his cologne. The same cologne from our date. Citrus with sandalwood. The familiar fragrance brings our night together to the forefront of my mind and images of our naked bodies pressed against one another take over my thoughts.

By the time he slides into the car, I remember what I was going to tell him.

"You don't have to come. You should be with your family."

His hand pauses on the keys before turning the ignition. "I know this is hard for you."

"How? You don't even know me." It comes out snarkier than I'd intended.

No one except for the girls has seen the real me. I mask my emotions well. There's no way I can be that transparent to this man.

"I have great instincts thanks to my job." He shrugs like it's no big deal. "It's in your voice. You don't have to admit anything to me. We don't have to call this anything other than a friend doing another friend a favor."

"So we're friends?" I ask, the term leaving a bad taste in my mouth.

"Well, since my brother is probably going to marry your best friend, I think we might as well try to be friends. We might end up godparents to my soon-to-be niece or nephew." He smiles and chuckles.

Maddie isn't pregnant, but I suspect he thinks much like me with the 'yet' hanging right after that statement. Maddie and Mauro are moving so fast, a jetliner couldn't keep up.

"I guess that's true." I place my hand on his where it rests on the center console. "Thank you for doing this."

He nods and pulls away from the curb. "You're welcome."

For the twenty minutes it takes us to reach the restaurant, the car is filled with conversation about the Spartan race and how Cristian forfeited first place. We talk about Ian and Tara and a few other competitors he's developed a friendship with.

I have a feeling Cristian makes friends easily. Another drastic difference between the two of us.

If it wasn't for Maddie and Lauren, I'd be a loner. During high school, I had friends who enjoyed backstabbing one another more than having my back. The guys were only interested in one thing. And since I had a workaholic cop for a dad who never took his eyes off of me, and a dead mother, I rebelled for attention. My reputation proceeded me as I continued to be too free with my body. Once Maddie and Lauren came into my life, and I escaped my dad's microscope, I finally figured out who I really am.

"If you just want to stay for a bit and then leave early enough to get back to your parents, that's fine." I ignore the shivers up my spine as he places his hand on the small of my back leading me into the restaurant.

"No, we'll swing by there after lunch."

Huh? I don't remember agreeing to that but how can I say no when he's doing this for me? Damn, I should've known there was a catch.

"Maddie and Lauren will be there. Well, Maddie will. Lauren might be in jail for domestic battery where Luca's concerned." He chuckles, opening the door for me.

"Is this weird for you? Having lunch with my dad?" I change the topic because I will figure out a way out of family dinner at his place.

"I like your dad. He's always treated me well. He pushed me to go on the date with you so I suspect he won't be upset if I'm with you today. I'm not going to jeopardize my chances of SWAT."

He speaks so proper sometimes and I wonder if it's because of his job. He can't very well approach someone in a car and be like 'Hey man, you were speeding. What's the fucking rush?'

I have no time to respond as my dad and his girlfriend, Vicki, are in the foyer waiting on us.

"Vanessa," my dad coos, his arms wrapping around me and kissing my cheek. "You look lovely as always."

This is where my relationship with my father gets tricky. His eyes speak his truth. He steps back from me, his strong hands on my upper arms as he stares into my eyes. Eyes that match the ones of the woman he lost. The brightness in his own eyes dims for a moment, then he blinks, vanquishing the thought...I'm the spitting image of my mother, just a reminder of the heartache he felt for so many years.

Cristian steps up next to me, holding out his hand. "Commander," he says.

My dad's gaze bounces over to Cristian and then falls back to me, questioning what's going on.

"Cristian," he says, shaking his hand immediately. "I have to say I'm surprised to see you here."

A woman clears her throat behind my father and he steps to the side, releasing Cristian's hand.

"Oh, Vanessa and Cristian, this is Vicki Sheridan." His hand falls to her lower back and for a second, I wonder if my dad gives her goose bumps the way Cristian does to me.

"Great to meet you." She holds out a Tupperware container for me. "Pumpkin spice cake. Your dad said you love this time of year and I love to bake so I thought it might butter you up. Not that I'm some evil woman who needs to win you over through your love of sweets. I mean you're not five..." Her face turns redder the longer she goes on and to my surprise, a warmness fills my chest.

"Relax, Vicki," my dad says with a chuckle.

Once I take the container, my dad brings Vicki to his side, kissing the top of her head.

They stare at each other like they can hold a conversation

without words. The same way I've seen Maddie and Mauro do.

"Thank you. My dad knows me well. Pumpkin spice is the way to my heart."

A big grin lands on her face and although I was worried about today, I sense Vicki is as nervous as me.

"Is your whole party here?" the hostess asks, approaching my dad.

"Yes." Again his hand falls to Vicki's back so she walks in front of him.

I follow behind her. Her hair is short and dyed blonde and she's wearing a nice pair of pants with a blouse. It's a cute outfit and I can tell that she put some thought into it.

Cristian and my dad make small talk behind me about the weather.

When we reach the table, my dad holds the chair out for Vicki and whether or not Cristian is doing it because of my dad, he holds the chair out for me before taking his seat. The restaurant overlooks a small lake in the suburbs. It's busy but we're lucky to get a table in a quiet area with no kids around.

"So are you two?" My dad points between Cristian and me.

"Friends," I answer.

"Friends? This isn't the charity date, right?" He unwraps his silverware and places his napkin in his lap. Vicki does the same.

"No, Sir, we already did that," Cristian says.

"Please, call me John."

Cristian nods but doesn't say his name. This has to be more uncomfortable than he let on earlier.

"So this is like a second date?" my dad presses on.

He'd love it if I was involved with a police officer, having never understood the downfall of the job himself. The late hours, the danger, the overtime and the fact you barely see one another. I've seen the strain it can put on a relationship and I don't want that for myself.

"No, Dad, we're just friends."

He sits back, his gaze floating between me and Cristian. "Okay. Well, glad you could join us, Cristian." His hand slides under the table and I notice Vicki's hand is gone as well.

My heart pricks a little bit at seeing my father use the same mannerisms he did with my mom with another woman.

You wanted this, my inner voice reminds me. *He's barely been on your case since the charity auction.*

"I have some good news, Vanessa."

I look up at my dad after straightening my napkin.

"Vicki is going to run Stan's Donut 5k with us this year."

I swallow past the lump lodged in my throat and try to hide my surprise.

I don't care what I wanted, this relationship of theirs is moving super fast.

"Oh. You're a runner?" I manage to choke out.

"Well, I've been training with your dad. He's a great coach." Again, she looks at him and the mutual adoration is clear in both their eyes.

Be happy for him. It's been years since Mom passed. Get over it.

I wish I could strangle the rational voice inside my head because I want to kick and scream like the eight-year-old who lost her mom. I want to pound on the table and scream at Vicki that she'll never replace my mother.

Instead of acting like a spoiled brat, I smile. "That's great. You guys will be way ahead of me."

"Have you been training?" My dad accepts the coffee from the waiter. "Remember you have to work your way up to it. I know it's only 5k, but Vanessa you can't leave it to the last minute."

My head is nodding, but he continues to talk.

"I'm sure Cristian could help you. He's always the top

runner in our fitness tests." My dad smiles at Cristian like he's his new son-in-law. Pump the brakes, Dad.

"I'll be fine," I assure him.

"When is Stan's run?" Cristian asks, the last to unwrap his silverware.

"It's next week." My dad hands Vicki a creamer.

He knows how she takes her coffee. Why does that make me sad?

Cristian's arm swings so it's around the back of my chair. "I can help you. Do you normally run?"

I'm sure he's offering because he thinks he can get in my pants afterwards. With the way his cologne has once again overtaken my senses, he might be right. After this lunch, I wouldn't mind a quickie to forget Vicki and Dad.

"It's fine, thank you." I put the packet of sugar into my coffee and grab a muffin from the basket in front of us.

"If you change your mind, I'm here." He winks and my insides turn to mush.

"Well, we have some more news."

"John," Vicki pleads.

Classic, I'm going to go full-on temper tantrum now because there are only four words that come from a lead-in like that.

"You're getting married?" I ask.

My dad smiles.

Vicki nibbles on her bottom lip.

Cristian? Well, Cristian grabs my hand under the table.

And somehow that gesture helps to quell the tears forming in the corners of my eyes.

"We're already married," my dad announces, all smiles.

My dad raises Vicki's hand, turning over a ring on her finger that's five rows of diamonds. Just a band. He then holds up his own hand.

My stomach feels like someone has poured acid inside it.

He never wore a band for my mom. Said that it told the creeps he arrested that there were people he cared about. People they could seek out to take revenge on him.

Now he's all smiles with a fucking gold band on his left hand.

Excuse me while I throw up.

I slide my chair out and place my napkin on the chair.

"I'll be right back."

I want some alone time, but do you think I got it?

Of course not.

One of the police officers at the table follows me right into the bathroom.

CHAPTER FOURTEEN

Cristian

"Excuse me," I say to the woman staring at me in horror when I followed Vanessa into the ladies' room.

Lucky for us, it's a bathroom with floor to ceiling doors and each stall is like its own little room.

"Vanessa," I knock softly on the door she just shut.

"I'm fine Cristian. I just needed to go to the bathroom and you following me in here is not helping my shy bladder."

I've never met someone with more defense mechanisms to keep someone out. It's like she permanently has her hand out at arm's length.

"Let me in." I lean against the wall in direct line of the door to the bathroom.

A woman walks in, stops in her tracks and stares at me.

"Please go ahead. I'm a police officer."

She quirks her eyebrow, not moving from the tile she's standing on.

I see this lady isn't going to be okay with me here.

"It's an emergency." I point to the door.

The woman, still not convinced, turns around and starts to leave. She stops before she lets the door close. "There's another bathroom downstairs. I suggest you lock the door." She waggles her eyebrows to reference that she knows what's really going on here. What the hell? She's my Ma's age.

But as Ma would say, 'Ma knows best,' so I head over to the door and lock it.

"Vanessa, it's just us. Come on."

She opens up the door and heads to the sink, turning on the water.

"Listen. I appreciate you coming today and following me in here, as creepy as it is, is a very sweet gesture. The news stunned me, but I'm good now."

Her red-rimmed eyes suggest differently.

"It's really ridiculous, I mean, twenty years and I'm hung up on my dad being with someone else."

She wipes her hands, her gaze never reaching mine. I lean against the door and watch. She says she's fine, but her body language gives her away—the slumped shoulders, the way the corner of her lips tip down, the set of her jaw...even her movements are more rigid and less relaxed than normal.

"It's not ridiculous. I can't even imagine how hard it must be."

She stares at herself in the mirror for a moment and I can't help but wonder if she sees the beauty I do. A girl who was raised without a mother and became a strong woman anyway?

She turns her head and meets my gaze for the first time since I came in here. "We're alone?" she asks, arching a brow.

"Yes."

Leaving her purse on the counter, she walks over to me at the door, her heels clicking on the tile.

"How long do you think we have?" She reaches for my

belt, loosening the leather from the metal. "Enough time to..."

"No." I place my hand over hers. "If your dad comes in here, I might as well be fired. I think he likes me, but I'm not about to screw his daughter in the women's bathroom while he waits in the restaurant."

"You were bold enough to walk in here." She steps closer, her breasts pressing against my chest.

I can't help it, my gaze dips to her mouth and I imagine what it would be like if she fell to her knees in front of me and wrapped those pink lips around my cock.

Fuck, quit it.

"We can't," I say and even I can hear that I only half mean it in my voice.

"Be that guy from the other night." My hand falls to the side and she unbuckles my pants and slides the zipper down.

My erect cock springs out of my pants, a happy guy. The logical part of my brain reminds me that she's hurting and I shouldn't take advantage of her like this.

"Vanessa," I sigh.

Her lips touch my neck, and I close my eyes as she works her way up my jawline. "You smell amazing," she whispers.

I could say the same. From the moment I picked her up, I haven't been able to get enough of her flowery scent.

My hands betray me and find her hips, molding around them as her fingers wrap around my length.

"You don't feel like a man who wants to turn me down." There's a playfulness in her tone. One I didn't hear that night at my apartment. One that suggests she uses sex in situations like this.

"Welcome to my constant state when you're near," I respond in a gruff voice.

I don't believe in playing games. And although Vanessa is playing a game right now, I'm not going to join her.

Her lips meet mine and yes, judge if you want, I allow her to slide her tongue into my mouth. She's a woman I can't say no to.

My hands slide up her back, pressing her chest into my body until my fingers are threaded through her hair. It feels like a fucking fantasy right now—the sweet taste of sugar from her coffee, her soft body along mine, her firm hand on my cock.

I'm not sure how long I lose myself in her, but soon there's a knock on the door.

Vanessa doesn't stop. Instead, she strokes me harder, her thumb spreading the dot of pre-cum along my tip.

"It's locked," a woman says from the other side of the door.

"Why would it be locked?" another woman asks.

"I don't know. If I knew that we wouldn't be out here."

"Don't be callous to me."

"Use your head, Ethel."

These two women are arguing about the door, meanwhile, I'm halfway to seeing stars.

"Excuse me!" one of them calls to someone. "The door is locked."

And that's my cue because as much as I want to bend Vanessa over the counter right now and watch her face in the mirror while I sink into her, I don't think her dad getting a glimpse of me fucking his daughter would make for a good lunch. It's not even the traffic patrol detail he'd stick me on that scares me the most.

Placing my hands on both of her arms, I push her back. My dick hits me in the stomach in a clearly pissed off pout.

I ignore the sting of rejection in her eyes. Tucking myself back into my pants, I make myself presentable for when that door opens.

"You don't want *me*, Vanessa. You just want a distraction."

"I thought you were down for some fun." She walks back to the counter and grabs her purse. "We could be friends with benefits."

"Not when your dad is right outside. Banging me in a bathroom won't change the fact that your dad is married."

She tucks her purse under her arm and heads my way. "Thanks for being the disappointment I expected you to be all along." She opens the door and steps out.

"Oh. Are you alright dear?" one of the women asks.

The door widens and they spot me.

"Yeah, she is. She's probably on cloud nine right now," the other woman says. "Look at him."

"Excuse me. Sorry for the inconvenience." I weave by them, keeping my head down.

"No inconvenience. I was hoping you were a perk of the restaurant."

"Oh, Ethel!"

The two women laugh as I follow Vanessa back to the table where her dad is paying the bill.

What a disaster.

———

"So, hold up a second," Luca interrupts me mid-story and stops doing bicep curls with Mauro's weights from when he was in high school. "You're telling me you actually denied her?"

We're supposed to be down here in my parents' basement talking about Ma and the fact that dinner was late getting started since she was too tired to get out of bed earlier. My dad didn't inform anyone until Mauro and Maddie showed up.

"We were in the bathroom with two old ladies outside. Her father, who is also my boss and oh yeah, carries a loaded gun, was a hundred feet away. So yeah, I stopped her." I pick at the ratty old plaid chair I'm sitting in.

"You're such a pussy."

I roll my eyes because whatever. The only way to impress Luca would be to have a threesome tonight. He's not worth my breath.

"I give you props." Mauro sits down on his old bed. "If Maddie would've had her hands on my junk I'm not sure I'd have had the willpower to stop her."

"Let's see if we can bump up her appointment. One of us has to show up and drive her," I say, trying to get us back on track. "You two have the most flexible schedules." I point to each of my brothers who have the luxury shifts of twenty-four on and forty-eight off.

"Hey, Maddie and I are looking for our next property," Mauro whines.

"And you?" I ask Luca who is back to doing bicep curls.

He doesn't answer.

"He curls for the girls," Mauro says.

Luca smirks and winks at us. "My thighs are as strong as my biceps, assholes. You need *all* the muscles to have the reputation I have."

Mauro and I both blow out an exasperated sigh.

"Can you take Ma to the doctor or not?" I ask.

"When? This is a bad week. I work and Nico is having a party."

I stare at him in disbelief.

"Okay, okay. Make the appointment and I'll make sure she gets there." He puts the weights back down in the corner with the dust bunnies.

"Now that the issue of Ma is taken care of, let's talk about you and Vanessa." Mauro raises his eyebrows up and down a few times.

"There's nothing to talk about," I say.

"Why would you go with her to lunch?" Luca sits down on the plaid couch across from me.

"Because she needed someone. It's complicated and really none of your business."

The two don't delve any further because they know I have a point. My brothers don't pry into lives that aren't theirs. Well, unless it's mine.

"I told you not to go back for seconds, but that and the fact that you denied yourself a hand job makes me certain we don't share the same DNA," Luca says, putting his feet up on the old coffee table between us.

"And just think those hands that were wrapped around my dick are upstairs making ravioli."

Mauro and I laugh, but Luca's face pales.

When we're done laughing, Mauro leans forward, resting his elbows on his knees and pins me with a serious stare. "Listen, Cris. I know you have a savior complex and that's why you agreed to lunch. Maddie hasn't told me much about Vanessa and I'm no cop, but I can read between lines. Controlling dad, lost her mother, I don't even know what she does for money. I just think that if you continue down this road, the chances of you getting hurt are at about one hundred and fifty percent."

Footsteps sound through the thin floorboards above us as our aunts and uncles arrive, which means the meal will be ready soon.

"You guys are making too big a deal of it. I can handle myself. Thanks for looking out for me guys." I prepare to push up from the chair.

"Push that savior complex into the depths of darkness and go find Betty Crocker's daughter."

I stand and head up the stairs, ignoring Luca. Just when I thought no one understood me more than my brothers.

Once I'm upstairs, I wind through the family members

speaking Italian, grabbing me for hugs and kisses until I find Ma in the dining room. She's sitting at the table, cutting a loaf of bread.

"Ma?" I ask, glancing at the kitchen door I'm so used to seeing her on the other side of.

"They make me come out here." She finishes cutting one loaf and moves on to the other.

I peek through the door to the kitchen, the steam and heat hitting me in the face.

Maddie, Lauren, and Vanessa are folding the ravioli as my aunt brings them the rolled out dough. Lauren doesn't seem really into it, she's spending more time talking to Vanessa than anything. Vanessa's eyes find mine in the doorway, but she doesn't smile. I know she doesn't want to be here, but that she felt obligated.

Shutting the door to the kitchen, I sit down next to Ma and hold my hand out for the knife.

"Don't you take my last job." She points at me with the sharp end of the knife.

I raise my hands in a placating way and let her continue.

"I like her," she says, concentrating on the bread.

"Yeah, Ma. We all know you like Maddie."

She places the knife down and pats my hand. "No, the blonde. She's not Italian, but neither is Maddie." She leans closer, lowering her voice. "I think Lauren might be Methodist."

I lay my hand over hers. "Vanessa is just a friend."

A soft smile lands on her lips and she's about to say something when my aunt and uncle start bringing in the food.

"I'm starving," Luca says, coming into the dining room with Mauro, who instantly finds Maddie. They're like two magnets.

Luca sits down at the table waiting to be served like the king he thinks he is.

"The girls made the ravioli." My aunt holds the plate out.

"Put them in front of Luca. He's been dying for some meat-filled packaged pasta." I slap him on the shoulder on the way to the kitchen to help bring in the food.

Luca gets up and runs to the bathroom.

"Is he sick?" Ma asks.

"Nah, he'll be fine."

My aunt goes to remove the plate of ravioli, but Mauro stops her. "Oh no, leave them. He'll be right back."

CHAPTER FIFTEEN

Vanessa

$\mathcal{T}$alk about mortifying.

He denied me.

Cristian insisted on driving me home because Lauren had an emergency and it was so dire she agreed to let Luca take her. So I know she wasn't pushing me to go with Cristian because Lauren would rather lose a limb than get in a car with Luca.

So here I am in his car on the way to my house after a family dinner where I dodged his gaze the entire meal. I sat between Maddie and Uncle Mikey who I think may have been trying to peek down the front of my shirt the entire meal.

"Thanks again for the ride," I say.

Cristian turns down my street and if it wouldn't be noticeable, I'd unclick my seatbelt and have my hand on the handle to flee this car the minute he rolls to a stop. But Cristian notices everything. So much so that he distracted his uncle

Mikey most of the meal after he saw me turn more toward Maddie. Still, I couldn't look at him.

"You're welcome."

Silence blankets the car once more and I count the seconds until this ride ends.

He stops in front of the house, and I see our neighbors outside in their small fenced-off front area, while the little girl rides her bike up and down the street.

"Well, see you around." I open the car door, but Cristian's hand lands on my one closest to him.

I close my eyes because I knew he wouldn't make this easy on me.

"Hold up."

I lean back against my seat but leave the door open a crack with one foot out to let him know I'm ready.

"For the race this weekend. Do you want a trainer? I work days but I'm off at three or four so I can swing by in the evening. I know it's only a week, but I'm sure we can get you to run at least half of it."

It's times like this I wish I wasn't so messed up. Cristian is one of a kind and if I let myself, I could probably get attached. But the truth is that it would never last once he found out what I did to get the money to start my clothing company it would shatter any foundation we had built.

"Thanks, but I'll be fine. I'm sure my dad will run with Vicki and I'll just walk."

He blows out a breath and runs his fingers through his hair.

"I'm letting you off the hook. You should be happy," I snip.

This is another one of my faults—I can be a little bitchy when I'm mad at myself and project that anger outward.

"I'm trying to be nice. Maybe I don't want to be let off the hook." For the first time since I've known him, he's raising his voice.

"I'm not sure what you expect, Cristian. You're the one who stopped me." I narrow my eyes at him.

"Because you were trying to get me to fuck you just to forget your dad was married. I don't play that way, Vanessa."

My hand squeezes tighter around the door handle. "You had no problem at your apartment."

"That was different. Unless you were using me then, too?"

"We were using each other." I shut the door because I don't want the neighbor's daughter to hear us arguing. Especially about sex.

"I wasn't using you. Damn it! I thought I could do it, but I can't. Fuck it." The cool and calm demeanor he always has on display crumbles in front of my eyes. "I thought I could be someone I'm not, but I can't."

"What are you talking about?" I have no clue what he's even talking about.

"You. Me. Sex. I can't do it without strings. Yeah, yeah, I get it okay? You're not looking for anyone serious. My brothers were fucking right." His hands grip the steering wheel so tight his knuckles are white.

My shoulders drop as guilt settles in.

He is the man I thought he was.

"Cristian," I begin, but he shakes his head.

"Don't say it."

"I just...it's me. I'm a mess," I say softly. "I'm not girlfriend material. I'm not even steady hook-up material."

He turns his head slowly in my direction, his gaze veering over to our neighbors. Reed and Victoria are watching Jade ride her bike, both of them laughing as they try to throw candy corn into each other's mouths. I'd be lying if I said my heartstrings didn't tug a little, yearning for what they have.

"Okay," he says, letting my words hang in the air. He

doesn't try to refute them like men before him have tried. "Just so you know." He returns his gaze to me and there's a hardness I haven't seen there before. "You can be whoever you *want* to be. I get that you've had a rough past and I suspect a rough go after college, but if you keep pushing people who want to help you away, sooner or later they'll stop offering."

His words are served cold and I suspect he meant them to be profound, but all they do is piss me off.

Who is he other than my best friend's boyfriend's brother and some guy I slept with? Him and his opinion of me doesn't mean anything.

You're lying to yourself.

I owe him nothing and for him to sit here and judge me?

Whatever. Screw him.

"Nice talk. See you later." I step out of the car, slamming the door behind me.

It hurts a little when he drives away without knowing if I got into the house okay. How can we have a fight when we're not even a couple?

"Hey, Vanessa," Jade says, squealing to a stop in front of me on her bike.

"Hey, Jade."

"Is that your boyfriend?" she asks.

I pat her on the helmet. "You're too wise for your years, but he was just a friend." I stop and think. "Or was a friend."

"Oh, you'll be fine. Henry and I got in a fight the other day because he said that only him and Reed could GP to the Bears game. He said it was a boy thing. I told him there is no boy thing or girl thing." Her little hands fall to her hips as she straddles her bike.

"You guys made up though?" I ask with a small smile.

"Yeah, he brought me home a Bears sweatshirt and apologized." She leans in closer. "I think Reed made him do it."

I look up to find Reed and Victoria watching our interaction. They each wave and say hello and I return the gesture.

"Sounds like Reed and Henry are good guys, huh?"

She rolls her eyes. "Yeah, Reed says the good guys get bad raps because women always want a man they can change. But he said nice guys have secrets, too."

I laugh at her wisdom from her stepdad or soon to be stepdad? I'm not even sure.

"Yeah, nice guys shouldn't always finish last," I say.

My own words crack the granite shell I've surrounded myself in practically my whole life.

Is that why I'm so eager to compartmentalize Cristian? I'm afraid he'll crack that protective layer?

Shit. Why am I always the last one to realize these things?

It doesn't matter though because me and Cristian are exactly where we should be—apart from one another.

CHAPTER SIXTEEN

Cristian

*H*aving a night to debate what transpired in my car last night with Vanessa sucks ass. Being at the district when her dad is only steps away makes it worse even.

The small voice that's not ruled by my dick in the far back of my brain says I did the right thing. That a girl like Vanessa isn't scouring Pinterest for the latest pumpkin spice recipes to bake. She buys them because she likes everything in her life to be easy and foolproof. Guaranteed results. That way her feelings don't get involved.

Going to college for criminal justice, I had my fair share of psychology classes. It helps me figure out a scene before anyone opens their mouth. I've been trained to see deception in the smallest of traits, and it's a hell of a lot more than gaze aversion and fidgeting. The longer you're on the force, the easier it becomes.

I'm six years in so I don't have the expertise, as let's say, Vanessa's dad does. So that leaves the question of how he can't see the signs that his own daughter's wound of losing her mother is now being transferred into her love life.

I guess that's what you don't learn in the academy—family ties negate all training. Sure, your partner will spot it, but you're like a blindfolded magician's assistant. Deep down you know it's impossible, but the magician is so fucking good even you get fooled by their trickery.

That's Commander John Flanagan right now. He's blind to his daughter's pain.

"Finished Bianco?" Jericho sits down at the desk across from me, putting his feet up and chomping down on a microwaveable burrito.

Bachelor.

"I would've been done a helluva lot sooner if you wouldn't have bothered to flirt with Klein. How many times does she have to tell you she doesn't sleep with people she works with?" I sign my name on the report.

"First of all"—his feet fall to the floor and he slides his chair up to the desk— "she's playing hard to get. Second, it's not like I'm her partner or her superior or anything. She works a different shift than me and everything." He takes another big bite of the burrito that I suspect is only a snack before he goes to dinner.

Jericho's been my partner since I graduated from the academy. He's got quirks and enough annoying habits to ensure he'll be single forever. Hell, he ruined his opportunity with a professional skier last year. Who does that? But, he's had my back more than once and whether I like him as a person or not doesn't matter. All that I care about is that I can trust him with my life.

Oh and he sucks at the paperwork. It's like my partner is Luca 2.0 with a shit-ton of viruses.

"Commander's going to be up your ass if she files a report," I say.

He swallows the last of his burrito like a human garbage disposal. The smile on his face holds his usual arrogance. "She won't because she secretly wants me."

"And now you sound like the guys we arrest." I stand up with the paperwork in hand to take to the supervisor.

"Speaking of the Commander, I heard a rumor," he sing-songs as he walks behind me.

All shift and not one word. A police station really is like a high school hallway.

"That Klein would rather eat ten of those burritos before going on a date with you?"

I place the report in our supervisor's bin. Jericho rests his hip against the desk. "That you're tapping the hot piece of ass that is the Supe's daughter." He punches me in the shoulder. "You sneaky devil. How did you get her because she's way out of your league."

"I tapped nothing."

"Come on. You finally went on the date from the bachelor auction, didn't you? I can't say I'm not hurt." He places his hand over his heart and throws his head back. "We've been together for eight hours in a damn car and you've been holding out on me."

As though I'd ever tell him about my sex life. He does it enough for both of us.

I look around because the last thing I need is Vanessa calling me up with the riot act.

"The date sucked. That's why I didn't mention it," I say in a low voice.

"Fuck you. I heard you were at lunch with Johnny, his new chick, and that hot piece of ass yesterday."

"Where do you hear this shit?" I head right into the locker room to get changed. Then I'll go home and try not to remember fucking Vanessa as I lay in bed.

Jericho follows me. Of course he does.

Gregory and Nichols come in from their shift, probably to write their own report. They each flash me the look. The look that suggests I nailed the Commander's daughter.

"What's up dick wads?" Jericho asks, smacking each one of them on the shoulder. He's known for his fourteen-year-old teenage boy vocabulary. Another reason I do the reports. Stops them from being sent back to us for corrections.

"Heard something about you, Bianco," Nichols says stifling a laugh.

"You heard wrong."

My phone rings in my pocket. Luca's name flashes across the screen when I pull it out.

"What's up?" I answer.

"It's Ma. We're on the way to the hospital. She passed out." The sound of sirens roar behind his voice.

"What?" I rush over to my locker, grab my shit, and forget about my street clothes. "What hospital?"

"Mercy. Fuck Cris, she's pale and her heart isn't in rhythm. I'm such a shitty son, I should've known." Luca's panicked voice isn't helping me stay calm.

Just as I have everything shoved into my bag, Shirley, a dispatcher, steps up outside the locker room door. "Cristian," she calls out. Her sweet face is riddled with concern.

I nod that I've heard. She obviously got the call with names and most people know my parents live in the area. I mean, Ma stops by with trays of food from The Sandwich Shop, so they all know her around here. Last year when there were a lot of robberies happening in their area, I asked patrol cars to make that street a regular on their pattern.

"Calm down, Luca. Let's just see what's going on. I'll meet you there."

"Okay, they're calling in a replacement for me."

"Good. I'll let everyone know I have to go, too."

I click off the phone knowing Luca won't call Mauro.

He was going to propose to Maddie this week and I pray he picked a better day than today.

"Your mom?" Jericho strips out of his pants and puts on his jeans. Never mind the fact that Shirley is still standing in the doorway. Jericho would streak across the field during the Super Bowl in a casual stride, stopping in the middle to do The Floss.

"Yeah, they're sending her to Mercy."

My gaze finds Shirley's. "Another ambulance was going and Luca tried to take the call. He got there before them and treated her. She's responsive and the ambulance says vitals are picking back up."

"Good. Thanks, Shirley."

"Anytime Cristian. Please tell her we're thinking of her."

"I will."

Jericho slams his locker. "I'll drive you." He slings his backpack over his shoulder.

"I got it, but thanks."

"I'll drive you." This time his tone is insistent and I don't argue as we walk out of the station and I slide into the passenger seat of his '69 Camaro. I'm sure you can imagine why he picked a '69.

I swear, all in all, he really is a stand-up guy.

———

I walk into the emergency room often when I'm on shift, but I don't remember the last time I had to for personal reasons.

Luca pushes off the nurse's desk when he sees us enter. He'll sweet talk his way into the operating room if need be.

"They're saying shit." He fist bumps Jericho. "What's up, man?"

My dad comes up to me, hugging me to his body for a solid minute. Whoever said real men aren't emotional never met my father. He wears his emotions for everyone to see, but we still fear him like he's Capone's twin.

"How is she?" I ask my dad.

"She just lays there. I couldn't get her to open her eyes." Wetness coats his own eyes, but he nods a few times without saying anything else and heads into the waiting room.

What would my dad do without my mother? I have no fucking clue.

"Dad's a mess as you can see." Luca huddles us together like we're about to hash out a winning play.

"You're not so great yourself." This is where Jericho is perfect. He says it so I don't have to.

Luca's eyes lock with mine and I have to say, it's unnerving seeing my usually overconfident brother filled with fear. "She's been having more symptoms. The arrhythmia was off, but I swear yesterday when I checked her out she was fine. I thought she's just getting older and doing way too much."

"She's only fifty-one," I say.

Luca stares at me like he doesn't understand my line of thinking.

"Cris!" Mauro bounds into the emergency room, dragging Maddie behind him because his footsteps are about twice the length of hers. Would've been easier for him to carry her.

Her eyes are swollen like my dad's and she spares us a quick glance before heading over to the nurse's station. It's funny that she thinks she'll get information we can't. The three of us are no strangers here. Hell, the head nurse has given Luca her phone number at least ten times hoping she'll win some Luca lottery at the end of her shift.

Glenda, the nurse on duty, points to the waiting room and Maddie beelines it in there.

"What's the word?" Mauro asks, and he appears about as disheveled as a hungover college student. His hair is a wild mess, the buttons aren't aligned on his shirt and his pants are hanging off his hips since he isn't wearing a belt. He's got slides on instead of actual shoes—in November. In Chicago.

"No mystery what you and Maddie were doing," Luca snips. "Ma's laying passed out on the floor while you're banging your girlfriend."

"Fiancée and I didn't fucking know," Mauro says with a glare.

"Fiancée?" Jericho says like he just said chlamydia.

Mauro doesn't even glance at him because I'm sure he's not in the mood.

"Congrats man," I slap him on the back.

I guess I'm the only other male in our circle who believes Mauro made the right decision on proposing tonight. Not that Luca doesn't love Maddie, but he'd never consider marriage. I'm sure Ma prays every night for him.

We file into the waiting room where Maddie's hand is clasped in my dad's, her other hand on top squeezing and then circling and squeezing.

"She'll be fine," she whispers.

I feel like a jackass that only Maddie figured out we needed to be a solid force for my dad instead of congregating in the hallway to form a plan over something that none of us have control over. Our Ma's health is in the care of the doctors now.

Mauro sits next to Maddie, wrapping his arm around her shoulder and leaning over to say something to Dad. The three do a little hug and my dad spots the ring on Maddie's finger. His eyes soften and he nods before kissing her on the cheek. "Your mama will be so happy when she wakes up."

Maddie sniffles and Mauro kisses her temple.

"He's her favorite for sure now," Luca mumbles next to me. "I should be stripped of the name Bianco. I'm supposed to take care of her. I should've seen the signs. I'm a fucking paramedic," he continues to beat himself up.

"Stop it. You're not a fucking doctor," I tell him.

"I should've been. Then I would've gotten her to the doctor sooner. Hell, I would have *been* her doctor."

I've never seen Luca beating himself up like this other than his senior year when his team lost state.

"Bianco family?" a doctor in a white coat says as he enters the waiting room.

We all stand and his eyes widen in alarm. Me and Luca are both in our uniforms and Maddie and Mauro look like they just wrestled a grizzly bear.

I guess Maddie kind of did.

"Before you see her, I want to go over a few things with you. I believe she has atrial fibrillation. It's late and we have her on a monitor now, but I'm going to schedule some tests. We won't have any answers until the morning. She's fine now. Alert and wanting answers. I don't have a ton and..." His eyes shift to Luca's paramedic uniform. "I don't want anyone panicking and trying to get their PhD on Google. As you probably know" —he directs his talk only to Luca now— "there are a lot of reasons for atrial fibrillation and we'll have to weed out results before we can get a solid diagnosis."

Luca nods, understanding way more than any of us.

"I'm sure you're eager to see her, so I'll have the nurse escort you down. We've set up a transfer upstairs for her since she'll be staying for a couple of days."

My dad holds out his hand for a handshake, which Mauro, me, and Luca all get in line right behind him in birth order. Maddie also shakes his hand and it's the first time I realize, she's practically a Bianco now, too.

A small smile comes to my lips. I never wanted a sister growing up, in fact, I felt sorry for our three cousins in New York when their younger sister Blanca was born. I can't imagine how many guys they had to scare off and keep their eye on over the years. But I think I'm really gonna like having a sister-in-law.

Jericho wishes us the best and heads out while the rest of us follow the nurse past half-drawn curtains with wallows of pain coming from behind them.

My Catholic upbringing comes in handy because I say a few short prayers on the way to Ma's bedside. She's the heart of this family and nothing survives without the heart.

CHAPTER SEVENTEEN

Cristian

It's after midnight and the only light in the room is a dim one right behind my mother's hospital bed so the nurse can see when she comes in. Maddie's curled up into Mauro's chest on the couch by the window, while my dad is in the chair closest to my mother, holding her hand. Luca went downstairs to grab a coffee and probably to bother the nurse for any word on Ma's test results. He's been a mess since we got here, practically crying to Mama about how sorry he was.

I sit in the desk chair, fiddling with my phone to stay awake so I can make sure I'm aware should anything change with Ma's condition. I kind of feel like Luca—we let Ma down. Here she has three sons who are certified in CPR, trained to handle any emergency and all of us didn't push harder for her to go to the doctor sooner. The woman who's kissed every scrape, dried our tears, patted us on the back, and been our biggest cheerleader our whole lives, and we let it get so bad that an ambulance had to be called.

"Cristian," my Ma's sweet, low voice pulls me from my thoughts and my gaze from the Twisty Road game on my phone.

I spring up to my feet and approach the bed. "Rest Mama," I say, covering her cold hand with both of mine.

She wrestles up, the wires making it difficult for her to fully sit up in the bed. Like everything else in her life, she manages and somehow keeps her other hand in my dad's because she wants him to sleep.

"You should go home. Sleep. I'm fine."

I'm shaking my head before she can finish. "We're here."

Her gaze falls around the room, spotting Maddie and Mauro and a soft smile creases her lips. Even in their damn sleep, they're smiling. "He loves her so much," she says.

Mauro told Mama the news in the emergency room, happiness stretching from ear to ear on his face. Mama took Maddie, looked at the ring and pulled them both in for a hug. I can't remember the last time I saw her busting with so much excitement. They talked about the wedding, and I know I wasn't the only one in the room praying that Mama would be there to dance.

"Yeah he does," I agree.

She squeezes my hand. "And what about your girl? Vanessa, right?"

I shake my head. "I told you. We're friends."

This time it's her shaking her head before I can finish speaking. "I see it in those eyes of yours. You might be able to keep a stiff lip, Cristian, but your eyes are always like glass."

"We're different."

Her vision shifts to my father who is now lightly snoring. "Your father and I are opposites. What's the term? Opposites love."

"Opposites attract?" I say with a small chuckle.

She nods. "If there's a saying for it, it must be true."

Go figure, Ma checkmates me.

"She doesn't want a relationship."

"And you do." She doesn't ask, she doesn't have to. She knows the answer.

Out of her three sons, I'm the relationship guy. Damn random genes. For the first time in my life, I wish I could have Luca's love for a carefree relationship and expect nothing from a woman other than for her to leave the next morning. Mauro wasn't a manwhore like Luca, but he rolled with whatever, never planning his future like I did. Looking ahead never scared me like it did my brothers.

"Sometimes people don't know what they want. How could she not love my boy?" She releases my hand and pats my cheek.

This is why we love our mama. Who else would say that and be genuinely confused?

"She lost her mom young. She tries to act like she's strong and doesn't need anyone, but I think she's afraid."

Mama's head tilts and it's the first time I've seen Ma's hair less than perfectly styled. I swear I would wake up in the morning and she'd have showered and dressed for the day. Christmas morning? Dressed and ready to welcome guests before the presents were opened. There are even pictures of her holding each one of us after delivery with a full face of makeup and perfectly styled hair. Now it's matted on the one side and her skin still has a slight gray tinge to it and that scares me. It means our family dynamic is shifting and we'll be taking care of them before long.

"You need to help her to see. Show her the man you are. She'll fall in love with you once she sees what's in here." Her hand moves to my heart. "Such an easy heart to love."

"Oh, Ma, you're supposed to think that."

"I would even if you weren't mine, but I feel extra proud that I did something right with you."

I smile, pride filling my chest.

Luca's one-night stands calling into my parents' deli come to mind and we all know what she thinks of that.

"I was never worried about you. Luca?" She shakes her head. "Dio mio. I may get a grandchild from that one, but no daughter-in-law. I worry about that boy. He needs to settle down with someone. Then I could stop worrying about him. Mauro found Maddie...If you think she's yours, Cristian, fight."

My hand covers hers on my chest. Nothing like your Ma to give you a pep talk.

"We'll see. Let's get you better first."

The smile falls from her lips. "No." Whoa, she transformed from sweet mama to 'why did you cut your brother's hair' ma. True story. I was six, Luca was five, it didn't end well. "If this should show you anything it's that time is precious."

Luca strolls in with no cup of coffee, confirming my suspicion that he was looking for information. Probably using that easy smile and flirtatious charm of his.

"Ma?" he says, his voice full of regret.

I stand so he can have some time with her.

He steps forward and takes my vacant seat. "I'm sorry." Luca's head falls and Ma's hand swiftly moves up to his cheek, urging him to look at her.

See what I mean about the difference between us siblings? As sure of himself as Luca likes to appear, he'll crumble if something happens to Ma. I'll be the one who arranges everything needed for Ma. Mauro will lean on Maddie who will support my father. We all have our roles and Luca's isn't to be the solid support beam holding us up. That's on me.

As I sit back down at the desk, ignoring my Ma's incessant pleas to Luca to stop being upset, I think about her words. Do I really want to lie down and die where Vanessa's concerned?

At some point that night while we wait for word on Mama's test results, falling in and out of sleep, I decide there's something between Vanessa and I that I refuse to throw away.

I'm going to show her what exactly she needs in her life—me.

CHAPTER EIGHTEEN

Vanessa

*T*he doorbell rings and I get up from my computer, grabbing my munchkins.

When I swing the door open, to my surprise Cristian stands there.

"Come to turn me down again?" I ask.

He grabs the bag of donuts and walks down the hall.

"Well, this is great. First, you deny me sex and now you're taking my donuts. You're kind of a buzzkill, Officer Bianco." I follow him because that box is half full and what woman wouldn't chase down a man for a donut.

"At least you're training for the race in your own special way." He tosses the box in the trashcan.

"Okay, I was willing to be nice, but you don't throw out munchkins and you certainly don't throw out pumpkin spice munchkins." I step toward the trashcan, but he moves in front of me, not allowing me to pass. "I'm enjoying this game of chicken, but you're ruining my afternoon."

"Go get changed."

He crosses his arms over his impressive chest. He's wearing a sweatshirt so I don't really see the chest, but I've felt it and seen it and I know it's drool-worthy. I have a good memory for things like that. When he leans against the counter and crosses his ankles, my eyes betray me and fall down his body taking in his compression pants with shorts over the top and his running shoes that are worn enough to say he's a serious runner.

It's impossible to deny how hot he is. That and the fact that I've been replaying our night while laying in bed by myself says he's under my skin.

"I'm working." I sit down at my computer, but he takes the seat opposite me.

"What are you working on?" he asks, seeming intrigued.

"A clothing line."

Jeez, I want to slap myself to shut up. Why am I so willing to tell him everything?

"Cool. Can you finish once we get back?"

"I'm not going anywhere."

He leans back in the chair, relaxed like he's not going anywhere. Why is he acting as if yesterday didn't happen? Like the sun rose and a new Cristian was born.

"I know you want to please your dad," he says in a smug way that grates on me.

"So you've pegged me for having daddy issues. Congratulations." I pretend to work when I'm really staring at a Buzz-Feed quiz on which Golden Girl I'm like between the sheets. I could save myself the time—totally Blanche.

I glance up and he links his fingers on the table in front of him. Now I'm not usually a woman who looks at hands unless I'm looking for a wedding band, but Cristian's fingers are long and thin. His nails are clipped and filed like he gets manicures on the regular. If I found hands sexy—which I don't—I might have to admit that his are.

"What cop's daughter doesn't have them?"

"I'll give you that one."

I glance up from my computer screen to find him smiling. All straight, white teeth on display. I wonder when they were all in high school how the girls picked which Bianco brother was the hottest? My vote would be Cristian if I'd gone there. Which I didn't, so why am I even pondering this?

"Why don't you tell me about it on our run?" His hand pushes the top of my laptop shut. "Forget this. I can tell you anyway. You're Rose in bed."

"I am not." I don't even address how he saw my screen, but then I realize he had to pass my computer after he threw out my munchkins. Sneaky bastard.

"Go get dressed and then I'll explain my reasoning to you."

"Are you going to leave if I say no?"

He shakes his head.

"Fine. But you better have a good reason because Rose seems boring in bed and if you tell me I'm boring, I might make it so that you'll never walk properly again."

He chuckles, not appearing the least bit fazed by my threat.

"And just so you know, I expect a replacement of munchkins if I do this."

I head upstairs not waiting for his answer because I can guess what it will be. And if he thinks some green concoction with a raw egg in it compares to a pumpkin spiced sugar bite of perfection he can think again.

———

Cristian is waiting by the front door stretching when I walk down the steps. I'm not exactly a workout girl so yoga pants, a t-shirt that says 'I Like Big Busts' with a picture of handcuffs, and shoes are the best I can come up with. Had I known of this impromptu run I may have splurged and bought a new outfit.

I beeline past him, grabbing my keys and walking out the door.

"You'll feel wonderful once you're done," he says, following behind.

"Yeah, you have your brother on speed dial I presume?" I pretend to stretch along the rod iron guardrail of our cement stairs.

"Mauro?" he asks.

"Luca. He might need to give me oxygen."

"Don't worry, I'm certified to give you mouth-to-mouth, too." His hands press on my back, moving me forward. "Get a deep stretch. You'll thank me tomorrow."

How does he always smell so good? It's not fair. Especially since I don't see his car anywhere.

"Did you run here?"

"I took an Uber. I figure we'd see how far you could go and I'll run home after."

I switch my legs and thankfully he's decided to stretch on his own now, keeping his hands off me.

"You said you'd tell me why I'm Rose in bed if I did this." I wince when I stretch my leg a little too far.

"You're right. A deal's a deal. You're Rose because at first glance you come across more as a Blanche, a little wild and crazy, throw caution to the wind. But it's only after someone has had you that they realize you're not entirely what they expected. You're surprising. There's more heart there than you'd like to admit. It means something."

I stare up at him speechless. He's right, but he's also wrong. Any of the many men before him would probably say that I *am* a Blanche. It was only with him, even in the midst of a raucous good time, that I felt anything.

"Do you think I'll pass out after a block?" I ask, changing the subject.

He bends his arm behind his head and let's be clear, I follow his lead because the most exercise I've done in the past year is bringing the donut to my mouth.

"No, I pegged you for at least a half mile before we stop."

"Oh you did, did you? I bet I can go a whole mile."

He jumps up and down a few times and then squats and stands a couple times. Already assured I'll be getting a side cramp in half a block, I figure we should get this over with.

It's clear from the first step that Cristian's pacing himself based on what I can handle. No wonder he'll be running home after this.

"You okay?" he asks a block later.

"Where is a half mile?" I pant.

He laughs because he has that much oxygen in his lungs while I'm one inhale away from passing out.

"Think of it this way. You see that fire hydrant?"

My eyes focus on the red object on the next block.

"Only think about getting there."

I nod because I don't want to waste my breath on words. Seriously, this is more embarrassing than when I threw myself at him in the bathroom. He's barely broken a sweat and my sports bra is already growing damp and I can feel the hair that's fallen from my ponytail sticking to the back of my neck.

We reach the fire hydrant and I slow my pace.

"Nope. Now look at that street light," he says.

I focus in, sweat stinging my eyes. "It's...three...blocks."

He laughs again because for some reason he finds torturing me funny.

"You can do it."

I half wonder what I look like running. Cristian looks

confident and sexy. Like the men in movies. I'm positive I'm Phoebe from Friends. Arms flailing and feet stomping.

A few minutes later I approach the light and thank goodness we have the big red hand to stop us from crossing. I love you big red hand. But Cristian jogs in place rather than standing to wait. Of course he does. Already feeling inadequate enough, I do the same.

"That's good. Now, you have two choices." His voice sounds as though we're sitting in a cafe enjoying a nice cup of coffee. "You've hit half a mile." He smiles like a proud father. I'd like to pat myself on the back, but I think I'd get a cramp if I tried. I didn't think I'd make it two blocks. Truth is, without Cristian guiding me along, I wouldn't have. "So, we stop and walk or you try to make it a mile."

Part of me wants to impress him, though I have no idea why.

"I'll go for the mile," I pant.

I really hope we pass a fire station so the paramedics can revive me.

"Thatta girl. I knew you were a fighter." He gives me a big smile and I hate that it causes a warm feeling to invade my chest.

The dreaded white stick figure appears on the traffic light and we cross the road. Cristian doesn't pick up the pace, but he talks the entire time about a domestic disturbance call he got the other day.

"She was crazy. She went after me with a high heel shoe... I had to arrest her in front of her son...I hate that...Luckily a grandma lived with them because...it's a hard day when social services gets called. I'm sure she'll get bailed out, but we have to draw the line...You can't disrespect the people who are there to help you...I know we get a bad rap and no one likes the police...Most of us are good guys who took this job to help...As it always is, a few bad guys give us all a bad rep...

Then again, I'm not the one issuing a lot of speeding and no turning on red tickets."

I enjoy hearing him talk about his job and I can't help wondering whether he's usually the type who keeps his day a secret. My dad told me nothing growing up. Sometimes I'd hear him talking on the phone to his partner or when he'd have poker night I'd listen in from the top of the basement stairs as they discussed calls they were sent on. Usually, I had a nightmare on those nights. As I got older, I understood why my dad wanted to keep me in the bubble he created. It's a sick world we live in sometimes.

"One more block, we're so close. You've got this, Vanessa." He switches conversation and I was so lost in my memories of my childhood, I didn't realize we'd already ran four blocks. He jogs up in front of me, showing off by facing me and running backward. I suppress the urge to roll my eyes.

"You want to hit me right now, right? You're done and want to quit?" He's egging me on.

I'd tell him I want to smack him if I could actually speak right now, but my throat is strangled for breath.

"Get to the end of this street and you can punch me in the gut if you want." He picks up the pace, turning back around and running a little faster.

I'm going to kill him.

I focus on the street sign until I reach it, pushing Cristian, the pain in my chest and my legs and everything else from my mind. When I reach it my feet come to a dead stop.

"Nope, keep moving." His hand lands on my upper arm, guiding me around the corner. "You can't just stop, you have to give the heart time to slow down a little."

We walk as I gasp for breath.

Yeah, I'd go back to the bathroom and allow him to physically remove his dick from my mouth because that would be less embarrassing than this. I might actually throw up.

"We'll walk for a little bit and then we're going to start running again. You think you can do it?"

"What am I getting for this again?" I manage to get out in a strangled voice.

He chuckles. "Your dad's respect."

I start to laugh, but it turns into a coughing fit.

Is this really that important? Is running alongside my dad and the new Mrs. Flanagan worth all this?

Sweat trickles from my eyes. It better be sweat, otherwise Cristian is about to see the complete mess that I am. And he wants to fix everything, including me. That's the last thing I'd be able to stand. A man who wants to save me. I'll save myself, thank you very much.

CHAPTER NINETEEN

Cristian

I've done ballsy things over the years. Things that could end my life. But showing up at Vanessa's, intent on persuading her to run with me was right up there with pulling my gun out during a bank robbery on my shift. I second guessed my decision in both instances. At least at the bank, it was because I didn't want to alarm the robber and get innocent people hurt. This time it was because I'd be the one to be hurt if she turned me down.

When I left her house last night I convinced myself we're too different, things would never work out between us. So the only explanation for why I'm walking alongside her right now is that my heart is leading me, not my head. Because my head knows there's a high probability, I'll completely fall for her and she'll still kick me to the curb.

She's trying to catch her breath and I'm trying to convince her to stick with me on this training thing. Even when a week to train for a 5k is absurd. She'll never be able to run the entire thing.

Heartbreak for me is on the horizon, so I enjoy the view of her ass as she's bent over as compensation.

Here goes nothing.

"I registered for Stan's race today."

Her head twists in my direction. "Why?"

"To support you."

She straightens out, standing in the center of the sidewalk while a grouchy old man huffs and winds his way around us, giving us both the death glare.

"Cristian, we need to talk. It's like you have multiple personalities. I'm not even sure what you want from me."

I continue walking because she needs to in order to prepare her body for the race. She'll be stiff and sore tomorrow if she doesn't.

"I'm not a games person, Vanessa. I know I've been saying one thing and doing another. We're probably as opposite as you can get, but the truth is, I can't stop thinking about you and me, and sure as hell can't stay away from you."

"Because you have a savior complex. My dad has it, too."

I roll my eyes. "That's not it."

"Why? I'm sure you must think I'm a mess. I mean I have some guy creeping around my house, you find me crying in a bathroom. What else has there been? A savior complex is the only reason you could be attracted to me."

I can't help but huff in amusement. "Let's be real for one moment." I reach for her arm and make her stop and face me on the sidewalk. "I'm attracted to you because you're five eight and blonde. You're gorgeous. I've wanted you from the first time I saw you at the district visiting your dad. But it's true that I'm not a guy who trolls for girls every weekend. I don't bring women back to my apartment with only the intent to sleep with them. Have I had a one-night stand? Sure. Do I prefer them? No. The reason I've been so hot and cold is because I know you don't want anything serious. Especially with a police officer. But for some reason, Vanessa." I take a step closer and her breath hitches. "I can't get you out of my head."

At this point, I have to let my gut lead me. It's what keeps me safe on a daily basis, so I'm going to lay out my hand right here on the street. She's trying her best to push me away, but I know there's something more between us. We just need the opportunity to discover what it could be.

"Cristian, you don't even know me," she says and starts walking again.

"I know you hate running, that you love everything pumpkin spice, that although you want your dad out of your daily life, you're not ready to see him with someone else. I know that you loved your mother and want to be a fashion designer. I know you have a small birthmark on the inside of your right leg that's shaped like a heart."

She bumps shoulders with me. "You noticed that?"

"I could probably sketch your body from memory. Or at least describe it to the police sketch artist since I lack the creative gene."

Her cheeks flush a slight pink and all the blood in my body heads between my legs.

"I don't do relationships, Cristian."

I stop us on the residential street, backing her up until she's pressed against a black iron fence that surrounds a newly constructed house. A few cars breeze down the street, most likely cutting through the neighborhood to avoid traffic.

"Try it. I'm not asking for much. You're not moving in with me and in fact, we don't even have to sleep together. But go on a date with me where you're not trying to get the waiter to spill a drink on you so you have an excuse to leave. Let's get to know each other and see where this goes. If it doesn't work out...we're both adults and we walk away."

She allows me to place my hands on her hips and I step in

closer because I'd love to seal this deal with a kiss. A kiss that might turn into more when I get her home, which if she agrees to I might just strap her to my back and run us both back to her bedroom.

"I don't know."

"Are you attracted to me?" I ask because the way her body reacts to my touch, I know for certain she is.

"I think every woman you come into contact with is attracted to you," she deadpans.

I tuck a strand of hair that's fallen from her ponytail behind her ear. "I've run into a few lesbians who aren't."

She smiles and inhales a deep breath, squeezing her eyes shut. "Okay. We'll see how it goes, but Cristian, I'm warning you. I'm not easy."

I crash my lips to hers because she's exactly what I want. I don't need easy. I wouldn't be a Chicago police officer if I did. But she's wrong about the fact that I want to fix her. I like her the way she is and I wouldn't ever want to change her, I just want her to open up. But that will take some time to prove.

She tastes like pumpkin spice mixed with peppermint and somehow that makes me smile as my tongue explores her mouth.

This kiss is different than our first one, it's rushed and urgent. Her hands wrap around my shoulders and she jumps up. I catch her and my hands cup her ass while her legs wrap around me. I kiss her hard, surrendering to the desire I feel for her. The frustration of trying to keep my distance wins the war in my head. We're finally both on the same page, so I don't stop, although it would suck balls if I got a ticket for public indecency. Especially with the Commander's daughter.

I push all thoughts aside because I have her in my arms again and she's agreed to give this thing with us a chance. It's like the little lottery balls just matched up with the ticket I'm holding. I'm cheesy as hell as I smile while my mouth descends down her neck and travels back up to her earlobe.

"Cristian," she pants. "We're in public."

Her words fall on deaf ears. I hear them, but the signal to my brain must not work because I don't stop. I can't.

"You're so fucking delicious." I inhale the salty scent of her sweat mixed with her perfume. The sweetness reminds me of walking into a bakery.

Her fingers cling to my shirt and I press her harder against the fence.

"Cris," she moans. "We've got to stop."

The seductive draw in her tone does nothing to give meaning to her words. Until she unwinds her legs from around my waist and slides down my body.

Finally, I come back to reality. God, she's right. What the hell was I thinking? I would've stripped her down right here in front of a stranger's house.

She makes me forget who I am.

"Come on. Take me home and we can continue this." She grabs my hand and pulls me forward.

Any normal hot blooded male would follow, no questions asked.

Too bad I'm not a normal male because I don't let her entice me. If we're going to do this, we're going to do it right. We want to be a normal couple then we're going to act like one and get to know each other better before we sleep together again.

"We need to run back to the house," I say.

Her entire body turns to Jell-O as she lets her arms hang in defeat. "I prefer to work out another way."

"Me, too, but Stan's Donut race isn't about how long you can fuck, so we need to run back to the house." I lightly smack her ass and start running.

"Cristian, you're such a buzzkill."

"I'll promise you something." I turn around and jog backward because I need to look at her.

"What?" She jogs forward, putting in the same effort a toddler does at cleaning up their toys.

"Working out means more stamina." I wink and turn back around before I embarrass myself and fall over a fire hydrant or something.

"Why do I get the feeling we're not headed back to screw each other?"

"Good intuition. I'm going to make you work for this body."

She laughs and nothing has ever sounded so beautiful to my ears. I could easily become addicted to hearing that sound.

"Total buzzkill," she says and jogs by me, smacking my ass like she won't be bent over in a block wheezing for breath. "I'm going to make it hard on you."

"I love a challenge."

She looks at me over her shoulder. "Challenge on."

Her coy smile sends a thrill right to my dick. I have a feeling I might've just bitten off more than I can chew, but I always rise to a challenge.

CHAPTER TWENTY

Vanessa

*O*ur third day of training and I run the entire mile by myself and only need pushing for the extra half mile. Yay me! It's not much, but I wouldn't have made it a block if not for Cristian.

That realization has kept me up at night.

I may have stopped at TJ Maxx on the way home from pitching myself and my clothing line at Rose and Ivy yesterday because if I'm running with the guy I'm dating but not sleeping with, I need to keep him intrigued. My pants might be a tad tight in the ass and my shirt should maybe be one size bigger, but yeah, workout clothes are meant to be fitted.

"Walk for two blocks and then we're going to run until the end of the street. Grab your visual goal and focus."

"You'd make a great Lamaze partner," I say.

"Is that an offer?"

"Since you're the one keeping sex off the table, I'm not

sure the father of my baby would want you in our delivery room." I smirk at him.

Cristian stops in his tracks and I slow my own pace down, glancing over my shoulder.

"I get that we're just starting out and don't want to get ahead of ourselves but please leave other dicks out of our conversation."

I laugh, grab his hand and tug him forward.

It's odd really. This ease that has transpired with Cristian since he caged me against the fence two days ago. It's nice not dissecting where we stand and even nicer not fighting my attraction to him.

Lucky for me, my phone has been clear of voicemails from certain other men, which is another reason why I'm floating on a cloud. Still, I can't deny how much Cristian has done to prepare me for this Saturday. I appreciate his help even if I'm reluctant to put myself out there and show it. I'd like to show it to him while we're both naked, but he's made it clear that's not happening yet. I kind of want to find out exactly how much stamina we both have.

"Jealous?" I ask with a quirked brow.

"I'm not too proud to admit I am."

He jogs by me and I watch his ass for a little bit before I join him. Just like the last two days he allows me to set the pace and just like the last two days I feel like a loser who's holding him back. But he took an Uber again and plans on running home so I guess he'll still get a proper workout in.

We finish the three miles and are stretching on the front steps of my house. Again, I follow his lead because he's the master in this area.

"Eat protein and no sugar tonight." He bends down in front of me and touches his toes.

He really does have a nice ass. Like your hands automatically just want to reach out and grab it. I didn't take full advantage of that when we had sex. I make a mental note to grab his ass the next time we sleep together. Well, if there is a next time.

"So like peanut butter then?" I ask.

I don't cook for myself. It's not like I stock up on chicken and beef at the butcher.

He turns around. The view of his front just as appealing as his back side.

"I was thinking a grilled chicken breast and vegetables."

The thought of staring at a rubbery piece of chicken with sad, overcooked green beans on the side gives me the heebie-jeebies.

I love food. I think about it constantly. But if I was eating what he just suggested, I might starve myself.

"Do you actually make dinner for yourself every night?" I ask, curious.

Maddie's told stories of Mauro cooking...or trying to cook. She jokes it's a good thing he knows how to use a fire extinguisher.

"I try." He stops stretching and stands up straight with a shrug. "After hockey, the guys usually want to head to the bar. I'm not some super health nut, but if I want to win, sugar and fried foods aren't going to get me there."

Am I really finding his dedication to reaching a goal a turn on right now?

"Well...thank you again."

Not moving from the bottom step of the stairs, his eyes focus in on me at the top. Like he's processing something or has something he wants to say.

"You're welcome. Same time tomorrow?"

I nod, ignoring the pull inside that has me wanting to ask him to stay. Maybe we could make dinner together. I'd have to go out and get some groceries since all I have are Frosted Flakes and some pumpkin spice Pop Tarts and I think we can all agree that that's not what gave Cristian Bianco his fantastic body.

He knocks his knuckles on the rod iron railing and steps down from the last step to the sidewalk.

Just ask him to stay.

"Bye." I wave, turning to my door.

As my key inserts into the lock, I swing back around.

Cristian is standing in the middle of the sidewalk staring at me. "Everything okay?"

I nod. "Yup." Turning back around, I get into my house and stand with the door still open.

He smiles and waves. "Remember to lock up behind you."

"I will."

Just let him go.

"Cris!" I call out and he spins back around to face me. "Would...would you like to stay for dinner?" I hold my breath and wait for his answer.

He smiles and walks back up the path, right up the stairs until he's standing in the foyer with me. "Took you long enough to ask." His chest brushes along mine as he shuts the door behind him.

As hard as I bite the inside of my cheek, I can't get the smile to leave my lips.

What has this man done to me?

"If you want to shower, I'll make the dinner."

"Okay, I'll be quick. You can go after me if you want."

He chuckles. "No offense, but I didn't exactly work up a sweat at the pace we were going."

I smack him in the stomach and laugh. "Okay well, watch TV or something until I'm done and then we can worry about dinner."

He passes me and heads into the living room, using the remote to switch the TV on.

I race upstairs and have the fastest shower known to man

and I'm back downstairs in comfy clothes and wet hair in less than ten minutes.

"That was fast," he says, turning the TV off and heading into the kitchen.

I follow him, happy he decided not to have a shower because I'm not sure I could stay downstairs knowing he was up there, stripped naked in a shower, without wanting to join him.

He starts looking around the kitchen like he's formulating a game plan.

"I'll help, but I don't really have anything..."

His shoulders slump when he opens the fridge and finds it bare. It's just me and Lauren and that girl can survive on black bean burgers and tofu.

"Well, you have some stuff." He grabs all of Lauren's food. "Tell Lauren I'll replace all this."

"How do you know they're not mine?" I ask.

He looks from the assortment of healthy items in his hands and back to me without a word.

"Point taken," I mumble.

He carries peppers and tofu over to the counter and opens the freezer. "What do you live on?" There isn't any judgment in his voice, just curiosity, which makes it easier to answer.

"Sugar."

His eyes roll up and down my body. "Well, I'd say for you, sugar does a body good."

"I can run to the store."

"Nope. We're good." He takes out a box of turkey burgers from the freezer.

I look at the three ingredients left sitting on the counter. We're screwed and I'll be starving by the time he leaves.

Cristian looks around the kitchen. "Mind if I make myself at home?"

He's always so polite.

"Sure. I'd love to help, but I don't know what I'm doing."

Digging around in the cabinets, he comes up with a cutting board, knife, and places a skillet on the stove.

"I'm a patient man." He winks and my stomach does that gurgling thing whenever he says anything remotely sexy.

"Okay, then where do you want me?" I head to the sink to wash my hands.

"That's a dangerous question."

He comes to stand next to me and doesn't wait for me to finish washing my hands before putting soap on his. Placing my hands in his, he slips the soap between our fingers.

"You have to wash your hands for twenty seconds. My Ma sings the Happy Birthday song in Italian."

Our fingers slide and weave together, sending bolts of energy through my veins all rushing in one direction. As if he didn't make hand washing erotic enough already, he begins singing the Happy Birthday song in Italian softly in my ear.

I think we're having a Ghost moment.

I hang on each word as his breath tickles my ear, I close my eyes, not wanting the song to end. *Another twenty seconds, please.* But sooner than my liking he places our hands under the warm water and rinses the soap off.

"That's step one." He leaves me breathing heavily at the sink, grabs two paper towels and hands me one.

I may have underestimated this guy.

"I'm going to defrost the turkey burgers. Why don't you cut up the pepper." Cristian places the red pepper on the cutting board with the knife.

He's overestimating my proficiency in the kitchen. I take the knife and slice through it. How am I supposed to get all these seeds out?

The microwave starts up behind me and seconds later Cristian's behind me, his chest to my back, and his hand on top of mine as he guides me through cutting the white stuff off the inside and getting all the seeds out. "You can always wash out the seeds if you can't get them all."

His deep voice so close to my ear is unsettling. Not in a bad way though.

Placing the pepper cut side down, he continues to show me how to complete my task. Somewhere during the process, I lose concentration and it's only his scent that I cling to. The softness of his hands over mine. The way his muscled forearm flexes lightly with every chop.

My head falls to his shoulder and I wish he was mine so that I could kiss him. This is a great moment for a thank you kiss. One little peck to his neck. But, my imagination doesn't stop at a kiss. My fantasy takes me on a trip of Cristian caging me against the counter, pushing the cutting board and pepper to the floor and propping me up. Our hands in a tangled mess of who can undress the other faster. His frantic lips exploring every inch of me. My head falling down onto the granite countertop, my eyes shutting as he pulls that thread inside of me tighter and tighter.

"There you go." He releases my hands and like a space shuttle that lost its fuel, I crash land back on Earth.

"Thanks," I choke out, swallowing the extra saliva pooling in my mouth.

The skillet sizzles to life a second later and even though we're in the same room, he feels miles away.

"Why didn't you ever you never learn to cook?" he asks. "I'm not judging. I mean, neither of my brothers do. After I moved out, I couldn't survive on burgers like Mauro could, so I taught myself."

One more sign of how different we are.

"Not sure. I just never did. But I can remember baking with my mom."

"Fuck," he sighs. "I'm sorry. That was shitty of me."

I turn around and smile. "It's fine, but if I had to peg a

reason, I'd say it's probably that. My dad got by but for about a year after my mom died, neighborhood women would stock our fridge for us. Casseroles galore and some would bring over freshly made dinners. After the first year, I think we lived off pizza and frozen meals. That's when I discovered my love for cereal."

He flips over the burgers, grabbing salt and pepper to season them. "What's your favorite?"

I step over to the pantry cabinet. "If you want any chance of getting me in bed again you better agree that Boo Berry is."

"I didn't even know they still made that." He abandons the turkey burgers to grab at the box I just pulled out. "I was a Count Chocula fan, but Boo Berry would be my second choice."

I open the box as he holds it, taking out a monster marshmallow. He opens his mouth and I toss it in. "Okay, if I'd known you had this I may have hopped on your train of having cereal for dinner."

I take a handful of the cereal and close up the box. "I'm awesome."

"I can't disagree there."

We each eat out of my hand. "They're only available during Halloween season."

"I bet you have a stockpile." He smiles and then starts in on the tofu at the cutting board.

"Maybe, I'll keep my eye out for Count Chocula, but he's usually the first to go."

"Because he's the best." He opens up his mouth. "Feed me."

I drop two pieces of cereal into his mouth and he goes back to the task of cutting up tofu.

It's arousing watching a man who knows what he's doing in the kitchen. I've never dated someone who knew how to cook anything other than heat and serve. I'm sure that's not surprising.

"Don't you find it hard in the city? Transporting all the groceries on the bus or the train. I've taken a taxi a few times."

"It's not New York, why don't you drive?" he asks, looking up from the cutting board.

Shit, I talked myself right into that one. Just another embarrassing fact to admit to the perfect guy.

"I don't know how."

CHAPTER TWENTY-ONE

Vanessa

"You can't drive? Like, you never got your license?" This time I do hear a tad of judgment in his tone.

I slide up on the counter. "I grew up in Chicago. My dad believed sixteen was too young for a license and said I could get it at eighteen. By then I was in college and Maddie and Lauren never seemed to mind driving. We only had so many spots at our apartment so I didn't have anywhere to park a car anyway. For the most part, I don't need one." I shrug. "The older I get, the more the whole thing kind of scares me."

"Scares you? How?" He seems surprised by my admission.

"The responsibility of it all. It's expensive and I'd have to get insurance and..." I could go on and on, but the bottom line is that it just scares me.

Cristian pulls the turkey burgers out and sets them on a plate and tosses the chopped up tofu in a pan. He looks through a few cabinets and the fridge again, looking for what, I don't know, but he eventually pulls out a bottle of soy sauce.

This sure is transpiring to be an interesting meal. Not that I'm judging. I don't throw stones at glass houses.

"I never chalked you up to hide from something you're scared of." He moves the tofu around in the pan, pulling back his hand when the oil splatters him.

"You don't really know me."

His eyes meet mine. "As you keep mentioning. Why don't we change that?"

"Because you probably won't like me once you find out my secrets." There's more truth in that statement than he'll realize.

"I'll tell you one of mine first."

He turns the burner down on the stove, flips the tofu over and as much as I hate to admit it, saturated in soy sauce it doesn't look so bad. He abandons the pan, coming over to me and placing his arms on either side of my hips. I widen my legs welcoming him between them.

"I lost my virginity to a teacher."

Whoa. Holy shit, I thought he'd tell me that he ate Mickey D's last night. He's going deep. I hope he doesn't expect me to do the same.

"Really?" I ask, eyes wide.

He raises both eyebrows and heads back over to the pan.

"Yeah. I should mention that I was eighteen, as embarrassing as that is to admit to you. She was twenty-four. Right out of college, her first year."

"Well, Bianco. As sick as it kind of is that a teacher seduced you, I have to say I thought you were a follow the rules all the time kind of guy."

Placing the tofu on a plate, he adds the pepper to the pan. "Your turn."

I stare up at the ceiling. It's hard to decide what to tell him. There's so many. "My dad was the one who got me drunk for my first time."

"What?"

Cristian looks like he might pass out.

"I came home from a party one night and he smelled alcohol on my breath. It was Jell-O shots and I only had one. The next night he sat me down and did shot for shot with me. It was a sick way to learn a lesson, but I didn't drink again until halfway through my freshman year in college."

"Damn, the Commander plays hardball."

"You have no idea. I puked so much that night. I think he switched his to water at some point. I was a lightweight back then."

"Oh, and what, you can drink me under the table now?" He fixes us two plates and I feel bad that I kind of slacked helping out.

"All this green stuff you eat, I bet you'd pass out before me."

"And would you take advantage of me?" He grins.

"Why do I feel like you're hoping that I would?"

He chuckles and his laughter fills the kitchen with a warmth that's absent when I'm here on my own.

"A man can dream right?"

I figure we'll eat at the breakfast bar, but Cristian takes the two plates over to the table.

"Wine?" I ask.

"Not until Saturday." He grabs two bottles of water from the fridge.

We sit down at the table and as much as I'm enjoying our time together, I try to convince myself I don't.

"Here's another secret, this is my first time trying tofu." I cut it in half, the consistency of the stuff not exactly winning me over.

"My secret is that I've never made a woman dinner."

I flip our conversation to lighthearted and he flips it right back to serious. This is the juxtaposition of us.

"I've never had someone make me dinner. I do have to say though that whoever cut up these peppers did an awesome job."

He smiles over his mouthful of food.

"That they did. Now you have a job for the next time we do dinner at home."

Home. A four letter word that means more than shelter. And it reminds me of another four letter word—love.

"You're pretty presumptuous." I place the tofu in my mouth and at first, I want to spit it out. It's like the inside of a tomato—gushy, mushy, and squishy...but then the spices come into play. The saltiness of the soy sauce, the heat of the black pepper.

"Try all three together," Cristian says.

I fork off a small piece of turkey burger, a small piece of tofu and then scoop up a piece of red pepper. As the entire mixture hits my mouth, I realize that it surprisingly works.

I place my fork down and wipe my mouth with the napkin.

"Did you just spit it out?"

"No." I show him my napkin. "I had my doubts, but this is good, Cristian. Ever think about leaving the force?"

He laughs, placing his fork down and taking a sip of water. "Is that a deal breaker for you?"

His question throws me and I don't answer right away, but he continues anyway.

"I know it's a risky job and you've lived with a cop your entire life. So I guess I want to know if me being a police officer is going to jeopardize my chances with you."

God, where did this guy come from? He doesn't even mean for his words to be so endearing. Chances with you? No one has ever wanted to put in the effort to really get to know me because—newsflash—I'm a hard person to get to know. Most men see my tits and my ass and my height. The blonde doesn't help, but even after I went brunette for a year, it was still the same. They want me in their bed, but not much else.

And no, I'm not asking for pity. I don't deserve any—things could always be worse. But just once it would be nice to think that a guy could like me for what's inside. Even if it is more like a jagged piece of slate rather than a clear, polished diamond.

I never wanted a man in blue until Cristian. So I find myself answering his question in a way I wouldn't have two weeks ago.

"No. I'm okay with it."

He smiles and it reaches his eyes, the deep brown sparkling. "Come to my hockey game tomorrow?"

Again, I respond by saying something that surprises even me.

"Yes."

———

The next night I'm in the stands of a recreation facility with Maddie and Lauren.

Cristian, Luca, and Mauro are across the ice with the rest of their team. Cristian has a clipboard in his hand and he's pointing his pen at a few of the guys.

"I didn't even know they played," Lauren says.

"Yeah, I guess since they were little. Cristian more so than Luca and Mauro." Maddie could win a Jeopardy category on the Bianco Family at this point. "Mauro said Cris even wanted to try pro at some point, but his parents didn't have the money to keep him in since it's so expensive." She elbows me. "But you probably know this. I heard he's been training with you. What's going on?"

Lauren sips her beer and bangs on the glass at the other

team practicing. "Twenty dollars to anyone who slams number fifty-four into the glass!"

The team stares at her like she's delusional. Which when it comes to Luca she kind of is.

I grab the bottom of her sweater and pull her down to sit in her seat. "Let's behave ourselves."

"Come on Van, I know you're not the kiss and tell type. We're not asking for specifics, but we're your friends." Maddie can load on the guilt like no other. "I told you about Mau—"

"It's nothing. You guys were right. He's a nice guy."

"And?" Lauren leans closer. "They had dinner last night. I came home to an empty fridge and Van washing dishes."

"Hold up." Maddie puts her hand in the air. "Vanessa was washing dishes?" She proceeds to put her wrist on my forehead. "Are you okay? What did you do with our friend?"

My friends laugh and I take her arm off my head.

"What was I supposed to do?" I ask.

"Leave them in the sink like you usually do?" Lauren says with sarcasm. "I have to say, the plate he left for me was mighty tasty. A hot police officer who plays hockey *and* competes in Spartan races *and* cooks? Come on Van, you got like the quadrulefecta."

"The what?" I ask.

"Whatever's like a trifecta but when you have four things," she explains.

"I don't think there is such a word," I say and steal a quick glance across the ice at Cristian.

"The man can do no wrong. He's perfect," Lauren continues on.

"Then you date him."

Lauren swallows down another sip of beer. "I'd never be willing to be a Bianco family member. Why would I sign myself up for the hell of being Luca Bianco's sister-in-law? It's bad enough with Maddie being engaged to Mauro now."

I roll my eyes. She's so blind.

"I think he's too perfect, you know?" I speak my own insecurities of dating Cristian. "But I will admit he's hot and how nice he is only makes him more attractive."

Maddie smiles wide, biting her lip. Right now she's picturing us married to brothers, co sisters-in-law. I know my best friend.

"Pretty soon we'll be swapping Italian recipes," Maddie says.

See. Told you.

"Speaking of Italian recipes, how's their mom?" Lauren asks, crossing her legs and disregarding the guys now that they're starting to play.

I thought she'd be pounding the glass screaming the entire game. It might have something to do with the fact that Luca is on the other side of the glass and is pretending he doesn't know Lauren is right here. Those two might as well strip down and fuck under the spotlight because it's clear to anyone around them how much they want one another.

"She has to wear a heart monitor for thirty days." Maddie cringes.

As Mauro skates by she jumps up and cheers. He does some trick with his hockey stick that probably has a name, but I wouldn't know it, and the buzzer goes off. Everyone on our side cheers.

"He scored!" Maddie coos.

Mauro comes to the glass and winks before skating away. Cue the sappy music now as she falls back to her seat.

"What are you guys talking about?"

Maddie and Lauren share a look and then direct their attention to me.

"She passed out Monday night. It has to do with her

heart, but they're having her wear a monitor for thirty days to figure out exactly what's going on. She passed the angiogram so there's no blockage. They think it's electronic. Talk about a rock. Cristian has been there for his mom the entire time. We all stayed at the hospital that night, but Cristian stayed up and then went to work the next day."

I sink down in my chair, mindlessly watching a game I don't understand. This entire week...all the stuff we've learned about one another and he never said a word. All the shit I've told him about not driving, my mom, and he didn't say anything about his mom being sick.

And here comes that feeling that I despise again. That one that makes me think I'm good for one thing. A nice accessory on his arm and a quick fuck in his bed.

Just when I start to believe that he was telling the truth about wanting to get to know each other better, I find out he's just like every other guy who's come before him.

CHAPTER TWENTY-TWO

Cristian

*A*s lame as it sounds, winning a recreation hockey league game fucking rocks. Especially when the girl you've been chasing bears witness. I mean I get that I'm not some Blackhawk making millions like I dreamed about at fourteen, but we schooled the other team tonight.

"We're going to celebrate, B2, bring the blonde." Mark pats me on the back as he exits the locker room, freshly showered. Using his ridiculous nickname of B for Bianco and whatever birth order we're in. Half the time he gets it wrong.

The ice rink we play at is a hockey house in the upper northside so yes, we have showers and a kick-ass locker room. No, we don't have names in front of our lockers and no one is placing freshly laundered jerseys in them for us, but it's top notch for a league like ours. Then again, it's the north side of the city. Everything is bigger and better up here. Especially the attitudes.

"I'll be there." I don't commit Vanessa to coming because I don't know what's going on in her head. That woman is hot and cold. The few times I could spare a look at the stands in her direction she didn't smile. Instead, she sat there looking bored. After last night, I thought we were on our way somewhere. Where? I have no idea, but not back to her strong-arming me away from her...again.

"How's Mama?" Mauro asks since he worked last night.

"She's good. Dad won't let her do anything which caused an argument," I say, shoving the last of my equipment inside my hockey bag. "She said that if she doesn't get her heart rate up, they'll never find out what's wrong with her. You missed a good one. They spoke Italian I've never heard before."

Mauro chuckles and my brothers and I leave the locker room, Luca immediately cozying up to some of the groupies who are always around when our team plays. The entire team is made up of first responders, so between everyone's schedules and shift changes, not everyone is able to make it to each game. It also means we have a shit-ton of players. These girls hang out for anyone of us that's single, but self-absorbed Luca believes they only come to his games.

Mauro slaps him on the shoulder, attempting to pull him along with us. Luca teeters but doesn't follow.

"We're heading to Brew Crew. Let's go," I say.

"I'll meet you there." His attention shifts to a woman wearing a short skirt. It's cold as shit in here so even though the view is nice—hey, I might want Vanessa, but I'm not blind—I've never paid any of them any attention.

"Don't worry about Ma on Saturday. Maddie and I are going to head over there. I know you have the race with Vanessa so take the day to yourself. Especially since you work Sunday."

I push open the door to outside and let Mauro slip out before I let go. "Thanks for the offer, but I'll probably be available right after the race though. I thought I was making some headway, but I don't know now."

"Why?"

The girls come into sight as we walk through the parking lot, but they don't spot us yet. Jericho has Lauren cornered against her Fiat. At least I know she can handle herself with him. Vanessa and Maddie are talking, and it looks serious from the expressions on their faces. Not at all like they're just casually waiting around for their boyfriends. I guess that'd just be Maddie anyway. Vanessa and I are unclassified.

"You got lucky. Maddie's like an open book. I need to crack a code to get Vanessa to open. Just when I have three of the four numbers correct, she spins all the numbers on the lock again."

Mauro laughs. My life is in a permanent spin cycle these days and he's on the delicate cycle.

"Can't say I didn't warn you, but if anyone can crack the code, it's you, brother." He slaps me on the back which propels us right in front of the girls.

Maddie jumps at him. "Good game hotshot."

There are those dreamy eyes I was talking about.

"Hey, Vanessa." We gravitate toward one another and step off to the side a bit.

"Great game," she says.

"Thanks." I smile, not able to read her mood yet.

"I'm sorry about your mom," she whispers.

I look at her in shock, unable to speak.

"You could've told me. I would've understood if you couldn't train me." There's an edge to her voice.

I grab her hand. "We'll meet you there," I tell the rest of the gang.

"But I came with Lauren." Vanessa fights me as I'm dragging her away.

"Lauren, I have Vanessa," I call out to Lauren, though I'm sure she's figured that much out.

"Cool, I'll head over with this gorgeous woman," Jericho announces.

Once we're secure in the car and I've dumped all my shit in the trunk, I don't turn on the ignition.

"I thought we were going out for a drink?"

"I told you I don't play games," I say.

"Yeah, I know..."

"Then why are you acting so defensive because I didn't tell you about my Ma?"

Her gaze veers out the window which is now only a dark parking lot with a scattering of cars and a line of dense forest next to it. Gotta love the burbs.

"Listen I get it. It's none of my business, but I told you stuff. Personal things I've never shared with anyone. And as stupid as it sounds, I felt...forget it." She shakes her head and moves her hand to the door handle.

I lock the doors.

"You're going to keep me hostage?" Her head swivels in my direction.

"Yes, because we're going to clear this up right now."

Her stern gaze meets mine and with the only light from the parking light shining through the windshield, I can't see them clearly, but I don't need to. I've seen those eyes more than once with her and they don't scare me now because under her hard exterior is treasure. Treasure I want to plunder and adore and cherish.

"There's nothing to clear up."

"The reason I didn't tell you is because I didn't want a pity date." If I don't lay it out, she'll go round and round with me and we'll get farther away from where we started instead of closer.

"What?"

"I thought that if you knew about Ma, you would've gone

out with me as a pity date and then paid a waiter to spill a drink on you again. Or some other equally ridiculous excuse."

The anger vanishes from her blue eyes. "Do you think I would do that?"

"I wasn't sure, but I didn't want to chance it. I was going to tell you at some point, it's just when it comes to you, I'm a little self-conscious."

"Self-conscious?"

I tuck a strand of her blonde hair behind her ear, staring into her eyes and cupping her cheek. "I really like you Vanessa and the more I find out about you, the more intense that feeling becomes. I'm trying not to scare you, but I want this to work."

Her eyes cast down. Not a good sign.

"You're so confusing... er... I'm so confused. You want something I can't give you."

I drop my hand and grip the steering wheel. "Put your seatbelt on, we'll just go to the bar." I turn the keys in the ignition.

"Wait."

I can barely hear her voice over the car radio so I lower the volume. "It's fine Vanessa, but I'm still keeping you to the date on Saturday."

"No."

"Fine." I throw the car in park. "Have it your way. But you should know that I would've treated you like no other man would. We would've been like Maddie and Mauro and you never would have doubted my love."

"Better," she says.

"What?" I whip my head to look at her only to find a grin spreading wide across her lips.

She unbuckles her seatbelt and climbs over the console and onto my lap.

"What are you doing?" I ask. This woman is giving me whiplash.

"You're right. You are a great catch and we'll be better than Maddie and Mauro." She presses her lips to mine in a hard, chaste kiss. "I like you Cristian. I thought maybe you were using me for sex because you didn't want to tell me about your mom."

"We're not even having sex, Vanessa."

She waves me off. "I know, and I realize how stupid that sounds, but like I warned you...I have issues. But you've been a solid force at my side since we met and I want to be that for you with your mom." She kisses me again, although way too briefly.

I press the button on the side of my seat to slide it as far back as it goes.

"I want you." She kisses me again, this time lingering longer and sliding her tongue in my mouth. "And it feels like you want me too?" She grinds her ass down into my huge erection that might bust my zipper if she keeps doing that.

"I always want you, but the next time I have you, it won't be in my car. I plan on feasting on you for days."

"Can we make out?" she asks like I'm not a member of the male species. I'd be a moron not to take her up on her offer, especially with her tits pressed to my chest.

"Let's just clear this up quick." My hands run along her sides and her hands play with my still damp hair.

She rolls her eyes playfully. "Always wanting to talk."

"You need to understand that you have one hundred percent of me."

The smile falls from her face.

"I don't say that to scare you. I just want you to know. There's nothing to question from my side so you can get that out of your head right now. You're not just a pretty face to me."

"Thanks." She buries her head into the crook of my neck which I think might be in order to hide her reaction to my words.

"You're an amazing ass to me, too."

She laughs and smacks me in the stomach. I hold her tighter, not wanting to ever let her slip from my grasp.

One day she'll be able to believe the words I speak. One day I'll look her in the eye and tell her how amazing she is, and she won't hide from me because she'll know I feel those words deep down inside.

"I'm completely yours, Vanessa Flanagan."

Her head lifts and her forehead falls to mine. Keeping her eyes closed her two hands hold my face in them.

"Don't say anything else," she whispers.

I shift her hips so her center grinds along my length.

"Just kiss me," I tell her.

And she does exactly that.

CHAPTER TWENTY-THREE

Vanessa

When I was six, my mom bought me a Belle dress. I wore that dress everywhere. As soon as school was out, I would change out of my Catholic school girl uniform and into the princess dress. I'd set up tea parties and play the soundtrack anytime I was in my room. My favorite song was "Something There." I would even lower my voice to sing the man parts.

One day my parents joined me for the tea party. My mom and I had baked her famous pumpkin spice cake with cream cheese frosting that afternoon and she prepared actual tea for us. My dad looked like the giant he is at my kid's table, sipping out of a small teacup and trying to eat daintily with a plastic fork.

My mom laughed as crumbs fell to the table. "You're my beast." She looked at him lovingly and caressed his cheek. I didn't understand the meaning then, but that night I asked her why she would call Daddy a beast.

"Oh, Van," she began, tucking in my sheets under my body. "One day you'll understand when you're older. Men and boys pretend to be tough, but many times it's just an act. When they fall in love that's

when you see the real man. That's when you know whether you really have a beauty or a beast on your hands."

"But?"

She kissed my forehead. "One day it will all make sense. Your daddy's not really a beast. I saw his true self even through his tough exterior. Now, get some sleep."

The fact that that memory picks now to run through my brain scares me. Am I the beast or is Cristian?

I wish my mom were still here to talk to. I'd tell her about Cristian with his kind words and gentle touches. The way he lives his life with his heart outside of his body—open for all to see, or hurt. It's admirable and impressive and it terrifies me. How long will he let me play these games and keep him at arm's length? How long until he says you're so not worth this effort?

"Jesus Vanessa." He's breathless as he kisses my neck. "You have no idea how badly I want you right now."

See what I mean? He hides nothing.

My fingers tighten in his dark strands, not wanting his head to move away. Not that he seems in any rush to.

"When we finally do it, be prepared for multiple rounds," I say, a little breathless.

His hands cup my breasts and his thumbs find my nipples, the cami not doing a great job of hiding how erect they are through my lace bra.

"You're trying to kill me, right? Like give me a heart attack?"

I laugh, and he pulls open my duster sweater, so it slips off my shoulders and pulls down the top of my cami and the front of my bra, exposing my breasts to him.

"I've missed these, but thankfully they visit me in my

dreams." He talks directly to my breasts and a laugh vibrates in my chest until he takes my breast into his hot, wet mouth, his tongue swirling around my nipple.

I almost suffocate him, pressing him into my flesh because it's been way too long. He doesn't seem half as eager as me. Although, if he fondles and sucks my breasts for the entire night I'd call it a win.

I rock my hips forward and the glorious friction of his erection sends me into overdrive.

The thought I won't have him inside of me tonight is depressing but not enough to stop our heavy make-out session. Grabbing at the hem of his hoodie, I pull it up and his mouth pops off my breast, helping me strip it off him.

My fingers graze down his abs. One day I will lick his stomach, I swear.

I strip off my sweater but leave my cami on mostly because Cristian's mouth and hands are back at me. I arch back, the steering wheel pressing into my back and I close my eyes loving the feel of him.

His knuckles run down my ribcage and he slides his hand under the waistband of my leggings.

"Fucking perfection." He doesn't hesitate but runs his finger under the edge of my underwear before his palm is flat between my legs, his fingers teasing my opening. "You want to ride my hand or my cock?"

Is this a trick question? Is he going to punish me if I say cock because I really want the cock even if his hand feels amazing.

"Cock," I whisper, always one to push the boundaries.

Our lips collide, our tongues sliding against each other's until he pulls away from the kiss. "Take me out then." There's a teasing note in his voice.

Before he can change his mind, I unbuckle his belt and

open up his jeans. His hard length springs out ready to play. Well, hello there big guy. The feeling is mutual.

His hand leaves my wet, warm center but only to pull my leggings down. We wiggle and shift until they're at my ankles. Since I have boots on, they aren't coming off.

Christian shifts the seat so he's more upright and I try to fight him because he'll never get fully inside of me like this. We manage to shrug his jeans down to his knees and I climb back up to be met with the glorious feeling of his dick sliding through my folds.

"I can't wait." I take his dick in my hand, ready to slide it into me. "Where are your condoms?" I shift to look in the glove box, but Cristian's hand slides behind my head and brings me down for a kiss.

He lifts his hips, the tip of his dick right against my clit.

I whimper and fall forward, my hands gripping his strong shoulders.

"Cris," I pant.

I'm so wet that he's able to continue sliding up and down, putting more and more pressure on my clit. He doesn't stop there, he pulls me forward and takes one of my breasts in his mouth while his two hands on my ass spread my cheeks apart as I slide along his rigid, slick cock.

I'm speechless and the only sound in the car is the panting and mumbles of incoherent words as he catapults me into the most intense orgasm I've ever had without intercourse.

My entire body stiffens as I cry out and my head falls to his shoulder, the weight of it too heavy to hold up.

Cristian cradles me to his body, but one thing I don't miss is the fact he didn't come. Which thank fucking God because if he had, we might be screwed. I'm probably the only girl I know not on the pill or with an IUD inside of me.

When I catch my breath, I wordlessly cross over the

console again, lifting my ass to pull up my underwear and leggings. Cristian must think we're done because he pulls up his pants and reaches into the back seat for his sweatshirt. As he's buttoning up his pants, I place my hand over his.

"You didn't think I was one not to reciprocate, did you?" I bend forward, smelling myself on him.

"You don't have to." He shifts in his seat.

"I know." My finger runs up the length of his shaft.

He arches off the seat and his eyes darken while he watches me with a gaze so intense I almost have to look away.

Wrapping my fist around his length, I use my other hand to slide my hair off my shoulder so he has a direct line of vision to what I'm about to do to him.

"As much as I can't wait to have this inside of me." I pump my fist up and down. "My mouth has been dying to be filled with your cock."

The darkening of his eyes turns sinister.

Wrapping my mouth over the tip, the saltiness of his pre-cum spreads across my tongue. My one hand continues moving up and down, and I start slow because I want him to remember this for reasons I'm still not sure of.

His hand reaches under me, kneading my breast. He murmurs praise of how good I am at this and how he's barely able to hold off. Going deeper, the tip hits the back of my throat and his hands shift from my breasts to my hair.

"Fuck...Van...shit."

There's nothing better than when a man can't form full sentences. The more swear words, the better.

I come up and then back down, deep throating him, and he starts raising his hips up off the seat, thrusting his cock into my mouth.

"Don't stop," he groans.

Like I would.

I increase my pressure and my suction, and that does the

trick. His hands unwind from my hair and he raises his arms grabbing the back of the headrest. "I'm coming, Van. Like right fucking now."

I understand his warning, but I'm not stopping now. Not that I mind a mess, but I want to give Cristian the full experience. I want it to be what's ingrained in his brain whenever he thinks about getting a blow job when he's jerking off.

The hot liquid squirts into my mouth and I swallow it down as his cock jerks a few times. I keep pumping until every last drop is out, lick him clean, and look up to meet his gaze.

He brushes his hand across my cheek, his thumb running along my bottom lip. "I think I blacked out."

I smile and make my way up to his mouth. Some guys hate to kiss after you go down on them, but I suspect...he crashes his lips to mine, holding the back of my head to keep me pressed to him. His tongue doesn't ask for entrance but takes it like I'm his. Which I kind of like, I realize. There's so much passion in our kiss that I can almost visualize us stepping over that line from 'I'm not sure what we are' to 'we're in a relationship.'

I've had sex with more partners than I care to admit, but I've never felt like I was claimed and taken care of all at once. Like he stamped me with his name and I stamped him with mine. That's exactly what it feels like in this car in the middle of a now deserted parking lot. Me and Cristian...the question is, can there be a happily ever after?

No.

Not until I tell him my secret.

CHAPTER TWENTY-FOUR

Vanessa

*C*ristian and I took the train to the lake for the race because parking down there is astronomical and he wants to show me somewhere after.

"You ready?" Cristian stretches his leg, holding on to a tree and I watch him surprised at my own calm in his vicinity.

Up until Thursday night, I'd be jittery and anxious when he'd be within twenty feet of me. I'm not sure if it's how open he is with me, or what went down in his car, but things are simpler between us. He hasn't really touched me at all today, but I know some people don't like PDA. It's not like I want us halfway to sex on a public bench, but I do enjoy his arm around me and the odd kiss.

"As ready as I'll ever be."

We both sport our pink shirts with numbers on the front.

"Love the medals," he comments to a volunteer hanging the gold donuts by a ribbon near the finish line.

"The donut and coffee is the real prize," I say.

My mouth waters for the sweetness. Cristian's been in

charge of my diet for the last few days which has left my stomach empty and my taste buds demanding compensation —in the form of sugar.

"I bet you can't wait to get yours." He smiles the one he usually gives before he pulls me into him or kisses me senseless. Right before he reaches me, he glances over my shoulder and his smile falls.

There's a clear shift in the carefree air and it's not the wind off the lake.

"What is it?" I turn around to see what he's looking at and my mouth drops.

What is going on?

"You didn't know?" Cristian asks.

His hands clasp my shoulders as a giant banner plastered with my mom's picture is carried by two men over to a small podium. Before every race, a representative from the organization talks about the food depository and all the money donated that year. So why the heck is my mom, who died so long ago all bright-eyed and smiley-faced on the banner?

"No," I whisper.

I turn to face him. "How did you know that was her?"

He smiles and gives me a look that says he knows me better than I think he does. He tucks a loose strand of hair behind my ear. "You're her. She's you. Looking at her is like staring at you."

It's true, I am her mini-me. Especially when the older version dies too young. I've seen the anguish in my dad's eyes when he's looked at me more than once.

"I just don't understand," I say, dumbfounded.

Cristian being taller than most people here, spots something over my shoulder...again.

"I'm thinking he can probably explain." Palming my shoulders, he twists me back around and sure enough, my dad and Vicki are approaching us.

My dad's always remained fit. He runs on a consistent basis and his diet is as bland as Cristian's. Vicki is in a pair of tight workout pants and her own pink t-shirt. She has one of those cute elastic headbands that never seem to stay on my head. A sweatshirt is tied around her waist and I realize for the first time how beautiful she really is. I'm impressed my dad scored her.

"Vanessa. Cristian." My dad wraps his arms around my shoulders. "What a beautiful day. It's like she's shining down on us."

Wha...What?

My dad doesn't talk about my mom...like ever. When I was actually in shape and able to run the entire race with him, we didn't talk about the reason we were here. We came, we ran, we ate donuts, and we left. I'd hide away in my room for the rest of the day and he'd go in the garage and build some new piece of furniture with uneven legs.

He releases me and Vicki tentatively smiles and leans in giving me a half-hearted hug.

"I guess we're the newbies today, Vicki." Cristian tries to bring humor to our tense bubble.

"How hard can it be to eat a donut?" She laughs.

I smile, tightly but my lips turn up.

"What's with the banner?" I ask, pointing behind him.

My dad puts his arm around my shoulders and leads me over to the podium. "We'll be right back," he calls out over his shoulder.

Cristian and Vicki's voices and easy conversation floats behind us until all the noise around me evaporates.

"Every year I give a big donation in your mom's name. They reached out to me this year and wanted to single out someone who's helped the cause so much. The banner was their idea. You know me. I'd rather it all be anonymous, but in making that donation every year, I knew somehow your mom's name needed to be on it."

Tears well in my eyes looking at her picture. I don't keep a picture of my mom out for anyone to see. My memories of her are tucked away in a box under my bed. In each one, her smile is bright and her face healthy before her illness stole that from her.

"She was beautiful," I say.

My dad rests his arm around my shoulders. "Yes and so are you. I'm a stubborn man, Vanessa. You know this. But when I make a mistake, I own it. It took Vicki coming into my life to show me how I might've steered you wrong. We should've celebrated her life after we mourned her. I should've told you stories about us instead of pretending she never existed. I can't go back and change what I did, but I never meant to..."

I lean my head on his shoulder and he looks down at me. Something I don't think we've done since her funeral.

"I'm sorry, sweetie." He kisses the top of my head.

"It's okay." I break down without warning. Uncontrollable tears fall from my eyes so fast I can't rein them back in.

My dad pulls me into him, patting my back. "I wish I could go back and do it differently."

"No." I swipe the tears from my face. "You did your best."

I'm not sure I ever believed those four words before today. I felt emotionally abandoned by my father the minute my mom was buried. I didn't lose one parent that day, but two. Or at least that's how I felt until this moment.

"I could have done better." He wipes a tear from my face. "I told Vicki and I know you're here with Cristian, but I want to run with you today."

"Oh Dad, I've been working hard, but I'll never be able to run the whole race. I'll have to stop and walk." My eyes cast down, ashamed.

His forefinger and thumb grab my chin to force me to

look up at him. "I don't care. I know I've pressured you in the past, but I just want to be with my daughter on a day that meant so much to her mother."

I step into his arms once more because I don't think I've truly been there since I was eight. Graduation hugs, birthday hugs, parting hugs. We had them, but there were no feeling behind them. If anything, I thought of them only as a step closer to escaping and getting farther away from him.

Cristian and Vicki head over to us. "Everyone is going to start congregating for the speech. I just wanted to let you know," Cristian whispers to the both of us and then backtracks.

A man walks up on stage and talks about Stan's Donut Run and what it supports. As he's talking about how much they've raised, everyone claps and cheers while I look at my mom's picture. My dad is right, her light is shining down on us today. I can *feel* her.

He says my mom's name and some kind words about her generosity. The crowd groans when he speaks of her passing nineteen years ago but quickly claps when he talks about my father and the generous donations he's given in her name ever since. At the end, my father and I walk toward the starting line.

Cristian comes up alongside me, his lips by my ear. "Vicki told me. So, I'll see you at the finish line. You've got this. Just remember every step you're closer to snagging a donut. I'll save you a pumpkin spice." He kisses my temple, but I grab him by the shirt and pull him back to me.

His eyes are wide in alarm and he takes a quick glance around, probably looking for my dad.

"I'd rather think I'm one step closer to you." I press my lips to his then release him.

"You call me a buzzkill, but you have the worst timing.

You pick right *now* to be all domineering and, dare I say, sappy?"

I laugh, glancing at my dad who is hugging Vicki.

"Yeah. I guess I'm feeling sentimental today. You caught me on an off day." I wink.

"I hope we can change it to be more commonplace."

I smile because he's so sweet. This time the nice guy is going to finish first.

"See you at the end. Kick some ass out there."

"Hope you brought your phone because I'm going to be awhile," I say.

"I'd wait for you forever."

"UGH...the lines. They're killing me." I don't really mean it. I love his openness, though I never would have thought I would.

"Do I get anything special if I come in first?" He winks.

"You're the buzzkill remember?"

He chuckles, wiggling his arms at his sides like he's loosening his body. "Not tonight. Buzzkill is clocking out tonight."

I bite my lip. Damn, I may just run a little faster to be done with this race.

The airhorn blows and Cristian takes off with Vicki at his side. My dad and I start running and hordes of people pass us immediately.

Throughout the race, we talk about all the races that came before this one. When I was just a baby and how he and Mom took turns pushing me. How she tried the baby carrier one year and which was a disaster. Another year I wouldn't stay in the stroller and they argued so bad, my mom ran off to finish and left my dad and me to walk. She later apologized. He's open and if he wasn't here in the flesh beside me, I'd think it wasn't him. He lets me dictate the pace and slows to a walk when I need to take a break. We're about a half mile to the finish line when he mentions the subject I knew would come up sooner or later.

"So, Cristian, huh?"

"Yeah. Is it a problem because you're his commander?" I ask.

He shakes his head. "No. There are enough people between us on the line of authority. But a police officer?"

Flashbacks of me screaming at him in high school about how I'd never marry a police officer because all they're about is rules and order run through my head. I'm older now and dare I say a little wiser, and I'm learning that not everything is black and white.

"Funny. I swore them off before him. It's early though. We haven't been seeing each other that long."

"He's one of the good ones. His partner's an asshat who couldn't find his way out of a paper bag. Cristian though, he'll treat you good."

I step around another participant who's stopped to catch their breath. "You act like we're getting married or already *got* married."

Yeah, so I cast that stone his way.

"While I'm apologizing for everything, let me apologize for that, too. I should have told you before we did it. It was a spur of the moment thing. We're going to have a reception. I shouldn't hide her because of what people might think."

"Dad, it's been nineteen years since Mom..."

So, it might take some more time to completely talk about her openly. It's still hard to say the words.

"Yeah, but..." He seems like he wants to tell me more. "I just hope she understands when I get to heaven."

I place my hand on his shoulder. "She'd only want you to be happy."

He cringes like he's not so sure. "Do you like Vicki?"

"She seems nice. I suppose I should be more welcoming to her."

"It would mean a lot to me. Come on, let's jog across the finish line."

"I guess it's the least I can do since you're accepting Cristian so easily." I jog alongside of him, using the trays of donuts set up past the finish line as my visual goal.

"I might accept it, but he's on traffic duty for the next two months." He laughs, increasing our pace a little at a time until we both cross the finish line side by side.

I'm bent over taking a breath when a pumpkin spice donut is placed under my nose. Looking up, I see Cristian there sipping a coffee.

"What did you say I get for first place again?" he asks, the donut medal around his neck and a cocky smile on his lips.

"You get me." I jump into his arms forcing him to have to drop the coffee and donut on the grass.

"Good because that's all I want." He walks over to a nearby tree, using it to prop me up and kisses me with tongue —in public.

"I'm fairly sure you don't want your commander to ticket you for indecency." My dad clears his throat behind us and I unhook my legs from Cristian's waist and he steps far enough back that you'd think we're strangers.

"No, Sir. My apologies. Your daughter..."

My dad and I laugh and I punch Cristian in the gut. He pretends to buckle over, and my dad praises my technique. Then we go and eat our donuts and coffee by the lakefront.

It's a day I'll never forget and I'm happy that Cristian was here to share it with me.

CHAPTER TWENTY-FIVE

Cristian

*A*ll my psych classes taught me that closure is a real thing. Seeing the change in Vanessa after she ran that race with her dad proves that theory right. They both crossed that finish line laughing. In all the years I've watched Vanessa interact with her father whether at a memorial service or just stopping in for lunch, she barely smiled, let alone laughed.

After the race, the four of us sat on rocks by the lakefront and talked and laughed. Vicki told the story about her first date with the Commander and how he took her to some taco dive. She almost called an Uber in the middle of it. Now, none of us would make the Commander look like anything less than Einstein at the district, so imagine my surprise when Vanessa laughs along with her father.

They hugged goodbye and as great as it was to see Vanessa so happy with her dad, a selfish part of me was happy to have her to myself.

On the way home, I figure I've been a good boy and waited long enough, so I send a text to my brothers.

Me: *Stay the fuck away from the apartment tonight.*

Mauro: *We're already here. Don't come in, I've got Maddie spread out on the counter covered in whipped cream.*

Me: *Gross and go to your own goddamn house.*

Luca: *Ma would be upset you're using the Lord's name in vain. If it means you're getting some, I'm happy to stay away. Maybe you won't have such a stick up your ass if you get some ass. LOL*

Mauro: *Not really funny, bro.*

Luca: *It so was.*

Me: *No it wasn't.*

Mauro: *You don't need to worry about me. Me and Maddie are bringing dinner to Ma & Pa's and spending our Saturday night playing games.*

Luca: *Maddie's nerd idea?*

Mauro: *Mine asshole.*

Me: *Let me guess, Boggle? Lol*

Mauro: *Monopoly.*

Luca: *And you're playing that with Dad? Good luck. I give him five minutes before he flips the board over.*

Me: *I say three. He'll try the whole hierarchy trick by saying he gets the best properties.*

Mauro: *Let's see how Ma is about skinless, boneless chicken breasts and steamed veggies.*

Luca: *I'm pretty sure she'd be the same as me. Spit it out on the ground like a toddler.*

Me: *What about some ravioli?*

Mauro: *LMAO*

Luca: *You guys are fuckers and whoever dropped them off at the station saying I forgot my lunch is an asshole.*

Me: *That would be me.*

Mauro: *Shit, why didn't I think of that?*

Luca: *Because all you think about is Maddie now.*

Mauro: *Jealous? Hey, speaking of jealousy, I heard Jericho went home with Lauren Thursday night.*

Me: *You've gotta be kidding me.*

Mauro: *Maddie was supposed to get the 411 today.*

Me: *Great, now I'm gonna have to hear about their fuckscapade for eight hours in a patrol car.*

Mauro: *Luca? Nothing to add?*

Me: *No smartass comment?*

Luca: *I don't give a shit what Hunt does.*

Me: *Anyway, glad we're all on the same page. No coming to the apartment tonight. I'm not joking. If you interrupt us I will pull my gun on you assholes.*

Mauro: *Threatening us with physical harm? We know you don't mean it.*

Luca: *Not to mention I can wrestle it out of your hands.*

Me: *In your dreams.*

Mauro: *I'm out of this convo. I got better things to do than have a pissing contest.*

Me: *I'm out, too. Stay away, Luca. I'm putting the latch across so you've been warned.*

Luca: *Watch out for Mrs. Johnson. Hate for the cops to interrupt you and the Commander's daughter. See how fast that gossip travels.*

Luca: *Cristian and Vanessa sitting in a sex swing, F-U-C-K-I-N-G, first comes off the clothes...*

Me: *You really are a dipshit.*

Luca: *Your life would be boring without me. You should thank Ma.*

Mauro: *We were happy without you.*

Me: *You know what they say about the oops baby...*

Mauro: *LMAO*

Luca: *That he's awesome.*

I tuck my phone back into my pocket and feel it vibrate a few more times.

Vanessa glances over at me. "Who are you texting?"

"My brothers. Telling them they aren't welcome at the apartment tonight."

She nuzzles into me while we walk down Michigan Avenue. I could get used to this affectionate side of Vanessa.

"Does that mean what I think it does?"

"And what do you think it means?" I ask, holding back a laugh.

"That you're removing my chastity belt...again."

I stop us in front of the art museum, guiding her by the chin to meet my eyes.

"Don't take my restraint as anything other than I like to torment myself." I kiss her lips and she leans into me so effortlessly the warm feeling in my chest spreads.

Is this all because she got closure from her dad? I don't know and I don't care. I'm just going to enjoy it.

"Take me home now," she whispers.

I lean in and kiss her again. "One more stop." I place a quick kiss on her nose.

"UGGGHHH... still a buzzkill, Bianco."

I drag her away from the building by her hand. "Promise I'll make it up to you."

Making our way through the downtown area, we end up in the alley behind my parents' deli.

"Is your fantasy to take me against a brick wall because..." She plays with the hem of her shirt. "I'm game."

"No." I laugh, stopping her hands because if my dad walks out of that store and sees Vanessa's tits, I'm not sure either of us could handle it.

"That's my parents' shop." I point to the closed metal door to our right. "That's their dumpster." I point to the smelly, beat-up metal bin.

"Is this a tour of Cristian past?" she asks. "Get it? Like Christmas Past from Scrooge?"

I chuckle at her lame joke and shake my head. "When I was in the academy, you get to know your classmates and at some point, everyone shares their story of why they decided to become a police officer."

"Oh." She loses her playful aura realizing I'm about to share something personal with her. This is something I've shared with very few people and I hope she can see that this means something.

"For some, the police force is a stepping stone into the bureau. Others were born into the blue family and think they have no choice. Some just want the power that comes with the badge and some want to help their community. Other people like that the job offers stability. Growing up, I wanted to be a hockey player. After my parents told me at fourteen they didn't have the money for me to join a travel team that was heavily recruiting me, I was pissed off."

I lean along the brick wall with her in front of me, her chin resting on my chest while she looks up at me.

"I came out here to throw a bag of trash in the bin, still mad about the whole thing and ready to go apeshit on the dumpster. I caught what I thought was a couple having sex. Remember I was fourteen and had zero experience, so it wasn't until the door slammed behind me that they noticed me and I saw the scene for what was really happening."

I look down and I can tell from the expression on her face that she understands where I'm going with this story.

"Her shirt was ripped and her skirt was up around her waist. He had his hand wrapped around her throat. Now back then I was a buck sixty, scrawny, and without my pads and stick, basically defenseless. Other than wrestling with Mauro and Luca, I'd never been in a fight. I went on impulse and yelled.

"The guy tried to fight me. He approached and punched me in the face. Then he pulled up his pants and ran. The woman fell to the ground, whimpering and crying. I didn't know what to do. I pulled my phone out and handed it to her. Telling her to call the police."

"And?" Vanessa asks, worry filling her stare.

"She refused to call. She said the police don't help people like her."

"What? Why?" She rears back so we're not touching anymore.

"I think she was a prostitute or an escort, but he was definitely not a client of hers."

"She never called?"

I shake my head with my lips turned down. "No. I gave her my shirt and she scurried away. Let the man just get away with raping her or attempting to rape her, I guess, I'm not sure. I was so mad after. Madder than I'd been at my parents before any of this happened. I called the police on her behalf, but they acted like I was an inconvenience and said if she doesn't want to file a report I can't do it for her. I didn't even know her name or anything anyway."

She nods.

"I guess." She steps in front of me again, entwining both our hands in the air between us. "I just wanted you to know why I chose this profession and why it's important to me. I do it so I can make a difference. So that I can be the type of officer who people will trust to help them, regardless of who they are."

"Cristian," she sighs falling into my chest, then kissing my neck. "Thank you for sharing."

I wrap her in my arms. "It's important for you to understand that I'm not someone who will try to control you. I didn't become a police officer to be a dictator."

Her lips press to my neck once more. "I don't think that."

We stay there for a few minutes, me remembering that night so vividly. I've thought of that woman almost every time I stepped out of here. I thought of her when I was sworn in and every time I'm first on the scene at a sexual assault call. I see her mascara-stained face in all the victims.

"Come on. Let's get out of here." I take her hand and pull her toward the alley's exit. "This isn't really going to get you in the mood."

"We're not going to see your parents?" she asks.

"No. They've got someone else working on the weekend. Regardless, today you're mine and I'm not sharing."

A huge grin spreads across her face and she jumps on my back. We get a few odd looks as I give her a piggy back through the busy city streets.

On the train, we're one of those annoying couples making out. I try to keep it PG, but we veer into voyeur territory for a minute. But no one can blame me for that. This woman is irresistible. I don't think there's such thing as getting enough.

CHAPTER TWENTY-SIX

Vanessa

I'm not too proud to say that I misjudged Cristian. He's not my father, or I suppose who my father was or who I thought he was? He was like a different man today after I let my guard down.

By the time we end up at his apartment, my body is coiled tight with desire. He unlocks the door and we step inside. It's a quiet Saturday afternoon with the sun beating through the windows onto the dark wood floors.

"Did you want to shower?" He toes out of his gym shoes, disposes of his keys and wallet on the table and heads right to the blinds, shutting the ones letting in the most sunlight.

"Sure. I suppose I should."

All the flirting and sexual innuendos all day have led up to this moment, but now that we're alone it's almost as if neither one of us is sure what the other wants. I've never been shy with a guy before, but I'm scared now what Cristian will think of me if I initiate something.

"I guess we should've gone to your house." He approaches

me, his hand resting on my shoulder and running down my arm until my hand is in his. "That's my bad."

"It's okay. I can borrow some clothes?"

"Of course." He starts to walk to the bedroom and I follow behind, my hand tucked into his, his thumb running circles in my palm. "Are you hungry?"

"I'm okay."

He turns to me when we reach his bedroom. The drapes are drawn, leaving only a hint of light from outside seeping through the cracks.

A dark bedspread covers a queen size mattress that's pushed up against one of the walls and his dresser has not much more than his cologne on it. Boys and their minimalist decorating. There are no picture frames and he doesn't even have a television in his bedroom.

His gaze meets mine and my heart pounds harder in my chest.

This is more stressful than when I lost my virginity.

His hand slides up my arm again and he steps closer, making all the air in my lungs rush out. This is it. We're going to have sex and it's not going to be anything like the first time, I can feel it. There's more weight, more meaning to what we're about to do.

I inhale his masculine scent before his two hands guide my face to his. He dips his head and I rise until our lips meet.

I thought it'd be explosive. We've been flirting all week, by now we should be ripping our clothes off ravishing one another.

But our kiss is slow and sweet and just...*everything*.

"Vanessa," he whispers against my lips.

How can so much emotion be conveyed in a single word from his lips? As if I'm some golden ticket he thought he'd never win.

He runs his nose up and down my cheek, his hands never

leaving my face as he steps closer. I cling to his t-shirt as if he might vanish.

"Please, Cristian," I say, not rushing us but verbally telling him, 'I'm in this and not just for the sex.' For us and everything we may or may not become.

Finding my lips again, his kiss grows hungrier and a moan slips from the back of my throat. Our tongues don't fight with one another, they slide in a gentle pace slowly growing deeper and deeper.

My hands slide under the hem of his t-shirt, pulling it up, loving the feel of his delicious tense muscles hidden underneath. His lips only leave mine to help me strip the shirt from him. Our lips collide once more, but this time it's him pulling my shirt over my head.

"Van." This time he's shortened my name like it'd kill him to take the time to say the whole thing. "Fuck." His voice holds frustration as his hands glide around to my back and find that there's no clasp on my bra.

A light laugh bubbles up out of me and my head falls into the crook of his neck.

"Sports bras are not my friend." He's laughing too as his strong hands try to wiggle me out of it.

Eventually, I stand in front of him, naked from the waist up.

"Those things are off-limits from now on."

He steps into me and his hot searing skin presses against my breasts and I lose all control. We kiss for another minute before he pulls back.

"Let's see if I can work these better." His fingers drag my workout pants down my hips and I slide out of them, taking off my socks, too.

"You should be easier." I pull down his shorts and realize he's got on those damn compression pants. "I love them, but they're like the male version of a damn sports bra."

He takes them off himself and his socks join the rest of our clothes. I take a moment to appreciate his body because I didn't last time. His rippled stomach, the perfect shape of a V on his lower torso, his amazing cock and strong thighs. He is lean muscle and all man. Pure perfection and he's mine.

No awkwardness remains when we embrace again, our lips feasting on each other. His bare cock presses against my stomach and makes me impatient to feel him inside me. Somehow, we end up on the bed with me straddling him, my center rubbing along his hard length, bringing back memories of us in his Audi.

He slides his hand down my ribcage and tucks between my legs, moving in slow circles across my clit.

"You're dripping." His voice sounds pained as if it's agonizing to feel me so wet.

I lift up from him and he takes the opportunity to push a finger inside of me and quickly adds a second. I throw my head back in a moan as he curls his fingers and presses against that perfect spot inside me.

Before long he rolls us over so he's the one on his knees, his mouth on mine, his fingers pumping in and out, spurring me on. I lay in complete bliss, a slave to the mastery of his hands and mouth.

"You're gorgeous," he whispers. "I've pictured this exact scene."

I reach between us and wrap my hand around his engorged length. As I pump, he thrusts into my hand.

A groan rumbles through him and he bends down, taking one nipple into his mouth. Suck, nibble, suck—over and over again, he shifts his attention from one breast to the other. The first flutterings of my impending orgasm tighten my core.

His lips and fingers leave my body and his cock slides out of my hand.

"No," I cry out.

"Don't worry, we have plenty of time." A devilish smile crosses his lips and the tip of his tongue licks down between the valley of my breasts, past my belly button and he situates himself between my legs.

His fingers torment me with pleasure once again and his tongue joins the cadence of his rhythm. My head falls back to the pillows and I relish the feel of him worshiping my body.

I've never felt as cherished as I do right now. There's no rushing. No half-assing the task. And the fact that he's enjoying it as much as I am is a total turn-on.

His arms slide under my thighs and he pulls me closer, burying his face in my wetness.

"Cris!" I grab his hair, the strands smooth and silky in juxtaposition to the raspy feel of his five o'clock shadow between my thighs.

He doesn't relent as I wiggle against him, my climax on the brink of exploding.

"Come on my tongue," he says. "I want to taste even more of you."

My body tightens, stiffens until I cry out, squeeze my eyes shut and shatter beneath him.

He kisses me right above my clit, reaches across the bed to the dresser drawer and pulls out a condom.

On his knees between my legs, he rips the condom open and slides the latex down his shaft. Fuck, I'll be reliving this moment again.

"I promise we won't always be missionary," he says with a laugh, his two arms caging me in on either side of my head, the tip of his cock at my opening, sliding in at a painfully slow pace. "I just want to be able to really see you this time."

He gazes down at me with reverence and once he's fully seated inside of me, he sucks in air through his clenched teeth.

It's like every nerve in my body is a live wire and we're surrounded by water. His lips fall to mine as his body drops on top of me. His pelvis thrusting deeper each time. He doesn't increase the pace, our lips unable to leave one another even through our matching moans, and my fingers scrape along his back.

Every time our lips part, we mumble a few 'more' and 'harder' and 'Jesus.'

I slide my hands down and take his ass in them as he clenches and unclenches, keeping the rhythm of the most glorious sex I've ever had.

I wish the clock could stop and we could stay right here forever. Raising my hips, I meet his thrusts and his mouth casts small kisses along my neck and ear, his deep unsteady breathing like a soundtrack to my heart.

He lengthens his body over me, pressing his chest to mine and stretching his arms above my head, grabbing something behind my head.

"Trust me?" he asks with a wicked glint.

I glance over to this hands and see that he's holding a pair of handcuffs. Just when I thought he couldn't get any hotter.

"I've been a bad girl, Officer," I say in a sultry voice.

He chuckles and locks the cuffs in place around one of my wrists then feeds the chain through the back rail of his headboard before fastening them around my other wrist.

"Are they too tight?" he asks.

I shake my head slowly. God, lying here while he's still inside me, looking down at me while I'm at his complete mercy has me ready to combust.

I wiggle my hips so he knows I'm ready to continue and he thrusts into me hard. I cry out from how deep he claims me.

"Fuck. I'll never be able to cuff a criminal again without

thinking of this right here. You spread out on my bed like a goddess."

His words leave me panting and arching into him.

"You have no idea what you do to me," he says as he grinds his pelvis against my core.

The sweat between us builds and he stares down at me, his searing gaze holding me captive as his movements become rougher. He takes me again and again until I'm there right where he wants me.

"Cris..." My back arches, my muscles coil, my thighs lock around him and I break apart beneath him.

He doesn't lose pace, hammering into me while murmuring words of affection. Seconds later he jerks inside of me in an awkward tempo and he's moaning out his release.

He immediately reaches over to his nightstand and grabs the keys for the handcuffs and releases me. I wrap my arms around him and he kisses my neck, his hands moving sweat-slicked hair off my forehead.

With a kiss to my forehead, he pulls out of me and my insides clench, not wanting him to leave.

"I'll be right back. Promise." He winks and I watch his perfect ass leave the room.

This must be what it feels like to be struck with Cupid's arrow. Because I'm a goner.

CHAPTER TWENTY-SEVEN

Vanessa

*T*wo condoms and a shower later, we're on opposite ends of his living room couch, naked with blankets draped over us, watching some cooking show and eating his healthy popcorn. We've chatted a bit, told each other funny stories and I mentioned to him how excited I am for my appointment at the Rose & Ivy boutique tomorrow. It's been a great day.

"Okay, you're ordering in some greasy, high-fat food tonight." I toss a kernel at him and he catches it with his mouth.

"I won't be able to perform if you make me eat foods that aren't good fuel for my love tank." He flashes me another grin and winks.

He really is gorgeous. Like the perfect male Adonis. Not one flaw.

"Do you have a flaw? An annoying little trait?" I ask.

His eyebrows crinkle. "If I did, I don't think I'd tell you."

"Why?" I throw a kernel at him again and this time he doesn't have time to catch it.

"Because then you'd obsess about it. What if it annoyed you so much you dumped me?"

I nod. "True."

"Come here." He opens up his side of the blanket and I scoot over and nuzzle into his side.

We watch TV for a few more minutes and it'd be easy to go on pretending there isn't something that still stands in the way of us successfully navigating this relationship. Hell, I managed to live in the moment all day and it was such a freeing feeling. But even me, with a doctorate for putting my head in the sand, realizes I'd only be biding my time.

"I've done bad things." The admission is out of my mouth before I can stop myself and shocks me probably as much as Cristian.

I really hope he's the forgiving kind—that his one fault isn't being unable to forgive and understand why some people do the things they do.

"We've all done bad things," he says with no note of uncertainty in his voice.

I get up on my knees so he can see what I'm really trying to convey here. The weight of what I'm telling him.

"I haven't always been good, Cris. I mean..."

He smiles. He fucking smiles. Like an ear to ear grin as if I'm some cute and cuddly teddy bear.

"Vanessa, it's okay. Did you murder someone?"

"No."

"Did you intentionally hurt someone physically?"

"No."

"Did you put a gun to someone's head?"

"No, but..."

"Relax." His hand squeezes my bare shoulder. "I'm not some priest you have to make a confession to. Just because

I'm a police officer doesn't mean I'm perfect. Don't go thinking that because you'll only be disappointed."

"But that guy..." I inch forward, desperate to let it all out but scared to say the words.

His back straightens. This gets his attention.

"What? Has he been around again?"

"No. I mean he wasn't an old boyfriend."

"He wasn't?" Finally, his expression turns more serious.

"It was more business related, but I'm out now. He hasn't been around."

The tension in his shoulders loosens a bit. "I'm glad to hear that."

"But..."

"Go ahead and spit it out because I can tell whatever it is, it's bothering you."

Finally, as I'm beginning to tell him, I clam up. Tonight is so wonderful and I could ruin it all by telling him what I did. What if he really can't accept me after?

"You know how I've been working to try and start a small fashion line of my own?"

"Yeah."

"It costs like twenty grand to get everything going. Fabric, designs, seamstresses."

His mouth turns down and his gaze searches for the answers I've yet to give them. I imagine he's dissecting every non-verbal thing I'm doing. Biting my lip, playing with my fingers.

"Okaaay..."

"So that guy in the town car...he was a guy who runs high stakes poker games."

"And?"

My stomach turns over on itself and I suck in a deep breath before pushing forward. "And I was the one who helped him."

"As in what exactly?" His face is void of emotion and I'm not sure what to make of that.

"I ran it for him. He has a few condos that he runs them out of and I was one of the girls who ran a game."

He pinches the bridge of his nose for second and closes his eyes before once again meeting my gaze. "I really don't want to ask this question, but I need to know. Did you sleep with men you didn't want to?"

"No!" My eyes widen and I shake my head. "It wasn't like that. It was me just making sure they had everything they wanted. A lot of men like to look, so I did dress kind of provocatively, but they don't touch—ever. The more cleavage, the more tips I seemed to come home with. Not like a stripper or anything. Just short dresses and high heels."

"Oh." His hand weaves through his hair. "And your dad has no idea, right?"

"No. God, could you imagine? But I have all the money I need now and I'm done."

He nods a few times and blows out a stream of air. "This is what you were so worried to tell me?"

I nod.

"I never want you to worry about my reaction to something. You can tell me anything, Vanessa. It's not going to change how I feel about you. I hate that you did that, but I understand you did what you thought you had to do."

"Really?" The weight on my chest lessens ever so slightly.

He laughs, pulling me into him. "Did you think I was going to kick you out?"

"A little."

"One day you'll figure out how much you mean to me. But you *have* to tell me if that man shows up again. I need you to promise me that."

"I did what I was supposed to for him. It's over." I kiss his bare chest. "Thank you for understanding."

"Always."

The doorbell buzzes.

"Who's that?" I ask.

"A smorgasbord of bad food. You deserve it after this week." He stands, grabs a blanket from the couch and wraps it around his waist.

As I shelter my own body in the other blanket, I smile, relieved that my confession is out of the way and that everything is working out.

The delivery man comes and goes, Cristian dropping the blanket the minute he latches the lock. Dropping the food on the counter, he walks over and cages me in on the sofa, his body pressed against mine, entwining our hands over our heads.

He's ready again and since I'm ready 24/7 for him, we use another condom before we eat and two more after.

Life is good.

CHAPTER TWENTY-EIGHT

Cristian

I'm trained to keep my composure. In high-stress situations, you won't normally see a reaction from me.

I like to think my training is coming in handy since I didn't blow a gasket that Vanessa allowed me to drive away from that dipshit the first night I tried to drop her off at her place. I also know that if he went to the trouble to wait around for her at her place, that she's wrong and it's not over.

Whatever he wants he's not going to relent until he gets it.

But tonight is our night and I don't want her to think I'm angry with her. I meant what I said, I get it, she did what she thought she had to do, regardless of the danger it put her in. And now I'm doing what I need to do.

Me: *I need you to drive by Lauren and Vanessa's house and tell me if there's a town car there.*
Luca: *What the fuck? Go yourself.*

Me: *I'll tell you the reason some day. Not today. Just do it. Black town car.*

Luca: *Like there aren't thousands of those in Chicago.*

Me: *Not on her street.*

Luca: *I'm just getting my pregame on.*

Me: *I don't need to know what you do before jacking off.*

Luca: *Isn't it YOU asking ME for a favor wiseass? Mauro's girl owns the house. What about him?*

Me: *Fine you're in starting line next week.*

Luca: *Sold. I'll report back.*

I've purposely been putting him on the third line because I knew I'd need a favor one day and sports trump everything in Luca's life.

I snuggle back into Vanessa, she fell asleep after I took her from behind on the couch. I'm not sure I'll ever get enough of her. My dick is already stirring again right now.

Her arms wind around me, and I slide us down to the chaise lounger on end of the couch, flipping through the channels.

This would be a good life.

Vanessa stays asleep and my phone buzzes next to me a half-hour later.

Luca: *No town car Detective.*

Me: *Okay. I'll head over in the morning before my shift.*

Luca: *Is this for Vanessa or Lauren?*

Me: *Don't worry about it. I have it handled.*

My phone rings and Luca's name flashes across the screen. "Can't talk." I click off.

The phone rings again and Vanessa stirs in my arms.

"What?" I snap when I answer.

"I'm outside their place and I know Lauren's home

because she's doing some sort of workout video with the blinds open. Is she in danger or something? You're being cagey." His voice is low and to my surprise, he sounds genuinely concerned about her.

"No. I mean...I don't really know. I don't think so."

"You don't think so. What kind of cop are you? You make me leave a pregame party and head over here and you won't tell me shit about why."

I should've sent Jericho.

"It's fine. Everything's fine, but I can't talk about it right now."

"Great. I'm going to freeze my ass off tonight waiting for a damn town car to arrive."

Click.

The line dies.

"Who was that?" Vanessa's eyes flutter open.

There goes my dick again, just one look at those icy blues.

"It was just Luca. Go back to sleep."

Her hand drifts down to my already stiffening cock. "I think I have other plans."

"I think you're going to be sore tomorrow."

"Good. Then I'll think of you all day."

Music to a man's ears. I flip the blanket over us, pick her up fireman style and take her back to my bed. Not sure why we ever left there to begin with.

I think we set a new world record today.

———

Shower sex was never high on my list, until five o'clock this morning when Vanessa insisted on helping me wash before I went to work.

Her hand slides up and down my dick, slippery from the

soap she's lathered. My lips mesh with hers while hot water cascades down my back.

"We need to make you clean for work," she mumbles against my lips before kissing me again.

"I prefer being dirty." I smile against her mouth.

We stop kissing and her laugh bounces off the glass encasing us. "Me, too. I like it when you're dirty."

"Should we play cop and criminal?" I tease, my hands grabbing both her ass cheeks. She squeaks. "Turn around."

Like a pro, she spreads her legs and puts her hands on the glass, leaning forward to give me the best possible access. I'm not sure if I love it or hate it that she's so skilled in the art of shower fucking. But we're adults and I can't say that I don't know what position works best either.

I creak open the shower door, a rush of cold air disturbing our hotbox, to snatch the condom I left on the counter. When Vanessa suggested a shower, I'd grabbed one from the night table hoping we'd end up needing it.

After I've rolled the latex down my length, I run my hand down her spine. She arches into my touch, her head falling back like it's chasing my hand. I slide one finger into her because one thing that sucks about shower sex is that it kills all lubrication.

Lucky for us, Vanessa is wet and ready which manages to blow my mind *and* feed my ego.

Aligning the tip of my cock with her entrance, I gently push inside her. Vanessa rocks back, eager for more. I give her what she wants, plunging into her deepest depths and savoring her moan.

"How am I going to go all day without you?" she pants out.

I'm glad her back is to me so she can't see how her confession affects me.

"I'll be thinking about you," she continues. "Fucking you... sucking you."

I thrust hard, and my fingertips dig into her hips, guiding us to a pace that has us both breathing heavily.

"Be ready tonight because I'm going to be hard after a whole day of reliving last night and this morning."

Her hand slaps the foggy glass, leaving a handprint. "Fuck, Cris," she hammers back into me, her ass colliding with my pelvis.

Clenching and thrusting I give it right back to her.

"More...Cris...Coming...Now...Ohh..." Her body limps forward, her tits pressed to the glass now, her hands leaving streaks on the steamed glass.

Vanessa is a woman who can't help but boost your confidence with her screams, her body language, her words. She's one hundred percent in the act with you and as lame as it sounds she makes me feel like a hero. Is this how great it feels to be a celebrity or a medaled Navy Seal? Someone who the world puts up on an unreachable pedestal? I don't care about the world, I just want Vanessa staring up at me like I'm *her* entire world.

She turns, putting one leg on the bench seat in the shower, her hand winding into the wet hair at the back of my head.

"Fuck me, Cristian," she whispers into the crook of my neck.

I push into her again and thrust for another minute, one hand playing with her tit and before long my balls tighten and I'm coming with a ferocity that surprises even me.

Neither of us moves right away. If I didn't have to be on duty in an hour, I'd stay like this for half the day.

Her fingers play with my wet hair and my hands slide up and down her torso. We kiss as though there's no clock dictating our eventual parting. Our tongues slide together in a slow dance delaying the inevitability of leaving the cocoon we've built around us.

One night wasn't near long enough.

"I guess I got you kind of dirty," she says when she pulls away.

I pull out of her, work an annoying tick in the back of my brain.

"I'll let you shower for real now." Instead of leaving the shower, she wraps her arms around my neck and kisses me one last time. "See you in your bed."

My dick pouts that his best form of entertainment is leaving and my heart aches for the time apart we'll have to spend today. Aren't we a great pair?

"Don't lie on my bed. I'll never get out the door," I call out after her.

Her jubilant laughter echoes through the bathroom as she leaves.

CHAPTER TWENTY-NINE

Vanessa

*C*hristian put up a good front last night when I told him about Bill's reappearance and the poker parties. But as we said goodbye earlier today at my front door, rocking back on his heels, hesitant to leave, I knew that my secret was like a third wheel in the room. I just hoped as I moved farther away from that life, it would be in our rearview mirror.

As I walk into Rose & Ivy later that day, I'm filled with nervous energy. I'm here to go over some plans for the clothes I'm about to send out to be made. So when the small hairs on the back of my neck stand on edge, I shrug it off.

"Vanessa," Adeline coos when I enter the shop. "I'm dying to see what you have."

The middle-aged woman sits on the couch in the middle of the sales floor. It's one of those boutiques unworried about wasting square footage on furniture instead of items to sell.

"I can't wait to hear what you think," I say, pulling out my sketches and samples of fabric for each design and setting them on the table in front of her.

"You look tired, but with those pink cheeks I'm guessing you had a good night last night." She shoots me a knowing smile and my cheeks feel like someone put a flamethrower to them.

"Well." I shrug and take a seat.

She waves her perfectly manicured hand in the air. "Don't be embarrassed. If I looked like you, I'd be having some hot sex, too."

She speaks as though she's not a successful business-woman who looks like she stepped out of Vogue magazine. Actually, that's likely one of the reasons we connected so well when we first met.

"Well... it's new," I say, a little uncomfortable.

She nods in understanding. "New explains the flush. This is what old looks like." She waves her hand across her body.

She's wearing skinny jeans and an oversized sweater that hangs off one shoulder. Not too much jewelry but enough to add a delicate touch to her casual outfit. Her rock of a wedding ring glimmers in the overhead lights. I'd be more than satisfied to look like her when I'm "old."

"Not that I'm complaining, he loves me, and I wouldn't trade him for all the hot sex you're having."

Adeline is the nicest person I approached about selling a line to. She said she started with a degree and nothing else. Lucky for her, the boy she fell in love with in college turned out to be a smart businessman who gave her this opportunity, but she's made it what it is today.

"I'm glad you're in a happy marriage," I say because I honestly don't know what to say.

She places her wild colored reading glasses on her face, touching a few of the fabrics, tracing the lines of my sketches with the tip of her finger.

While she looks over all my designs, my mind wanders. I'm riding high on my Cristian cloud and I think forward to when I'll see him tonight. Wait, I will see him, right? We never actually made plans. I realize that I have no idea what his expectations are...what it means to be his girlfriend. Will we see each other every night or just a few times a week? Does he expect me to prepare dinner for him? Or pick up his uniform at the dry cleaners? My mind conjures up a million what-ifs until I can't think straight.

Stop the insanity.

"I love it, Vanessa." Adeline's voice finally draws me from my mental cage. "You really have a great eye and the fact that Rose & Ivy will have your debut collection...we're honored."

I release a relieved breath. "I'm so happy to hear that. Do you have any suggestions of what you think will sell better?"

"Try not to go too young. I know you can wear next to nothing and look great, but my regular customers aren't willing to show a ton of skin. Everything you have here is perfect for my clientele. When do you have it projected to be ready? I'd like my spring lines to be in store by February because a lot of my clients vacation around that time of year."

"It shouldn't be a problem. I wanted your okay and as soon as you send me a purchase order with how many of each in what size, I'll send everything to the manufacturer. They predicted it would take about a month or so to complete, so I should have everything right after Christmas."

She claps. "That's great. Since I love this, why don't we get started on a summer line for you, too. I'm going to put you on the right side of the window. Do you have a logo and promotional materials? Maybe we can do a coming soon display. If you could get an outfit from the spring line in short order, we could do a 'don't miss out' tease or something. I want our clients to be as excited about this launch as you and I both are."

Adeline is talking a mile a minute and as much as I love her enthusiasm, the amazing feeling I had vanishes because I don't have any of those things. I didn't even think of a logo or promotional materials. I've been so focused on the cost and execution of having the clothes made.

"Also, you'll need a website where customers can go and see what you'll be offering." She practically bounces on the couch. "I'm so excited. Can you tell? Grant, my husband, always tells me to calm down, don't put the cart in front of the horse, but Vanessa, I can't wait to help you bust your way into this business." She stands and I watch her head behind the counter as I sit there silently, still trying to take everything in. "Wine? I know it's not dinner yet, but I have some small muffins I picked up from the bakery this morning."

"Oh, I..."

"They're pumpkin spice."

"Sold."

She laughs, bringing two glasses of white wine and a tray with four mini pumpkin spice muffins over to the couch.

"Now that we have business over with, tell me all about this new guy."

I lean farther back into the couch, more relaxed than I was a minute ago. Cristian is a topic I could talk about for hours. "Well..."

For the next half an hour before her staff comes in and she opens, I tell her about Cristian and how I have no idea how it all transformed, but I can't seem to tell him no.

———

When I leave Rose & Ivy, I check my phone since I heard it buzzing a few times in my purse during my meeting.

Cristian has text messaged me four times.

Cristian: *How did it go?*
Cristian: *She'd be crazy not to love your designs.*

Funny since he's never seen the designs, though I do appreciate his support.

Cristian: *My dick misses you.*
Cristian: *Should I name my dick? I've never done that but I have a feeling I'll be talking about him a lot with you. ;)*

Just as I'm about to type out a response, a new message pops up.

Cristian: *Scratch that. I've spent way too much time with Jericho today.*

I chuckle on the street corner, my fingers ready to hammer a text back when I notice a black town car come to a stop beside me in my peripheral vision.

I try to tell myself there are hundreds of them in the city, until the window rolls down and Bill is opening the back door.

Tucking my phone back in my purse, I hold my portfolio tight against my chest.

"Vanessa, let's go for a ride."

His tone of voice makes it clear it's not a request. He slides over and my heart rate picks up. Cristian comes to mind and I wonder if I should text him?

And have him be my savior once again? I'm sick of being the damsel in distress. I handled this *before* Cristian, I can do the same now.

"I'm in a rush, Bill. What do you need? I left. Remember?" I lean down and peer into the car seeing him in his classic plaid shirt with silver buttons and worn jeans over a pair of cowboy boots. The back of the town car smells like a distillery and cigar smoke.

"Thomas will drop you where you're going."

Inhaling a deep breath, I repeat the rules in my head I've been told my entire life.

Don't get in the car. Don't get in the car.

What do I do? I get in the car. I need this in our rearview mirror permanently if I'm ever going to move on with my life.

Thomas presses the gas before my door is all the way shut. Bill says something to him and Thomas apologizes and mumbles something about a bus behind him.

"So..." His word hangs in the air. His eyes fall over my body from head to toe and back up.

I shiver under his gaze—not the pleasant kind. His attention unsettles me and it's the reason I left. It was an easy gig that paid exceptionally well and yes it was illegal, but it's not like I was the king pin or anything. But it was a common occurrence where Bill recruited beautiful women with the promise of money but eventually tried to sleep with them. I saw the signs and when I refused him one night, the anger in his eyes was a stark reminder that I needed to get the hell out.

"I told you I was finished."

"Oh Vanessa, the guys are wondering where their favorite girl is. I haven't found anyone who can remember drink orders, let alone the names of their kids. They miss the easy conversation with a gorgeous woman."

"I wish I could help you, Bill, but I'm finally moving forward with my life. I just had a meeting and someone is picking up my line." The excitement bursts from me, but Bill lights a cigarette and cracks the window a fraction.

"If you stay with me, you can have a whole shop. Hell, you'd make enough to be in New York or Paris or wherever you want."

"I'm sorry Bill. I can't." I shift in my seat, hoping he'll realize there's no way to persuade me.

Thomas winds out of downtown and I really hope he's driving me home.

"I think you should reconsider."

"No."

"I've seen the guy. A cop, Van?" He tosses his cigarette out the window. "He's not the one for you. What are you gonna be? Pregnant and barefoot in the kitchen fetching his beer every night? That's not you. You're a star and he's going to suck all the shine right out of you."

He turns in his seat, but I shift my legs toward the door.

"Leave him out of this," I say, panic making the hairs on the back of my neck stand on end.

"Why? Afraid he'll get hurt? I don't make it a habit to hurt people," he says, his voice low because he's bent his head to my ear, the stench of smoke nauseating me.

"I just..."

I've seen Thomas hurt people. People who went too far. Owed the house. Disrupted a game. Those people were used as an example to not screw over Bill Versavich.

"You like him."

I say nothing.

"It's clear the way you press your body to him. The way you allow him to kiss you against a fence in broad daylight. You're a needy bitch wrapping your legs around his waist. You throw yourself at him." His tone is caustic.

I reach for the handle. Bill has never been mean to me, but I see now that I've crossed some imaginary line and he's revealing his true self.

"We're moving, Vanessa. Use that pretty head of yours."

My phone beeps in my purse, but I ignore it.

"Is that Prince Charming now?" His gaze flicks down to my purse.

"I'm sorry, but I gave you notice and I'm out."

Thomas stops at a red light and I'm relieved to see we're in my neighborhood. My hand finds the door handle and I thrust the heavy door open. But Thomas slams on the gas and the door falls shut and I fall to the cushion of the backseat before escaping.

"You know what I've always loved about you, Vanessa? Your sweet innocence. Did you think I didn't know I hit gold when the daughter of a commander in Chicago's finest wanted to come work for me? I celebrated with three hookers that night. Your first week, I actually thanked the man upstairs for bringing you to my doorstep."

He found me, it should be added. Through a girl I worked with at a grocery store.

Pulling out a file I didn't notice from the other side him, he tosses it in my lap. "How do you think Daddy would react to these?"

Inside are pictures of me talking with different men as they placed bets. Me counting money and handing it over to a winner. Me in a short, slutty dress and fishnets bending over and a customer's hand inches from my ass. That guy might have got a broken arm for the move, but it was purposely recorded for this purpose.

It's clear to me now that I am in over my head.

"Please, Bill. Can't we just figure this out between us?"

"We can." The car stops and my eyes see the safety of my house. Lauren's outside with our neighbors, throwing a softball to the little girl. "I'll pick you up Wednesday night at seven. Dress extra slutty, I have big clients flying in for this one and I need it to go well."

"One and I'm done?" I ask.

His head wavers back and forth like he's thinking about it.

"I need you for five nights. And you train the new girl for

me. Make sure she knows the ropes and how to fleece more money outta these guys."

I put my hand out. "Promise?"

He stares down at my hand. "You know you can't trust my handshake, right?" He laughs at me in a way that makes me feel like a foolish child. "I'm not some old-school businessman but you give me this weekend and I'll finally let you go."

I retract my hand. "Fine. Wednesday at seven."

I step out of the town car and the slamming door alarms Lauren who watches me climb out with distaste clear in her features. Keeping her eyes steady on the town car, she watches it drive down the street, the softball still in her hands.

"Lauren?" Jade calls out to her.

I wave and walk up the stairs to our house.

"I'll be right back, Jade." Lauren follows me up the steps.

"I'll throw," I hear Reed say.

"You're a boy, you can't throw a softball."

Reed laughs. "You know who should be throwing with you? Uncle Dean. Did you know he used to play baseball?"

"Really?"

The door shuts, leaving Reed and Jade's conversation behind it.

Lauren starts in on me immediately. "Tell me what the fuck is going on because I thought you were with Cristian last night. This time I'm not taking the brush off. It's time you finally come clean!" Her voice just about rattles the windows.

"Call Maddie," I say in a dire voice and walk up the stairs into my bedroom, happy to hide out for as long as I can until I have to face reality.

CHAPTER THIRTY

Vanessa

"Oh, Van," Maddie sighs in reaction.

She's still in her overalls with paint splattered all over them. Lauren called her and even though she was painting one of the rooms in her new place, she came right over here, stopping for a dozen donuts on the way. What a great friend.

"What the hell were you thinking? He's not going to let you go. Don't think that if you work this weekend, it's over." Lauren paces around my room, scolding me like I'm her child.

"He said and I—"

"What? Can trust him? Because I think he said you were out once before and now he wants you back. And he's black-mailing you. And following you around. Christ Vanessa. Why do you love to push the boundaries so much?"

I pick at my nails feeling like the disappointing daughter for the umpteenth time in my life.

"Relax, Lauren. You screaming isn't going to fix this."

Maddie the rational one joins in, picking at a donut in the box.

"I told Cristian. He knows about before but if I tell him this, I'm afraid of what he might do."

Maddie's hand runs up and down my thigh.

The doorbell rings downstairs.

Maddie and I startle while Lauren bolts for the stairs.

"I hope it's that son of a bitch because I have some things to say to him. He thinks he can fuck with my friend's life? Well, my size six is going to look magnificent up his sleazy ass."

"Laur." Maddie chases after her.

Lauren whips the door open without caution and there's a man standing there. A man I don't recognize wearing jeans and a sweatshirt.

"Hi, I'm Jack. Cristian sent me."

Lauren turns to look at me at the bottom of the staircase. I shrug.

"I'm here to install an alarm system," Jack says.

Maddie sighs.

My eyes widen.

Lauren cracks up laughing and then shuts the door in his face. Opening it halfway again, she sticks her head out through the crack. "One minute, we just need to verify."

"You *should* be afraid, Van. Cristian doesn't even know yet and he's installing an alarm system."

I walk over to the entryway table and pull my phone from my purse. Sure enough, there's a text message from him, as well as three missed phone calls.

Cristian: *I wanted to talk to you first, but I have a friend coming over. He works at the fire station with Mauro and does alarm systems on the side. I know what you said, but I'd feel better if you had an alarm. I hope you don't feel like this is me trying to control you, I just*

feel better when I know the person I care so much about is protected.
Call it a cop thing. ;)

I bust out laughing at a time when I should be chilled to the bone.

"Open the door," I instruct Lauren, who does as I ask. "Come in."

"Good for you girls not letting any ole' Joe in the door." He steps inside and another guy comes in from behind the door.

Maddie lets out a startled yelp. "Trevor?" she asks.

"Hey, Maddie." He smiles at her.

This guy is younger and in the same t-shirt as Jack.

"Sorry, I'm just a little on edge. Guys, Trevor works at the station with Mauro, too," Maddie says.

"Oh please, I'd be scared if Trevor was coming into my house, too," Jack jokes. "Don't worry. He's been warned..."

"This is Bianco's girl." Trevor nods in Maddie's direction, stopping Jack from continuing.

He walks over and shakes her hand. "Hey. I've heard your name so many times I hit Mauro in the stomach when he says it." Maddie blushes and chuckles. "Nice to finally meet you. I always seem to miss you at the station."

"Well, I'm happy to hear that my name isn't far from his mind."

"Yeah, I swear he murmurs it in his sleep," Trevor says.

"So, let me get this straight. You're dating Mauro and you're dating Cristian." Jack weaves a finger between us, circling around with the finger pointed to Lauren. "That leaves you with Luca?"

Us three girls laugh.

"Not a chance in hell," Lauren says. "I caught him spying on me last night." She crosses her arms over her chest.

"What?" Maddie and I say in unison.

"Okay, I'm pretty sure I don't want to hear this because I'll give Luca hell for stalking a chick...er...girl...woman. And I have to remain professional, so come on Trevor." Jack walks by us. "We'll be in the basement looking at your panel first. Should take us about three hours."

"It's down the hall to your left." Maddie points and they head in that direction.

"So spill it. He was spying on you?" I pull Lauren by the sleeve of her sweatshirt over to the living room and mute The Bears pregame.

"I was working out and I saw him through the window. Or his car. I mean you can't miss that thing. Then he had his phone out which lit up his face."

"What did you do?" Maddie asks, a smile already on her lips because we both know this is gonna be good.

"I stomped down and banged on the window. He didn't even try to get away. He made some excuse about Cristian needing something. I only half listened because I thought he was probably banging that chick across the street. The twenty-two-year-old who prances around in those short skirts and tight shirts."

"You mean, Amara? The one who still lives with her parents and goes to church every Sunday?" Maddie asks.

"Oh, you know those Catholic girls."

"Excuse me," I say, offended since I'm a Catholic girl myself.

Lauren dips her head and raises an eyebrow.

"Okay, fine," I say and plop myself down on the couch beside Maddie. "It's not like I was sleeping with everyone." I roll my eyes.

"Amara is heading to medical school next year," Maddie chimes in. "She's super sweet and I doubt she's Luca's type."

"Luca's type is anything with a cup size over a B," Lauren says.

"Maybe," I say. "But I still don't think he's seeing our neighbor.

Lauren throws her arms up. "Forget Amara okay? I just assumed that since the man can't keep his dick in his pants, that he was on our street for some reason. Especially since his brothers were nowhere to be found. But now I get it. Cristian asked him to come here and as pissed as I am, I can't believe Luca was keeping watch on me." She falls to the chair, pulling her legs up to her chest.

"Anyway, yeah I'm pretty sure that has Cristian all over it. Now he's having an alarm system installed."

"You gotta tell him, Van." Maddie's hand rests on my knee again. "You can't keep this from him. It'll only cause problems. You were strong enough to tell him last night."

I throw my head in my hands. "Yes because I thought it was over. I'm such a basket case. How can someone like him actually want to be involved with someone like me?"

Lauren gets up from the chair and sits down on the couch next to me. Maddie's on the other side, both their arms around my shoulders.

"He's lucky to have you," Maddie whispers.

"You're a great catch. You did what you had to and he knows it. Want us to tell you some embarrassing stories about him from high school? You know he wasn't always this stern, mysterious, hot guy," Lauren says.

A reluctant smile creeps onto my face. "Sure."

Maddie gives Lauren a look that asks 'what the hell are you talking about?'

"Okay, I think he taped a kid's butt cheeks together in the locker room."

"Lauren, that was a movie," Maddie says.

"Oh. Well, he failed a science project and—"

"Same movie," Maddie sing-songs.

"Okay, forget high school. Forget him. The only thing that

matters is, he cares about *you*. He wants *you*." She points at my chest. "He sees that special thing inside that we both do. That thing that makes you your unique, stubborn, sugar craving, reluctantly affectionate but ultimately a big-sap-inside self."

I let a small laugh escape.

"You have to trust him, Van," Maddie adds. "Trust that he'll stick by your side and everything I know about Cristian says he will."

"URRGGHH!" I scream into my hands.

"Okay, I'm going to install a camera on the porch." Trevor passes by the room awkwardly, gawking at us like a car accident.

"You can tell him after Sunday dinner." Maddie slaps my knee.

"Sunday what?" I ask.

"At the Bianco's. All the aunts and uncles are preparing the food, but I need to go over there because I know Mama will try to do something. She keeps going on about how she's supposed to get her heart rate up for the monitor. I'm picking up Mauro, you two can come with me."

"Yeah, I'll be taking my own car." Lauren shakes her head. "Actually, I don't need to go. I'm not a Bianco or a soon-to-be Bianco. Have fun ladies." She removes her arm from around me, reaches for and presses play on the remote. "I'll be here watching the game while these boys finish their job."

Maddie doesn't argue because Lauren has a point.

"I'll ride with you," I say to Maddie, hoping Cristian will be okay with me joining in. "Can we make a stop on the way? I want to pick her up some flowers."

Maddie's face lights up and she squeezes my shoulders. "You know the way to a man's heart is through his mama, right?"

I roll my eyes, though I'm sure in the Bianco family, that's true. They treat her like the queen of Chicago, but I'm going over there because...well...because I like Cristian and...whatever. I'm just going.

CHAPTER THIRTY-ONE

Cristian

"When is this shit gonna stop?" Jericho sits next to me, his fingers wound tight around the steering wheel. "I mean if another firefighter loses—"

"I know. I know. It's like the department is doing nothing. They know it's arson at this point."

A third warehouse has now burned to the ground. Firefighters stumble out while the building is still succumbing to the flames.

Pulling out my phone, I seek out the engine numbers before texting Mauro.

Me: *Looks like there's another arson fire. They've pulled everyone out.*

The three dots appear.

Mauro: *Motherfucker. Don't tell Mad, okay? She's practically becoming a cling-on on the days I work.*

Me: *Sure, but Luca is here and you know how he is.*

I look up to see Luca sitting in the back of his ambulance, giving a soot-faced firefighter oxygen. I switch over to my conversation with my youngest brother and type out a new message.

Me: *Luca, zip it about the fire at dinner tonight. Ma doesn't need to worry about Mauro right now.*

Blaming it on Mama will help entice Luca to keep his mouth shut...hopefully.

He doesn't answer, because at the very least, he's a professional at work.

"Let's get back to the station." Jericho starts the cruiser up. "I have a date tonight."

"Sounds good."

We're a mile or so to the district when the possibility of what—or who—Jericho could be doing tonight dawns on me. "It's not Lauren is it?"

Jericho crinkles his eyes at me like I'm talking in a different language.

"Vanessa's friend Lauren. The one you met at the hockey game."

"Oh, the little one. She's spunky." He grins.

Oh fuck me. He's going to blow this and Lauren's going to beat the shit out of him.

"So tonight...your date isn't with her, right?" I shift in my seat to better face him.

"No. She's hot as fuck, but she's also a fucking tease. Once we got to the bar, all she cared about was playing darts and ragging on your damn brother."

I let out an exasperated sigh. "Yeah well, they have a weird relationship."

"A kinky one I bet." He waggles his eyebrows.

"Why do you say that?"

Hatred I see. Flirtation, not so much. Still, there's this undercurrent between them I can't quite decipher.

"They seem to get off on pissing each other off. All that frustration is bound to lead to sex."

I roll my eyes. "You think everything leads to sex."

He shrugs, turning into the district parking lot, putting the cruiser into park. "Everything *should* lead to sex." He chuckles, turning off the engine and climbing out of the car.

Another text comes into my phone.

Mauro: *You coming to dinner?*
Me: *Nah. I'm going to head over to Vanessa's.*

Because I won't allow her to sleep there alone even with a new alarm system.

Mauro: *That's a shame because Vanessa's over here.*

What? She's at my parents' house without me? Jesus, what are they telling her? They better not be telling her how I used to dress in Ma's high heels or how I would only eat peanut butter sandwiches for every meal for three months straight when I was four.

Me: *Then I'll see you in 30.*
Mauro: *Yeah, that's what I thought. #pussywhipped*

———

I park along the curb of my parents' bungalow. The park across the street is now a state of the art masterpiece with cushy foam instead of wood chips and plastic instead of a metal equipment. Specific swings for babies and no sharp corners or materials that will cause third-degree burns after a day in the sun. Where are the poles to fly down like a firefighter or the roundabout where you became king of the playground if you spun it fast enough to make someone throw up? The baseball fields are locked now and reserved for only organized teams. Kids these days don't know what they're missing.

I look up to my parents' house and see the silhouettes of everyone through the foggy windows. It's chilly out here, but a Bianco gathering means it's hot inside. Christmas lights are lit up on a spattering of houses on their street. I'll need to come over this week and get that done for my parents.

I walk up the driveway and open the door to the house to find everyone congregated in the living room, watching football. Well, Mauro and my cousins at least, or the few who still live around here. We used to run around this house playing tag, then we hid in the basement because our parents were lame, then most of them moved out of state and explored careers outside of Chicago. My parents always say how lucky they are that their boys stayed close.

My gaze scans the room for a blonde in the mix of brunettes. I spot her at the dining table, talking with Ma and my aunt. She can't see me because her back is to me, but Ma smiles at me over Vanessa's shoulder, her hand touching Vanessa's in a sweet gesture to say, I'm here.

Vanessa turns and all the bullshit from my day evaporates. I forget about the damn reports, the arsonist lighting fires throughout the city, the man who beat up his wife, the kids throwing stones from the overpass. All that disappears with only the slight turn up of her lips.

She's here. In the flesh without any pestering from me. That has to mean something, right?

She says something to Ma and my aunt. They nod in

understanding and she slides out of the chair, walking toward me.

She's beautiful, stunning and I lose the ability to breathe as she grows closer.

"Hey," she says in a quiet voice.

I take my finger and tuck a strand of her hair behind her ear. "Hey."

Her gaze falls down my body. "Out of uniform, huh?"

I stare down at her because although she's tall for a woman, I still have quite a height advantage.

"Thinking about playing cops and robbers?" I lean in and whisper.

"You could show me your old bedroom."

I laugh, pulling her into me. At some point, my family will have to see what we are and what better time than now.

"Follow me." My hand runs down the length of her arm until her hand is securely in mine.

I stop briefly to kiss Mama on the cheek and then my aunt before we sneak off to the end of the hallway where my old bedroom is.

Shutting the door, her eyes take in the room that hasn't changed since I moved out many years ago.

"Not one naked picture?" she asks, sitting down on my double bed with the same blue and red plaid bedspread I used as a teen.

"Are you kidding? Ma would never allow that. The magazines are hidden in the back of the closet in a box labeled 'confirmation stuff.'"

"What? You put nudie magazines with religious stuff?"

"Ma won't bother looking in there and if she does, it's under the blanket they baptized me in."

She shakes her head. "And I thought you were one of the good ones."

I hop on the bed, the dipping mattress moving us both to the middle, and I pull her down to me.

"So." I inhale the scent of her shampoo. "Any visitors today?"

She swats at my stomach but kisses my jaw.

"Two actually. Uninvited." She props her chin on my chest and I tuck a hand behind my head for leverage to see her.

"Really? Who?"

"Oh, just some guys who came to install a security system."

I laugh and she kisses my neck again. Those kisses are addicting.

"Thank you, but it was unnecessary."

"Nah, it wasn't. I want you safe and Lauren, too."

She takes a deep breath sits straight up, looking down on me. "Cris?" She says my name as though it's a question, but there's an undercurrent of dread. Suddenly her shortening my name doesn't sound as good as it did the other night.

"What?" I sit up and she turns, putting one leg between us, and picks at her sock. "Van." I place my finger under her chin and pull her gaze to mine. "You can tell me anything, remember?"

"I saw Bill today."

A mask of red slips over my vision like a curtain. "What? At your house?"

I'm on my feet, pacing, my hand in my pocket and gripped around my phone. Ready to call the station, ask a few guys to do me a solid and check out my girl's place. To get the plate number so I can beat the shit out of the man myself.

"No, he found me after I left Rose & Ivy." She bites her lip. "He said he wants me for one more weekend. That the girl he found to replace me isn't working out. I wanted to be straight with you..."

I stop midstride, staring down at her so hard, her vision

shifts to the right, away from me.

Knife to the fucking heart.

"You're not actually thinking you're going to do it?"

She shrugs. "It's just until the end of next weekend and this can all be over."

"Please, Vanessa, please tell me you aren't this stupid." The calloused words rush out of my mouth before I can soften them.

Her gaze no longer veers away, it's squarely on me now.

"Stupid?" she asks, her body rigid and preparing for battle.

"I didn't mean that *you* are stupid."

"Really? Because that's what you said."

I throw my hands up in the air. "I'm sorry, I'm just pissed off."

"Stupid," she murmurs to herself, her fingers knotting along one another.

I fall to my knees, my hands sliding between her legs to part them for me. "I really didn't mean that. I'm just...it's a bad idea is all. Please...forgive me." My hands find their way to her hips and I lower my head to find her eyes. "Really, I didn't mean..."

"He has pictures," she whispers. Thank God she's letting the stupid comment go, but what she says doesn't make me feel any better.

"Pictures of?" The feeling of hot lava burns a trail down my throat to my stomach.

"Pictures of me in short dresses, men hovering over me with their hands close to my ass. Me counting stacks of money, handing it over to men. Serving drinks, lighting cigars..."

"Oh."

"I didn't let them touch me, but the pictures make it look like it's possible. He said he'll send them to my father and his superiors if I don't do what he says."

My head falls to my chest and my ass to my legs. Still sitting in front of her, I blow out a breath. I need to come up with a plan.

"I'll just do it. He'll pick me up on Wednesday night and I'll be done on Sunday. It will be over and done with."

I stand, running a hand through my hair.

"Do you honestly think I would let you go?"

"I don't remember this being your decision." She stands. "I'm not asking you to fix this, Cristian. I'm telling you out of courtesy because Lauren and Maddie thought I should. I can fix this myself and I plan to do just that."

Her abrupt change in demeanor throws me at first. I'm not supposed to be thrown. I'm trained to stay calm and collected, to think fast. Vanessa takes what I learned and runs it over like an eighteen wheeler.

"I'm not some asshole who tells his girlfriend what to do, but I'm not letting you go into a situation where you're not safe." I stand now, too. "Who do you think I am?"

She swallows and raises her chin in defiance. "I started this, I have to finish it. I don't want you playing hero and saving me."

Can we rewind the tape and start this conversation over? Because what's happening right now is pissing me off.

"Vanessa."

She shakes her head. "I'm going Wednesday. Either you support me through this or this is over."

I'm stuck, albeit temporarily. She doesn't understand. No way she can.

"Fine. If that's your choice," I grind out between clenched teeth.

"I'm glad we're on the same page."

I wrap her in my arms, laying my head on top of hers. Yeah, we're so not on the same page, but she can think what she wants. She will anyway.

CHAPTER THIRTY-TWO

Vanessa

*C*ristian has been by my side for the past few days. He had Tuesday off, so we spent the day at his apartment, having sex and lounging around. He tried to push me to run, but I had to work on making sure all materials and patterns hit my manufacturer on time. Not to mention figure the whole website thing out.

The only time we were apart all day was an hour and a half while he went on a run. I'll tell you, but don't tell him...I missed him. I want to throw my head in my hands and cry or laugh or scream. I can't believe I'm here, in a relationship with Cristian Bianco, Mr. Honest and Noble, missing him after only an hour and a half away from him.

I like the fact he's allowing me to handle this thing with Bill on my own. It shows he won't be controlling, albeit I was surprised he was so easily convinced. But he's given me no reason to think he's not one hundred percent on board.

I hear a key insert into the door and speak of the devil,

my gorgeous police officer walks in sweaty and sexy from his run with a brown paper bag in his hand.

"How was your run?" I ask from where I sit with my laptop at his kitchen table, complete with a bowl of fruit in the middle.

What bachelor has a bowl of fruit? That would be my guy.

"It was okay." There are lines indented on his forehead that weren't there when he left. His dark eyes aren't sparkling like they usually do either. "I picked you up something."

"Oh." I stand and walk over to him.

He holds the bag above my head and pulls me closer by my waist.

"Where's my thank you?" he asks, dangling the brown paper bag above our heads.

"I have to see what's in it first." I reach up, but he only holds the bag higher. I manage to get a finger on the rough paper, but he shifts it behind his back.

"Do I smell pumpkin? And spice?" He inhales against my neck. "Or is that coming from my beautiful girlfriend's pores?"

I laugh trying to reach the bag with my hands around his waist, but soon my back is pressed to the counter and his thigh is parting my legs. I grind on his muscular leg like a dog in heat. I'm insatiable with this man.

"Hmm…" he growls, putting the bag on the counter behind me to free both of his hands.

With his hands on my hips, he directs me in an arousing rhythm that ignites my core like flint to steel.

"You're sweaty," I say.

"And if I'm lucky I'll be even sweatier soon." He smiles down at me and captures my lips with his.

We've kind of perfected this slow dance of our tongues that speeds up and slows down. Right now he's matching the same rhythm of his thigh. With every plunge of his tongue,

I'm rewarded with a push of his thigh to my center. The seam of my jeans only causes the desire to ripple through me faster.

He rips his mouth from mine. "What's it going to be? Me or some pumpkin spice?"

"Hmm..." I moan into his mouth, my hands desperate to unclothe him.

He steps back and eyes the bag behind me. "Come on, answer the question."

Taking the hem of his t-shirt, he strips it off his body. He kicks off his shoes and flings off his socks in a pile on the floor. He's mouth-watering and calendar-worthy. Hell, he could fill an entire calendar all by himself. I lick my lips.

"I'm a little offended you're still over there."

I giggle like the teenage girl he turns me into. I put both my hands in the air like I'm weighing my options.

"You're bruising my ego." He loses the shorts and compression pants and look-see there, he doesn't wear anything else underneath.

"You're playing dirty." I step forward.

"By all means see what's in the bag." He takes a few steps back, leaning on the back of the couch, and strokes himself a few times, not at all embarrassed about his nakedness. I wouldn't be either if I looked like him.

"Shut up. You know whatever is in that bag is only worth one orgasm. You're worth at least three." I strip my t-shirt off over my head and push down my leggings. Two can play at the not wearing underwear game.

"You know I like to undress you, but" —his eyes darken as he takes in my body— "this'll do."

He pulls me to him, and we fall back down onto the couch. Me on top of him, our limbs tangled.

Life has never been sweeter.

———

Remember that phrase about life being so sweet?

All was good until Wednesday night at six-thirty when I walked down the stairs of my house.

"Just take the taser." Lauren opens my clutch and shoves it in. I don't bother arguing.

"Let me give you a little self-defense course." Mauro stands in the center of the kitchen. "Act like you're going to seduce me." He moves my hand to his chest like a man would grab a woman's boob.

I go along with the act but he quickly twists my arm behind my back and my heel almost breaks. I cry out.

"Thanks for that lesson," I say once he releases me.

"No prob." He grabs a piece of pizza from on top of the stove.

It's like this is some party before I head off. I went from no one knowing to everyone knowing.

"Use the taser. Don't be afraid to scream either," Maddie says.

"Guys, if Cristian isn't worried, why are you?" I ask.

Cristian called a bit ago. He's stuck at the district and said he'd see me when I got home—that he'd be waiting with his gun loaded in case that asshole tries anything.

Mauro glances at Maddie who looks at Lauren who stares back at me.

"He's still trying to win you over," Lauren says.

"And he's being a fucking pussy because of it. If I was Cris, I'd have that guy in handcuffs or a body bag," Mauro says around a mouthful of pizza.

"Definitely a body bag," Luca joins the party.

"How the hell did you get in here?" Lauren asks.

"Your door is unlocked, which I'll be nice and keep that from Cris. You're welcome." He winks at Lauren who rolls her eyes and takes a big sip of wine.

They have wine and beer out. I hate that I have to go do

this and not hang out and party with all of them. Cristian could meet us here and we'd play games and drink and laugh. Well, four of us would. The other two would either kill each other or fuck each other.

Operation L & L is bound to combust sooner than later. That's dumb, I need a better name to get those two together.

"Here." He hands me a small switchblade.

"Luca!" I scold. "I don't want to carry this thing."

He purses his lips and shakes his head like I'm an idiot. "It'll buy you some time if things go bad."

"What the hell are you doing with that?" Lauren asks, but the look on her face says she's kind of impressed.

"It's just a knife, not a bomb, Hunt. Relax." He disregards her and turns his attention to me. "Please take it just in case. People like this guy aren't anyone to mess around with."

I put it in my purse next to my taser. "Thank you all for everything."

"Remember." Maddie stops me right before I'm about to walk out the door, her hands on my shoulders, her motherly eyes on me. "Self-defense. If he does anything to you, you can get off on self-defense. I'm sure Reed knows some excellent lawyers."

"Thanks." I flip around to face them all, my hand on the knob of the back door. "You guys are worrying about nothing. I handled this guy before. It's no big deal." I almost believe that myself.

All four of them look like I'm a five-year-old on my first day of kindergarten. They want to encourage me, but they know it's going to be tough.

"Hold up." Luca runs over and takes my hands and bows his head. "Please watch over Vanessa because she's the only girl in the world who would want to spend a lifetime with Cristian." He straightens his back and uses his finger to make the sign of the cross over his chest.

"LUCA!" Maddie comes over and smacks him on the back of the head.

He holds his hand to the spot. "Jesus Mauro, are you sure she's not Italian?" He rubs it a few times. "That was like Nonna."

"Bye guys." I sneak out while they're all telling Luca he's a pussy for thinking Maddie hit him hard.

Walking down the stairs to the back of the house, a path I took most nights for the past year, feels worse than it did before. Before I was doing it for a purpose—my future. Now, I'm a pawn in someone's game and as much as I don't want to admit it to myself, it scares me. Bill has never spoken to me like he did two days ago. Then again, he never had a reason to. I was there willingly.

Like clockwork, the black town car pulls up to the garage and my hand moves to the car door.

It opens with the click and I tuck inside, finding Bill in his usual attire. Ripped up faded jeans over cowboy boots and a plaid western shirt. His hair, or what he has left is slicked back.

"I'm surprised." Bill's gaze roams my body, concentrating on my boobs that are one string away from being out on display. I should've worn my coat. It was stupid not to.

"What?"

"I thought for sure your boyfriend would try to find me."

"If you keep to your word he doesn't need to be involved." I turn away from him to face the door.

A creepy laugh rumbles out of him. Way too many cigarettes in his lifetime. "He doesn't scare me."

A dark form approaches the car and I close my eyes in frustration. Why are Luca and Mauro getting involved in this? Trying to be saviors for their brother?

Only when the door opens, it's the other Bianco brother.

CHAPTER THIRTY-THREE

Vanessa

*H*e's not in his uniform, but dark jeans and a jacket that I have no doubt has his holster underneath.

"Hey babe, slide over for me." I do which only puts me closer to Bill. "On second thought, I'll take bitch." He lifts up and I slide back over to the window for him to sit between us.

"What the hell is going on?" Bill sneers.

"I just thought you might want to see some of the blackmail I have on you since you're so willing to share yours with Vanessa. Come on, I'll show you mine if you show me yours." He pulls out a manila folder from the inside of his jacket.

How? What could he have? He's never been to the poker games.

Bill opens the envelopes and looks through the pictures and a few other pieces of paper that look like bank deposits. "This proves nothing. It could be a friendly game."

"Jeez, it's stuffy in here. Mind rolling down a window or

something?" Cristian leans over Bill to press the window button.

His presence is so commanding, and I hate to admit it, but I'm growing a little damp between the legs. Then I remember the dress I'm wearing and I stretch the fabric at the bottom to cover myself. I look like a slut and that's exactly what Cristian will see me as in this moment.

The stench of a Chicago alley hits us as the window descends.

"I'm going to give you two choices," Cristian continues in a calm, friendly voice that somehow still conveys that he means business. "You let Vanessa go and get rid of any evidence she worked for you, or two cop cars come in both sides of this alley and arrest you for running an illegal gambling ring."

"You have no proof. This isn't going to put me in jail for more than a day until my lawyer can get me off." He drops the manila folder on the ground.

"Lucky us, we have a key witness. Yeah, you might not go to jail, but I'm sure once the D.A. starts poking around they're likely to find tax evasion, maybe some other illegal activities you have your hands in. Not to mention the fact that you'll lose every customer you have. Every client will wonder if they'll be the one on the front paper the next morning. Wondering if you can actually provide them with the privacy they need to play cards for money. We've looked into it. Your client list is extensive and exclusive. Those are the kind of people who don't want to be putting their hands up in front of flashing cameras."

I look from Cristian to Bill, wide-eyed.

"She wouldn't go on the stand, her father would lose all credibility," Bill says with smug confidence.

Cristian shrugs. "Small price to pay to make sure your daughter isn't tied to the likes of you for an eternity. The city could spin it however they want. Plus." He leans in close to Bill. "Who's to say she's the witness?"

Bill pales and the only reason he would be concerned is if someone else left on bad terms. He stews and says nothing for a full minute while Cristian continues to stare at him. Never once averting his gaze.

"Fine," Bill chokes out. "She's done, but you better not go back on your end of the deal."

"I'm a man of my word. If you had been, we wouldn't be in this car." Cristian reaches over and opens the door for me. "Go ahead, Van."

I step out of the car, but Cristian closes the door before retreating himself.

There's no sound, no yelling, nothing coming from the town car and because of the tints I can't see what's going on inside.

Not knowing what to do, I stand there with my arms wrapped around myself, the cold air chilling me through the small amount of fabric covering my body.

A minute or two later, Cristian's big body emerges into the dark night, only a dim streetlight and a few house lights for me to know it's him.

The door isn't even shut before the town car drives down the alley, turning right.

Relief wells up inside of me until Cristian wraps his arms around me.

"Let's get you inside. It's cold out." His big hands run up and down my bare arms.

I nod and allow him to guide me by the small of my back up the sidewalk to our back door. The noises of the girls and the other two Bianco brothers laughing and carrying on inside finally pulls me back out of my fog. We reach the door, but I don't open it, instead circling back around to him.

"I would've handled it," I say.

"I know, but this way you don't have to work and let's be honest here, he never would've let you loose. He would've dangled the carrot in front of you for who knows how long."

Does he think I'm stupid? His comment sure implies he does.

"You think I would have just kept on working there?"

He shrugs. "I don't know what you would've done, but it's over now. I handled it."

My heartbeat picks up pace at the same time my blood boils hot. He handled it? Is this how he expects to handle our life for ever and ever?

"I told you I'd handle it!" My voice grows louder.

He takes a step forward. "Your way wasn't the best way. I don't get what I did wrong here. I thought you'd be happy. I pulled strings to get those pictures and that intel. A lot of people helped me save...get you out of this situation." He crosses his arms over his chest.

"I never asked them too."

"No, I did," he snaps.

"And you had no right."

He raises his palm to me. "I didn't have a right? You're my fucking girlfriend, that means I take care of you!"

No words.

Nothing.

I'm speechless.

"You don't take care of me. I'm a grown adult. *I* take care of me." I point my finger at my chest.

He blows out a stream of air that's illuminated by the light above us.

"Okay, you do, but I wanted to fix this for you." He steps forward, his arm already out and ready to wrap around my waist. "I couldn't stand the thought of you in that room. In this." His gaze moves down my body, disgust heavy in his eyes. "With those men. I'm sorry, but I wasn't cool with it."

I throw my hands up and step back. "Then why did you say you were okay with it?"

"Because I knew you'd fight me on it! I knew what I was doing."

"You know what? This whole thing." I wave my finger between us. "It's too fast. You shouldn't be putting your career on the line for me. Neither should those other officers. You just want someone to fix. Some woman who needs you to keep her together. I get that when we met, I was a little broken, but I'm not now. I would've gotten myself through the situation. But you're just always going to sweep in and act like a savior. God knows what you'll do when we have kids."

"You think about having kids with me?"

It's like he doesn't hear me speaking.

I ball up my fists at my side. "You know what Cristian? Thank you for what you did and I do mean that. I appreciate all the effort you went to, but I wish you would have respected my wishes. I think I need some space." My hand touches the doorknob and since it's the first moment of silence between us since we started arguing, I notice that there's no more talking inside.

Cristian says nothing and I wait for his calculated words before I can retreat to my room.

"How long?" he asks.

"I don't know."

An empty hollow chill fills the late autumn air. "No."

"No?" I ask.

"No. You know what, I'm done." He slides his palms over his cheeks. "I can't do this. I can't keep sitting here like some loser waiting for you to pick me. I did what I did tonight because during the short time we've spent together, I fell in love with you. And I guess I'm not the right guy for you because when I love someone I want what's best for them and I'll do whatever is in my power to make that happen. It's not me controlling you, Vanessa, or thinking you can't handle it on your own. It's the fact that if we're together, you don't *have* to handle it on your own. You're not some charity case and I don't have a savior complex. This is me loving you. It truly is that simple. Ever heard the term I'd take a bullet for you?"

He doesn't wait for me to answer and the distance he's keeping between us somehow feels so thick that we'll never get back to where we were.

"Well, I would. I'd take a bullet or wrestle a fucking lunatic who could tear me limb from limb if it meant you were happy and safe. That's me and I'm done apologizing for who I am. So, you go on inside and keep yourself bottled up in that jar of bulletproof glass because I can't be with someone who won't let me love them the only way I know how."

Tears prick the corners of my eyes, but I blink them back. "Cristian," I sigh. "I only asked for time."

He takes one step down the stairs and circles back to me. "You know where to find me if you decide you can live with me loving you. Me and you. No bullshit." He jogs down the stairs and disappears into the dark night.

CHAPTER THIRTY-FOUR

Vanessa

I open the back door to four eavesdropping trolls.

They all pretend they're looking at the floor molding by the window that's coming up. Yeah, I don't buy it.

"Hey, Van. That was quick." Lauren is the first to speak. Typical.

"Shit, Mauro. I totally forgot. We have that thing tonight," Luca says.

"Oh crap." Mauro kisses Maddie quickly on the lips. "I'll call you later."

"Sure. Okay," Maddie squeaks out and the two men leave through the back door instead of the front.

I think it's fair to say that they could've just said, we're on Cristian's side so we'll be with him.

The door shuts and Lauren lays into me immediately, following me to the cupboards. I grab the package of pumpkin spice Oreos that Mrs. Bianco gave me because she heard I loved pumpkin spice and she said she doesn't bake with pumpkin, and because I haven't had time to get the real Oreos and I need some form of sugar right now.

"You've completely lost your mind." Lauren sits down on a stool across from me. Maddie keeps her distance trying to find some articulate advice to give me.

"It's none of your business." I take the Oreos and head upstairs.

Four footsteps follow me.

"It is our business because we care about you and you're about to throw away the first guy you've ever loved."

I try to slam the door to my room, but Lauren's hand slaps it and the door springs open again.

"I don't love him. I'm about to start siding with Luca, you are crazy."

Lauren gives me the finger and flops down on my bed.

Maddie takes a seat in the chair in front of my vanity. "I think she's trying to say the first guy you might care for not, you know, not lust."

I slip off my high heels, unzip my dress, and disappear into the closet.

"I lusted Cristian for your information." I emerge in my panties and bra and head to my dresser.

"I'm going to keep my lips zipped because you're hurting," Maddie says.

I dig out a pair of yoga pants and an oversized sweatshirt, put them on, then sit on the edge of my bed and chomp down on three Oreos. Black crumbs fall to my chest. I guess these things aren't that bad.

"Okay, Vanessa, you need to get real right now," Lauren says beside me.

Maddie shakes her head at her.

"What Lauren's trying to say is that Cristian was just doing what men do. They like to be the hero. They want to take care of you. Just last week, Mauro called the electrician to read him the riot act because the guy was being condescending to me. I had to explain to him that I can handle myself and don't need him interfering where I'm in charge. He still thinks he did the right thing. Men." She rolls her eyes.

"I think—" Lauren tries to speak, but Maddie interrupts her.

"You seemed really happy with Cristian. Were you?" Maddie asks.

I finish chewing my cookie which is hard when it feels like there's a boulder on my chest. "Well...yeah."

"But you wouldn't use the word love?"

"No!" I balk. How could she even suggest that? I've known him for a hot minute. "You guys are failing to realize I didn't know Cristian in high school. We only met a short time ago."

"That doesn't matter. Love doesn't really know time."

There's the Maddie I know.

"You should write for Hallmark." I shove another Oreo into my mouth.

"Okay, forget the love thing, but you guys were on your way to something special, don't you think?" Maddie presses.

"What do you want to know? I like Cristian. There. I *really* like Cristian. I let him see me for me—imperfect, flawed parts and all. I thought we had something, yes." The boulder on my chest feels heavier with my admission.

"But..."

"But nothing." I leave the Oreos on the bed and step over to the window. Our street is dark and I notice a few snowflakes beginning to fall to the ground in the light of the streetlamp.

Our first snowfall of the season.

We couldn't even make it to the first snowfall.

"Alright Maddie, nice try, it's my turn." Lauren sits up on

her knees on the mattress like she's preparing for battle. "Vanessa, get your head out of your ass and see the damn light. Not a lot of guys would put up with all this bullshit. And don't go putting words in my mouth, you're worth every ounce of energy Cristian has given to make this work, but now it's time for you to go the distance. You need to step up. Show him you're in it to win it. No one is asking you to accept a ring or change your name or be the cowering little Mrs. who follows the Mr.'s orders."

"Whatever Lauren, you can't even admit that you want Luca," I snip.

"Want him? I don't even *like* him."

Maddie and I both shoot her a sympathetic 'whatever you say' expression.

Lauren just rolls her eyes. "I know you're mad at him and it's okay to tell him he overstepped, but you have to try to understand where he's coming from. My guess is that he's gotten you this far kicking and screaming."

I cross my arms over my chest and look up at her a little sullenly, then shrug.

"You're always working so hard to keep people out, Van. Imagine what might be possible if you really opened yourself up and let him in." Lauren lets her statement hang in the air.

"He decides he doesn't want me anymore and I end up broken-hearted," I whisper.

"You need to decide whether you want him in your life or not," Maddie adds in a gentle voice. "I have a feeling Cristian doesn't mess around and he won't wait forever. You can't expect him to. The last thing I want is for you to come to your senses and for it to be too late because he's already with someone else."

"Some cute blonde who makes him dinners and makes his bed," Lauren adds. "One he has hot sex with. One who he plays cops and robbers with."

The boulder on my chest feels like it's rolled down into my stomach at the thought of Cristian with someone else. "Lauren," I sigh.

"Do you guys play that?" she asks, getting off topic. "If I were dating a cop I'd be all over it. I totally get it if that's your thing."

"Shut up." I stare out the window, the snow mesmerizing me and all I can think is that I wish Cristian were here to share it with me, his arms around my waist, his chin resting on my shoulder.

"We'll leave you alone now." Maddie stands to leave and drags Lauren off the bed by the arm.

They leave and I don't move from the window. I glance over at the Oreos his mom gave me, and I think about if I was working with Bill right now. How miserable that would have been. Several minutes pass and then my phone beeps so I grab it off my nightstand.

Dad: *I have some stuff of Mom's I wanted to bring over.*

I click the home screen and there's the picture of me and Cristian. From the race. When was the last time I felt that happy? Looking back, I feel the smile that never left my warm face from the sun. How happy we were. How at peace my body was. How everything made sense in my life.

Darn it all to hell. They're right. I can't let him slip away because of my stupid pride or my fear of rejection. Some things, some *people*, are worth the risk.

I swing the door open and Maddie and Lauren are standing along the wall, Maddie swinging her keys around her finger. "Time?"

"Time." I nod and they run to me, jumping and down screaming. "Okay, but let's go before he finds that other blonde," I say.

"How about I drive?" Lauren says, running down the stairs first.

"I'd like to get there in one piece."

We rush out the back door and race across the yard, the snow falling onto us, and get into Maddie's car.

"Wait I don't know where he is?" I say, panic pricking my stomach.

Maddie glances over at with a 'come on' expression. "It pays to date your best friend's fiancé's brother."

CHAPTER THIRTY-FIVE

Vanessa

*M*addie slowly backs out of the garage, presses the button on the opener again and watches the metal door until it's almost closed. Then she shifts from gear to gear until the D lights up.

"MADDIE!" I yell.

"What?" She looks over at me as we're in the middle of the alley.

"I'd like to hurry this up before he has time to convince himself that he's better off without me."

"First off, I almost ran over a stray cat the other day. Second, Cristian knows you're the woman," she says.

Finally, putting her foot on the gas, we move forward down the dark alley and she turns right to get back on to our street. Even though I can't drive, I kind of wish my hands were on the steering wheel. Then again, I'd probably drive into the side of the Warner's garage.

"Maddie, I get the whole safety of animals thing and that

Cristian is probably not even to his apartment yet but, come on," Lauren adds her two cents in from the back seat.

"Maybe you'd like to drive?" Maddie says, looking at Lauren in the rearview mirror.

"Perfect. Pull over."

"I think Vanessa would like to be alive and unharmed when she tells Cristian—"

"Nope. Don't say it," I warn her with a finger. "I don't."

"OKKKAAAYYY." Maddie turns away from Irving Park Road which means it'll add on extra minutes to the drive. Minutes that I don't want to add, but having no license and no car means I'm at her mercy.

Her phone dings on her console and she takes a quick peek at it before setting it back down with a small smile on her face.

I sit back and try to be appreciative that she's driving, but when she pulls up along the curb in the front of *our* house, I lose my self-control.

"MAD!"

She laughs, parks and takes the keys out of the ignition.

"What are you doing?" I turn to face her, my back to the window.

"Brilliant," Lauren says from the back seat.

"What are you British now?" My head twists sharply in Lauren's direction.

Her finger points out the window and her smile would make you think she just screwed Chris Hemsworth.

"What?" I shift my gaze to the window and if a heart could soar out of a chest, mine would be lifting me to the clouds.

Cristian stands at our front door, his hands in his pockets. His two brothers are at the bottom of staircase talking.

Maddie honks and all three heads turn in our direction.

"Whoops. My hand slipped." She shrugs.

Even with only the brightness of our porch light, I see the relief in Cristian's eyes. He jogs down the steps until he's halfway and jumps over the rod iron railing to the sidewalk, not stopping until he's outside the car.

"This is where you tell him everything." Lauren's hand touches my shoulder. "Don't hold back, Van."

He doesn't open my door, but his gaze stays locked on me through the window. With a deep breath and a burst of courage, I open the door and step out, shutting it behind me to keep Lauren inside.

Which doesn't work all that great because the car doors on the opposite side open and my two friends speak in hushed whispers as they head to the house.

"Hey." I'm looking down admiring my shuffling feet.

He bridges the gap, places his finger under my chin, and I meet his gaze. His deep brown to my bright blue. The anger from an hour ago is absent, replaced with the admiration that usually shines through.

"I'm sorry," he says.

"No, I am. You're right—I haven't met you halfway."

"You have. I should've given you more time. You've had a rough road and I know I can't change all that in a few weeks." His hand drops from my chin and my body chills from not having his touch.

We stand inches apart from one another and as much as I want us to be flush together, I have to put my big girl panties on and admit how I feel.

"This." I wag a finger between us. "I'm in. I care about you."

A smirk emerges. I haven't really seen Cristian smirk a lot. Smile. Yes. Grin? Yes. Smirk, not so much and it's sexy just like every other facial expression of his.

"Care for me?" He raises his eyebrows.

My shoulders deflate. "Yes. You know what I mean." The

words I'm really trying to say feel like sandpaper in my windpipe.

He wraps his arm around my back, pulling me to him. My hands splayed on his chest.

"So you forgive me?"

I nod. "But more than that, I understand why you did it."

He stares down at me, the smirk disappearing and I know there's something serious going on in that head of his right now. "I'll apologize for surprising you by hopping in the car, but I won't apologize for helping you. That's me, Van. I'll always protect you. But I'll always support you, too. I don't see it as exerting control over you. It's what you do when you...care...for someone." The smirk reappears. "I just want you to understand that before we end this fight with a kiss and some hot make up sex."

I dip my head and chuckle into his chest, then meet his gaze again. "I understand, I'm just scared...about how much I feel for you, about how vulnerable that makes me. So when I thought you disregarded my feelings and were trying to control the situation, I was upset." My arms entwine around his neck.

"It's not that. It's just you're everything to me and I'm a cop for fuck's sake. It's in my blood to protect. And when it's the person I...care for, that urge is even stronger."

I inch closer, rising to my tiptoes. "You care for me?"

"Very much."

"Do one thing you weren't planning on doing tonight?" I ask him, my lips millimeters away from his.

His fingertips dig into my hips and I don't think we'll make it back to his apartment.

"Are you making me work for another date?"

"No, you've got me."

He kisses my forehead. "I think this time you should do

one thing you weren't planning on doing if you want to ditch these guys and go back to my apartment."

"Well." I tighten my arms around him.

"I'm kidding. Come on. I want you away from spying eyes." He breaks us apart and his hand finds mine, leading me away from Maddie's car to his.

I blame Cupid. Who would've known that little man in a diaper had such power? Because just like that, I'm ready.

"Officer Bianco," I call out and his feet stop, turning his attention back to me.

It only takes him a second to figure out what I'm doing—taking us back to that night at the bonfire.

"Miss Flanagan?" He steps into me.

"You want me to do one thing I didn't think I was going to do tonight?"

His hands cup my cheeks and he brings us chest to chest, heartbeat to heartbeat because he knows. "More than anything," he whispers.

My hands cover his on my face and I lock eyes with the man who makes me the happiest I've ever been. "I love you."

The smile of all smiles brightens his face. "About damn time."

Then I smile like I will on my wedding day and the day I have a small piece of Cristian bundled in my arms. The same one I'll have on our fiftieth anniversary and every day in between because the man in front of me isn't my savior, he's my rock.

EPILOGUE

Cristian

I slide behind Vanessa on the kitchen floor, pulling her into my body exactly where she was meant to fit.

"Watching it bake?" I ask.

She giggles like the little girl she's acting like. It's endearing.

"I remember doing this when I was a kid. I was always so eager for the cake to be done, I'd watch it rise."

I kiss her shoulder and lean my back against the cabinets of the breakfast island. "Thanks for letting me be part of it."

She turns her head and stares at me for a moment, gifting me with a smile that melts me like butter on warm pancakes. "I wouldn't have done it if it wasn't for you. You've dug this whole other woman out of me."

Flipping around, she gets on her knees and puts her hands on my cheeks. She's still wearing her running gear.

Yes, I said that right. She's committing to three point one miles. Nothing more. But I just like it when we run together.

The tank top she was wearing under her sweatshirt hangs at the neckline giving me a glimpse of her cleavage which has my dick twitching because I seem to be at my horniest after I work out. For some guys it's morning wood, for me, it's post-workout wood.

"Thank you, Cris." She kisses my mouth, but I slide my hand to the back of her head, slipping my tongue between her lips and deepening our kiss.

She moans, and I flip her on her back, pressing my body down on hers. Her legs part for me to nestle between them even though the floor can't be the most comfortable for her to be splayed out on.

I close the kiss and grind into her. In the tiny bit of time we've lived together, she knows how much I crave her after a workout, especially when I've had to stare at her ass and hear her small whimpers for miles on end.

"How about I distract you a different way while the cake is baking?" I offer. My hands slide up under her shirt, the damp sports bra sticking to her chest.

"I'm open to suggestions." I circle my hips again and a laugh falls from her lips. "Is that your suggestion?"

I cup one of her breasts, kneading it between my fingers.

She inches up and smashes her lips to mine. I guess exercise is becoming an aphrodisiac for her, too.

That's when things get out of control.

Clothes get stripped off while we cling to each other with roaming hands and wandering mouths. Pretty soon she's screaming, I'm grunting and we're gasping for breath.

Like the champs we are, we both fall down into an exhausted mess just as the oven timer goes off.

"See, now wasn't that much better than watching the cake rise?" I ask, getting up to throw away the condom.

Since Vanessa's moved in, I've stashed them in places you'd never think of. Imagine my horror when Mama came over to bring us soup and found one in the silverware drawer. Of course, Luca had to fucking be here for that one.

Vanessa uses the hot pad to pull the cake out. An open oven, baked goods, and her naked. What a sight. How great is life?

She tiptoes up to me, and I hand her the pile of her clothes. "I'm going to shower so we're not late. We'll frost after it cools."

I kiss her. "I'll see you in there."

"No, Cris." She swats at me as I follow her down the hall. "It's bad enough your mom knows we have sex thanks to your squirreling practices with condoms. If we're late, she'll think it's *because* we were having sex."

We step into the bathroom. "I don't see the problem. It gets her that much closer to a grandchild. You know we have to beat Maddie and Mauro if we want to be Mama's favorite."

"I'm okay with second." She turns on the shower.

"Do you not know me at all?" I follow her into the shower.

"Cris." Her hand is on my chest.

"What? I just want to make sure you're clean. Think of it as me helping."

Another dick twitching laugh rumbles out of her and she puts her head under the spray of the shower. I watch, my cock growing hard again. I step closer and her eyes pop open.

"I said no. How can you even want to again?"

This time it's me who laughs. "I'll never have enough of you."

"Good, because I don't think I'll ever get enough of you either." Her thigh winds around mine and I grab her ass and lift so she can lock her legs around my waist.

"Fuck."

My dick pushes against her opening.

"What?" She grinds along my hardness.

"No condom." I rest my head on her shoulder.

Her hand reaches up on the edge of the shower and a gold packet shines in her hand.

"Look who's being resourceful now?" I take it from her, opening and rolling it down on myself which is pretty impressive with one hand if I do say so myself.

"Well, I know how much you want to be Mama's favorite, so I have to make sure you don't trick me and knock me up." She rocks her hips, waiting for me, but we need to hold up here.

"You don't think..."

She stops me, her hand on the back of my neck. "No, Cris, I know you wouldn't. It was a joke."

"Good." I thrust into her for the second time in a half hour and it's like the first time all over again.

She clenches and with the steam building in the bathroom, I lose myself in her. Vanessa Flanagan is my whole world. She's all I can see, smell, hear, touch, and taste. And I wouldn't have it any other way.

———

"It's lopsided," Vanessa complains, holding the cake in her hands.

"It's fine." We walk up to my parents' house. "It's our first time."

"Hopefully it tastes good. I feel like we should've done a trial run." She waits for me to open the door.

"I'm really rubbing off on you, huh? Trial run?"

I open the door happy that it's only my immediate family since Ma has surgery scheduled for tomorrow. The procedure is supposed to be simple. An ablation but they still have to get to her heart. The one muscle that keeps our bodies alive. Not to mention the anesthesia.

Everyone is a little on edge, but the doctors assure us it's nothing to worry about.

"Don't get your hopes up. I'm still never making dinner," she says.

"Good, because I like cooking for you." I kiss her on the cheek, take the cake from her hands, and open the door.

There's no garlic and basil scent. There's no heat and humidity inside from a day spent cooking. Ma is on the floor looking through photo albums, my dad watching the Bears game.

"Hey," I announce our arrival since for the first Sunday in my life, this house feels cold and distant.

Ma looks up and then I see her makeup is smeared. Wiping her face with the hopes we didn't catch it, she stands and rushes over to us.

"Vanessa," she coos and hugs her, kissing both of her cheeks.

Moving to me, she does the same and then glances down to the pumpkin spice cake with cream cheese frosting.

I'm sure Vanessa saw her questioning look.

"I baked a cake." I hold it up higher.

"You?" She points to me.

"Yep."

"No!" Vanessa smacks my arm. "We did it together, but I think I did something wrong."

Ma takes the cake and places it on the dining room table. "Come Vanessa."

Taking a fork from the table, she slides it through the frosting and the cake and eats it.

Vanessa glances back at me, biting her lip.

"It's good. Look doesn't matter. Taste matters." Ma grabs another fork and hands it to me.

She's smart and she knows this cake means much more to Vanessa than me.

I do what Ma does and she's right. My eyes widen. "It's great." I hand my fork to Vanessa and she does the same as Ma and I both did.

She nods, clearly surprised the cake tastes so good.

Then I spot a tear falling from her cheek.

"Why tears?" Ma asks, stepping forward, her hand on Vanessa's arm.

I've told my parents a small part of Vanessa's past, but I want Vanessa to share what she wants when she wants.

"It was my mom's recipe," she admits. "I haven't tasted it since before she died."

Ma's small body takes Vanessa in, her hand running up and down her back. "I'm here. Maybe we can make the cake together."

This is Ma's attempt at a fix. She's not trying to replace Vanessa's mom, but I'm afraid Vanessa could very well take it that way. I wait for Vanessa to shoot me a look over Ma's shoulder. One that suggests she overstepped.

Instead, her eyes close and she nods into Ma's shoulder. "That would be great."

Ma pulls away keeping her hands on Vanessa's arms. "I'm here for you always. Even if you and Cristian don't work out, I'm here."

"Ma?"

Ma looks back at me. "What? She needs a mama, I'm a mama."

I roll my eyes and walk over to my dad, leaving the new mother-daughter duo to themselves. As I sit down next to my dad in the family room, I pretend to watch the Bears game while watching Vanessa and Ma. She shows her the china her mother brought her over from Italy for their wedding. They laugh, they touch and they get along. How did I ever think Vanessa didn't want to fit into the Bianco family? It somehow feels like we weren't whole until now.

A half hour later, Mauro and Maddie show up with the catering order of chicken and beef. We're just setting it out on the dining room table when a blast of cold air rushes through the front door and Luca walks in with some short brunette.

Idiot. Why is he choosing today to bring a girl home?

It's not until I do a double take that I notice it's Lauren with him.

"Lauren?" Maddie asks, separating herself from Ma and Vanessa's circle around naked pictures of the Bianco babies.

"Hey, everyone." Lauren puts up a small wave of her free hand since her left one is locked in Luca's.

"Hey guys," Luca booms, sucking up all the attention in the room like he usually does.

Ma approaches him with a kiss on each cheek and a handshake for Lauren. "How's my baby?" She lightly smacks his cheek because we all know Luca is the crazy one.

Maddie finds her way to Mauro and Vanessa to me, the four of us staring at whatever is transpiring in front of us.

"Guess what, Ma? Your baby is getting married!" Luca winds his arms around Lauren's waist and kisses her on the cheek.

All of our mouths drop open.

I blink.

I blink again.

Luca and Lauren are engaged?

The End

COCKAMAMIE UNICORN RAMBLINGS

Well that's a wrap! Another Bianco brother book done, but we have a feeling you're all dying to get your hands on Luca's book now.

We were astonished at the love Flirting With Fire received from readers. Not because we didn't think our M&M deserved it, but because we didn't anticipate just how much everyone would love the Bianco family. The brothers came to us back with Break the Ice last February, so it's been a long wait for both us and you. All of that makes us thrilled that so many readers want to be honorary Bianco babes, too!

The love for Maddie and Mauro made us worry that readers would find Vanessa too cold and they wouldn't connect with her. The two best friends(Maddie & Vanessa) and two brothers (Mauro & Cristian) couldn't be more opposite in their approach to love. In our minds, she's just a young woman afraid to open herself up to vulnerability. Which is why she needed someone like Cristian to draw her out. Someone patient and kind, someone who doesn't quit because things get hard. We knew he was the man for the job!

Which brings us to Cristian. Even our assistant, Shawna, doesn't understand the compression pants aka man leggings. It's a running joke between the three of us and Rayne constantly trying to change Shawna's mind that they are all the trend with a lot of hot guys. That's the fun of everyone having different preferences though. They might not be for everyone out there, but it made Cristian's character a little unique and we strive to make our heroes and heroines not cut from the same cloth. Plus, Piper still laughs when she thinks about Luca calling Cristian Christine when we introduced his 'man leggings' in Flirting with Fire.

Oh, and for all your pumpkin spice lovers out there, this book is for you. ;)

Now, fasten your seatbelts for Lauren & Luca's book because it's time for the baby brother to grow up.

We need to thank the regulars who always support us:

Letitia from RBA Design for the awesome cover.

Wander Aguiar for his magnificent photography skills and making Andrew Biernat our Cristian Bianco.

Ellie from Gray Inks for her excellent editing skills.

Shawna from Behind the Writer for her stellar eyes on proofing.

Dani Sanchez and the whole Inkslinger PR gang for their proficiency and spectacular organization skills to get Crushing on the Cop in the hands of readers and bloggers.

Bloggers who decide to wiggle us in their already packed schedules.

ARC readers for always being on top of it with posting your reviews right away.

Our Unicorns, who we'd be nothing without. You are our rocks. The ones that keep us writing and inspire us to top your favorite heroes and heroines because we live for those posts after we release where you tell us how much you fell for our characters. Our thank yous don't convey the love we have for those posts and what they mean to us.

XO

Piper & Rayne

ABOUT PIPER & RAYNE

Piper Rayne, or Piper and Rayne, whichever you prefer because we're not one author, we're two. Yep, you get two USA Today Bestselling authors for the price of one. Our goal is to bring you romance stories that have "Heartwarming Humor With a Side of Sizzle" (okay...you caught us, that's our tagline). A little about us... We both have kindle's full of one-clickable books. We're both married to husbands who drive us to drink. We're both chauffeurs to our kids. Most of all, we love hot heroes and quirky heroines that make us laugh, and we hope you do, too.

www.piperrayne.com
Amazon
Goodreads
Facebook
Instagram
Pinterest
Bookbub

ALSO BY PIPER RAYNE

The Modern Love World

Charmed by the Bartender

Hooked by the Boxer

Mad about the Banker

The Single Dad's Club

Real Deal

Dirty Talker

Sexy Beast

Hollywood Hearts

Mister Mom

Animal Attraction

Domestic Bliss

Bedroom Games

Cold as Ice

On Thin Ice

Break the Ice

Charity Case

Manic Monday

Afternoon Delight

Happy Hour

Blue Collar Brothers

Flirting with Fire

Crushing on the Cop

Engaged to the EMT

Book: 2

9 781987 925456